DASTARDLY DOINGS ON ALLHALLOWS EVE

A.J.A. GARDINER

Contents

1	1
2	10
3	23
4	33
5	47
6	57
7	70
8	83
9	93
10	106
11	115
12	123
13	131
14	145
15	153
16	164
17	177

18	190
19	201
20	213
21	224
22	232
23	242
24	252
25	262
26	274
27	289
28	302
29	318
30	328
31	337
32	343
33	352
34	364

AUTHOR'S NOTE 375

1

A scuffle of movement in the surrounding shrubbery makes me grab Daisy's arm. 'What's that?'

She shoots me a sideways glance. 'It *could* be a rabbit. *Or*...' her voice deepens '... d'you think it's the Bogeyman?'

Daisy can mock all she wants—but after some of the horror films I've seen, it's hard to be rational about this.

It's seven p.m. at the wrong end of October, and the path to our detective agency is a crawling mass of inky shadows. There *are* posts fitted with solar lights on both sides, but they're only useful as guides to ensure we don't stray—and do nothing to disperse an all-enveloping, shiver-inducing gloom. Now and again, an errant sliver of moonlight reveals the vague outlines of what are *probably* bushes. Occasionally, a soft breeze makes them rustle menacingly.

Suddenly, a twig snaps underfoot—unfortunately, it wasn't under either of *our* feet.

When a hooded figure jumps from behind a cluster of hydrangea, even Daisy can't hold in a muted squeal. Naturally, I trump her by letting out a full-blown howl of terror. Well, you do—when faced with someone in an ivory-white rubber mask with wide slanting eyes. Its scariest feature is an opening where the mouth should be, shaped like an exclamation mark, giving the impression of a scream.

In fact, that's where I've seen this mask before—in *Scream,* the classic slasher movie featuring "Ghostface" who typically has his long-bladed hunting knife held high and ready to strike.

Just as this one does

Ghostface dances closer, cackles, and I sense his gaze settle on me. Then, without warning, he rounds on Daisy and his knife flashes down in a blur.

When its blade disappears into Daisy's chest, every last molecule of breath wheechs out of me.

Ghostface howls gleefully, then turns and stampedes away along the path.

My eyes must be bulging in their sockets as I stare at Daisy. Her lips move. 'Get a grip, Sam.'

'I did *not* enjoy that one bit. It was terrifying.'

Daisy giggles. 'Yeah—good, innit?'

She brushes at an indentation in her sweatshirt left by the knife's retractable blade. 'Didn't that hurt?' I babble.

'Naw—the blade's made of plastic. And being lightly sprung, it retracts into the handle with virtually no resistance. Hey, "Murder-Meals" has outdone themselves this time—don't you think?'

"Murder-Meals" is the company who stage our murder mystery evenings twice a week at the Cairncroft Hotel. (Or "The Murder Hotel", to use its proper moniker.) They're doing a Halloween special tonight, which includes pre-dinner scariness in the hotel grounds for those brave enough to venture out. Pumpkin lanterns set at various points along the pathways add an extra element of spookiness, but the pièce de résistance is a team of "ghouls" (such as the one we just encountered) who are out scaring the pants off our guests. (And us.)

A shiver of relief runs through me when we reach the old stables, now headquarters to The Cairncroft Detective Agency. While Daisy unlocks the door, I suddenly remember and twist my wrist to see what time it is. 'Beggar—it's after seven.'

'So?'

'Davy said he'd phone at seven.'

Daisy shrugs. 'He must have forgotten...'

'No, you don't understand—I haven't got my phone with me.'

Her expression changes to long-suffering. 'Why not?'

I flap both hands. 'Well, it's in my bag—which I didn't bring. Can we go back? Now?'

She hisses through pursed lips. 'Sam, I need those files. It'll only take a minute to find them...'

No, it won't. I know Daisy—while searching for the files, she'll come across "x" number of other tasks that can't wait. Which means we're looking at a minimum of *ten* minutes. My relationship with Davy has been strained enough lately without standing him up on a scheduled phone call. Oh, nothing else for it...

Daisy reads my mind. 'Just go—I'll see you at the hotel.'

'What if there's more of those... things... on the way back?'

She chortles. 'Let them stab you, say "thank you" nicely, and carry on.'

'But...'

It's no good. I have to do this. Yes, I know they're only actors dressed up, but that whole experience was terrifying—I'm the one who disappears behind the sofa during horror movies. And yet, I can't leave Davy hanging. He might think... 'Fine, I'll do it. You're right—there's nothing to be afraid of.'

Shrugging on a new, steel-clad resolve, I set off down the path. Daisy's voice wafts after me. 'I'm *fairly* it's only actors out there...'

I DON'T LIKE THIS

A couple of minutes is all it takes to get from our detective agency to the hotel, but tonight the track feels endless. I know pleasure makes time pass quicker, but hadn't realised how much terror slows it.

Out here in the countryside, everything's deathly silent at night—except for noises I'd rather *not* hear. They *could* be bushes moving in response to airflow, or small animals who are more scared of me than the other way around. But being the *only* sounds amplifies them—imparting a more sinister persona.

What really does it is the gloom. Darkness, after all, is the domain of imagination's scariest creations.

Then I stumble, flail wildly to keep my balance, and scream again.

Idiot, I castigate myself. It's only a loose shoelace. Although "only" is a relative term when your left leg's a prosthetic from the knee down—that could have been nasty.

I carefully manoeuvre my left knee to the ground. Luckily, it's the right-hand lace that came undone, logistically an easier proposition to fix than the other way around—when getting back up would put painful pressure on my stump. Maybe I should look on Amazon for laceless trainers?

Reaching to retie my loose lace, I barely register a sudden footstep behind before something cannons into me. Not wanting an unplanned nose job, I thrust both arms out in the nick of time and end up on my hands and knees, like an overgrown toddler. After shuffling onto my bottom, feeling not a little indignity at finding myself in this position, I squint to see what tumbled over me—and crash-landed on the path.

Despite the sight that greets me mere feet away, and although my heart's thumping, I don't feel the panic of our previous encounter because Ghostface is now a familiar figure.

I can't tell if this is the same Ghostface or a compatriot. Poor fellow's sprawled flat out, shaking his head to try and clear it, and his demeanour's more pathos than threatening.

What I think happened is he came at me from behind, intending to stick his pretend-knife in my back (no doubt accompanied by a blood-curdling howl) at exactly the moment I crouched to tie my lace. Silly beggar must have gone straight over me, like they used to do in slapstick comedies. I actually feel sorry for him—bet he's feeling a right dork.

A glint of reflected moonlight draws my gaze to his knife, which landed on the ground beside me. Scooping it up, I'm surprised how realistic the prop looks and feels. Heavier than I expected, for starters, and it's hard to believe that wicked-looking blade is made of harmless plastic.

Ghostface clambers up and peers down at me, his breath coming in laboured puffs. I wink. (Well, I try to, but winking is a skill that's always proved elusive and from Ghostface's flinch, still is.) Feeling bad that I may have given the impression of being miffed over what was just a silly accident, I hold out his knife.

Ghostface jumps back. Now he thinks I'm making angry gestures at him with his own knife? Oh dear—I'd better reassure the poor chap. Carefully, I reverse the pseudo-weapon and offer it handle first. This time, he leans in and grabs it...

... at the same moment alarm bells go off in my head. Because, when I touched it, that blade didn't feel like plastic. No, I realise belatedly, what I felt was hard metal—steel.

Craning back, I cower as Ghostface towers over me and raises his knife. My blood runs cold even as I struggle to cope with the obvious conclusion.

That's a real knife—and he's about to stab me with it

'SAM.'

Ghostface's head snaps up. Then he whirls and crashes into the shrubbery. A moment later,

Daisy appears. 'There you are. The files were lying out on Liz's desk, so I was only a minute behind you. Em—why are you sitting down there?'

2

'Did you get through to Davy?'

I nod, my mind still with the phone call. 'Yes, and he says "hi".'

'Anything wrong? You're acting funny.'

That snaps me back. 'Anything wrong? You mean apart from the fact somebody just tried to stab me?'

Her eyes roll ceilingward. 'Sam, your imagination's running amok. No way was one of our Ghostfaces carrying a real knife.'

'I'm telling you, that blade didn't feel like plastic. Anyway, it was too heavy...'

'But its weight could be all in the hilt, and you only touched it for a second—those props are dead realistic, you know.'

Oh, maybe she's right. Between worrying about Davy, and the state our first "slasher" encounter left me in, my brain *was* fried. Yet I'm still sure that knife *didn't* have a plastic blade...

The residents lounge is buzzing tonight because our special Halloween "spooky mystery" is a sell-out. About half the crowd is in fancy dress—it's strange to see people dressed in suits and glittery dresses mingling with vampires and werewolves. Morticia Adams catches my eye and makes for our table with a blood-stained Carrie trailing behind. I nudge Daisy. 'Is that...?'

'Yeah, Rebecca. And Liz.'

Thought so. Rebecca's easy to recognise—despite her Morticia-inspired outfit, goth-style makeup (which isn't *so* different from what she usually uses), and a long black wig—the clue being her neckline plunges so deep it makes Angelica Huston's look like a polo neck. Also, Morticia Adams did *not* wear a miniskirt over fishnet tights...

Carrie at least is decent in her full-length prom dress, although methinks she went overboard with the ketchup.

Rebecca sinks into one of two remaining chairs around our table and Liz bags the other. They're both drinking tonight's special cocktail, which Colin spent hours creating. (I suspect a lot of "tasting" was involved.) It's a vile-green concoction with drops of blood on the glass's rim—just what you'd expect Frankenstein's monster or Dracula to tipple on. Amazing what you can do with absinthe, cava, and an eye-dropper of tomato juice.

Daisy squints over her pint glass. 'What does that taste like?'

Rebecca giggles. 'Liquorice champagne. Quite nice really, but awful strong.'

Liz scowls. 'Actually, it's yeuch. Wish *I'd* got a beer, now.'

'How's the flat working out, girls?' I put in.

They answer in unison. 'Great / love it.'

Liz is the Cairncroft Detective Agency's newest recruit, having taken over as receptionist to free up Rebecca for more detective work. About a month ago, the girls moved into a flat in Donstable together. I sense Daisy wondering the same thoughts as me. She's also aware Liz's previous flatmate refused to have her back—because food, clothes, and cash were going missing on too regular a basis.

Employing Liz was a gamble, having only met her because she tried to rob the hotel. But the girls became friendly after, and Rebecca insists Liz is a reformed character—I'm reserving final judgement until her trial period's complete, although I was happy to give the lass a chance. Daisy feels Liz is worth the risk, working as she is on a "set a thief to catch a thief" premise. (Quite how that applies to the agency's *receptionist* escapes me.)

I'm trying to figure out a non-offensive way of asking whether they have a system for keeping their food separate when Daisy beats me to it. 'Has Liz started tea-leafing your grub yet?'

Daisy shrugs apologetically when Liz turns beetroot (even though it's obvious she couldn't give a damn) but Rebecca just laughs. 'We put money in a pot for shopping, so the groceries belong to both of us. Saves any arguments.'

'Mm.'

Daisy doesn't quit so easily. 'What about clothes? Liz's last flatmate is still looking for her favourite jumper.'

Rebecca's fingers flap dismissively. 'Oh, she borrows my stuff all the time—but that's alright, because I do the same to her.'

Sounds like a marriage made in heaven

I'm about to change the subject before Liz is embarrassed further when Daisy jumps up and points. 'There's Wilf—and Harriet. C'mon, Sam. I want you to meet them.'

'Have a good night' I only just get out before Daisy seizes my hand and drags me across the lounge towards a short, slightly dishevelled middle-aged man (who still manages to pull off a "spiffy" look) and his mousey female companion.

'Who's Wilf?' I hiss, halfway there.

Too late—Daisy accelerates and suddenly I'm shaking hands with "Wilf"—who, I now notice, has blue swastikas inked on his knuckles. He sees me looking and reddens. 'Sorry—really should get those removed. I used to be a bad boy—but not any more.'

Daisy nods sadly. 'Wilf got his tattoos in prison. He doesn't do that stuff any more, though.'

Not another one. What does Daisy think we are—a Battersea for ex-criminals?

Harriet shyly extends a hand and I'm relieved to see she's wearing neither tattoos nor brass knuckledusters. Wilf beams at her. 'Was her what reformed me,' he confides. 'It was Harry turned me straight as a die. Well, her and the army.'

'You two should get on like a house on fire,' Daisy burbles. Then, when both Harriet and I look puzzled, adds: 'You know? Sam—and Harry.'

Oh, I see what she means. And that makes us blood-sisters?

'So you're in the army, Wilf?' I conclude, seeing he said so.

'No, that was years ago. These days I'm self-employed.'

Shall I ask what doing? No—maybe not

Wilf clears his throat noisily, then: 'Anyway, Sam. Understand you've got a below the knee prosthetic?'

Wow. And I thought Daisy was outspoken

I gape at him and he shuffles awkwardly. 'Sorry, didn't mean to... it's just, my dad was the same. He died a couple of months ago.'

And you're wondering when I'm due to pop my clogs?

'No,' Wilf goes on. (Did he read my mind then?) 'What I'm trying to get at is, I don't know what to do with Dad's leg. The artificial one,' he clarifies.

Harriet looks pained. 'It's in the under-stairs cupboard, and I keep telling Wilf what a waste that is if someone could use it.'

'So you seemed the right person to ask,' Wilf adds hopefully.

'Ah. I see.'

After I explain what's involved in fitting a prosthetic (making a cast of the stump, for starters) Wilf nods sadly. 'So it's no good to anyone else?'

'Not really.'

The hush following that little exchange is deafening—obviously neither Harriet nor Wilf are hot on conversation (and Daisy's more than comfortable with silence) so I guess it's up to me. 'Um—Wilf. How did you and Daisy meet?'

He winks with an ease I could never master. 'Daisy came to me for lessons a while back,' he says. 'Star pupil, she turned out to be.'

"Lessons"? Daisy's number one interest is unarmed combat, which I can't imagine Wilf being an authority on. There again, he *was* in the army—but looking at him, my first guess would be the cooking corps. Not a commando unit.

Daisy has the grace to blush. (If barely discernibly.) 'It was Wilf showed me how to pick pockets.'

I grip my bag a little tighter. 'And do you still...?'

Wilf shakes his head firmly. 'No—all behind me now. These days, I'm on the side of the angels.'

So long as that isn't the HELLS Angels

Daisy slaps my arm. 'That's why I wanted you to meet Wilf. Reckon he could be a real asset to the agency.'

'Um... we've only just taken Liz on. The agency isn't really in a position to...'

Wilf grins at me. 'Don't worry. Like I said—I'm self-employed. Only get paid when I'm needed.'

'Ah—so you work with other detective agencies, then?' That makes more sense—but Wilf shakes his head again.

'Naw—at least, not yet. Luckily, I was able to put some cash away before having to give up my job, but it won't last forever. So I'm looking to use my... other skills... legitimately.'

'What *was* your job?' I regret asking before the words are out of my mouth.

'Slaughterhouse,' he says without a blink. 'Got paid by the kill, and I'm good at slitting throats. Learned in the army,' he adds.

Oh—not the cooking corps, then. Or, I suppose, it still could have been...

Wilf's starting to make me feel uncomfortable. 'So what happened—why did you leave the slaughterhouse?'

Harriet answers, slipping an arm through Wilf's. 'I persuaded him to turn vegan.'

I can't help a sense of relief when Kat waves to us from a stool at the residents bar. 'Oh, look,' I announce, trying to sound reluctant. 'There's Kat. We'd better say hello.'

On the way over, I bend to Daisy's ear and hiss: 'Who else are you friendly with? Harold Shipman?'

KAT'S NURSING HER USUAL GLASS OF PINOT GRIGIO—THE green goo obviously didn't appeal. 'This is a great do, guys,' she enthuses.

Daisy scrutinises her. 'What are you supposed to be—a solicitor?'

She pouts. 'I thought fancy dress was optional? Dad wouldn't have come at all if it weren't.'

I notice Kat's started calling Mr M "Dad". Well, he is... though she only found out a few months ago. Looking around, I ask: 'Where is he?'

Kat's eyes do a quick sweep of the room, then she points. 'Back there—talking to Graham and Sadie.'

Daisy goes on tiptoes and peers. 'Cor, Sadie looks scary. What *is* that costume? Oh, wait, it's the same clothes she always wears... hey, isn't that Miss Dobie with your dad?'

On a second look, I spot the grey bun bobbing about on Mr M's far side. 'It is. I didn't think she did this sort of thing. Or any sort of thing, for that matter...'

Kat frowns. 'Dad talked her into it and bought an extra ticket—expect he feels sorry for her. But it's a pain, because I was hoping he would "out" his new girlfriend tonight.'

'He has a girlfriend?' I exclaim. 'A real one this time?'

When Kat first arrived on the scene, everyone thought Mr M was her "sugar daddy"—rather than the genetic version it turned out. Not that Kat did anything to dissuade that misunderstanding—she took delight in fanning the rumours.

Kat nods. 'I'm sure he has. The old stud's been going out without telling me where. On Saturday he was away the whole day, then came in looking all hot and bothered.'

'Wow—any idea who it is?'

'No—hence my high hopes that tonight would be her first public appearance. Might have been, too, if dozy Dobie had stayed at home like she usually does.'

I *have* to call her on that. 'Kat, don't be rotten. Miss Dobie's lovely.'

She holds up her palms. 'Oh, I know she is—ignore me, I'm just desperate to find out who Dad's new squeeze is.'

'How're you settling in, Kat?' Kat recently joined Mr M in his solicitor's practice as a full partner. The man she believed, through childhood and beyond, to be her dead father was Mr M's original partner in Dougall & MacLachlan. Since Kat kept her maiden name when she married (three times at the last count), Mr M's decision to keep "Dougall &" on the firm's letterhead proved predictive.

'Love it,' she replies instantly. 'The pace of living up here is so relaxed compared to London. Looking back, I don't know how city life didn't do my head in years ago.'

'D'you think Mr M will retire, now you're here?' Daisy asks curiously.

'He's showing every sign of slowing down, so it wouldn't surprise me if the old beggar made his part-time hours official. When I say "slowing down", that's only in the office—his golf handicap's plunging faster than the stock market.'

'Maybe Miss Dobie will cut *her* hours, too,' Daisy grins. 'They must be about the same age.'

Kat leans in closer. 'Oh, I hope so. Don't get me wrong. Sam's right, Miss Dobie *is* a kind hearted soul—despite her eccentricities—but *very* set in her ways. Some fresh blood in the front office wouldn't be a bad thing. Anyway, I'm off to the restaurant—nearly time for dinner. You coming?'

I shake my head. 'No. Daisy and I are ordering a takeaway later.'

Kat stops, half-on and half-off her stool. 'How come?'

Daisy develops a sudden fascination with the far wall as I explain. 'It being so busy tonight, we set aside one six-cover table for senior staff and compos. Since Logan and Jodie weren't interested in coming, that left four complimentary tickets going spare. Guess how many brain of Britain here gave out?'

'Um—six?'

I nod, and Daisy scowls.

Kat colours. 'Now I feel guilty.'

'Don't—it was me who told her to give one each to you and Mr M, and I'd already said Rebecca and Liz could have the other two. Then she went and invited her tame ex-con and his wife.'

'That's business...' Daisy protests, but I speak over her.

'Actually, I'm fine with it. Louis has done a magnificent job of putting together Halloween fare, but the eyeballs are way too realistic for my taste.'

'Eyeballs,' Kat splutters. 'What are they made of?'

Daisy crooks a finger to bring Kat closer. 'You'll find out soon enough.'

3

Although not eating here tonight, Daisy and I suss out an inconspicuous spot in the restaurant where we can loiter to watch the show. On our usual murder mystery nights, "Murder-Meals" players enact a short crime drama after the guests finish dinner. Our erstwhile amateur detectives take notes during the performance and afterwards, the cast present themselves for "interview".

Murder-Meals also gives everyone participating a sheet of puzzles—the solutions point towards hidden clues. Anyone who's still stumped next day can hire a private detective from our on-site agency to "gather" more information on their behalf. (For which purpose Murder-Meals furnish us with pre-printed "reports".)

Tonight, the "murderer" is Ghostface, and our guests are tasked with unmasking him. The expertise involved in compressing dramatic performances into a clue-laden twenty-minute slot is the reason we use "Murder-Meals", and not for the first time I'm glad we farmed these productions out from the start. After seeing the professionals at work, there's little doubt we'd have fallen flat on our faces trying to do it ourselves.

'Who do you think it is?' Daisy whispers, as another innocent falls victim to Ghostface's knife.

'It's obvious there are only two suspects, but I have a feeling narrowing it down further is going to involve solving some puzzles.'

She nods. 'You're right—Ricky told me that earlier. He also says tonight's puzzle locations will make the guests feel as though they're on "I'm a Celebrity". Lots of creepy-crawlies involved, from what I gather.'

I stare in horror. 'Creepy-crawlies—in a hotel?'

'Don't worry, they're plastic. And clockwork. I've only seen the giant spider, but it's a doozy.'

'Mm... Just so long as no one has a heart attack.'

The lights dim—a sign that another murder is imminent. This'll be the third and Daisy's bored now. 'So how are things with you and Davy—*really*,' she emphasises.

I decide to give in gracefully. 'Davy didn't sound happy tonight—the company he's working for seems to have an overrated opinion of what he's capable of. Davy says they keep sending him out on jobs he hasn't a clue how to do—and the bosses are getting narky about it.'

Two months ago, a big building firm in Glasgow offered my fiancé a plum job. Which gave *us* a problem, because I love Davy—but couldn't stomach the prospect of leaving Cairncroft. Thing is, neither could I let Davy pass up what he called his "chance of a lifetime".

By mutual consent, we chickened out of making a final decision about "us"—and he left for a twelve-week trial period in Glasgow on a "let's wait and see how it pans out" basis. Now we meet up every second weekend and between the reality of maintaining a long-distance relationship, plus inflated expectations on the part of Davy's new employers, my poor fiancé's becoming progressively more depressed.

Which should make me happy—because if Davy's dream job doesn't work out, he'll soon be back in Cairncroft permanently. But I can't feel good about it—not after seeing how miserable he was last weekend. It'll kill him if he gets his marching orders for not being up to scratch.

'Do you think it's that Leslie's fault?' Daisy asks. 'After all, it was her who got him the job. Maybe she overstated his qualifications to the bosses.'

'Why would she do that?'

'Because she was sweet on Davy all along, even if he didn't realise it, and wanted to guarantee getting him to herself in Glasgow.'

'Trust you to come up with something so ridiculous.'

'It fits.'

I hate to admit this, but she's right—it does. Was I fooled by bouncy Leslie when she insisted netting the best man for the job was her sole motivation in headhunting Davy? They *were* sweethearts at uni.

Maybe I'll have a wee word next time we get together… go into this business of his bosses thinking he can do stuff that's beyond him and try to figure out what's really going on.

If it is down to Leslie's scheming—I'll kill her

I suddenly realise Daisy's waiting for my reaction. 'No, that's nonsense. Probably just teething problems—oh, look. They're gearing up for the finale.'

My friend snorts loudly and turns back to the performance. The "stage" is somewhat makeshift—we absolutely need to organise something better. Currently, the actors perform on a rectangle painted on the floor—behind it, hanging from "hospital-bed-style" rails, black curtains form an area for them to "hide out" between appearances.

The kitchen door is ideally placed to double as a "stage" door, which was our original plan. Until Louis heard we were intending to annex a (little-used) corner of his kitchen. In deference to our chef's blood pressure, we went with the curtained area.

Maybe the mystery of Ghostface's identity isn't so clever as I thought, because all the indications are that one of my two suspects is about to become the next victim. That being Mr Fortescue, the bank manager.

Sure enough, Mr Fortescue is all alone when ominous music starts up—grating on everyone's nerves like a badly played violin.

Mr Fortescue is immersed in a document that may or may not be relevant. He's reading it aloud "to himself", but of course the information thus shared could be another red herring. Daisy jabs me with her elbow. 'Here he comes,' she whispers.

Sure enough, Ghostface creeps up behind Mr Fortescue with his knife raised and ready. Cue the *boom boom boom* "Psycho" music as Ghostface's blade plunges into Mr Fortescue's back. The poor man screams as his legs fold beneath him and—wham. Everything goes black.

The lights stay off for about ten seconds to let Mr Fortescue and Ghostface get themselves offstage and into their hidey-hole. Then the owner of Murder-Meals (a personable young chap called Ricky Malvern) will give some final instructions before our amateur sleuths begin their investigations. Meanwhile, Daisy and I have a date with the Chinese deliveryman.

'Sam, look.'

I am—and can't believe what I'm seeing. The lights just blazed back into life, but Mr Fortescue is still there. Worryingly, he's lying in a pool of blood. Ghostface (played, we now know, by Ricky Malvern) hasn't moved either, except to take off his mask. Poor Ricky looks horrified.

Daisy's already halfway to the stage and I hobble in her wake. Louis must have heard the commotion because he comes flying out of his kitchen and rushes to Mr Fortescue. Daisy joins him and together they search desperately for signs of life in the fallen actor. Ricky staggers backwards—I think he's in shock.

After a minute's frenzied activity, Louis replaces Mr Fortescue's limp arm on the floor and stands. He bows his head. All the colour drains from his face and he trembles uncontrollably. Daisy, still in a crouch, glances round and (subtle as ever) draws a finger across her throat.

I freeze, my mind racing.

"Mr Fortescue" is really dead?

THE NEXT TWO HOURS ARE A NIGHTMARE.

Paramedics arrive (and pronounce "Mr Fortescue" beyond help) followed closely by the police. Meanwhile, I have a hotel-full of traumatised guests to deal with. Not to mention Logan, who's convinced this will ruin us.

Free brandies at the residents bar go a long way towards calming our public—and assigning Logan to assist Colin with passing them out gives him something better to do than flail about bemoaning our imminent decease. (Metaphorically—as opposed to Mr Fortescue.)

Inspector Wilson arrives in the wake of an influx of uniformed police, with Jodie trailing behind. Since she returned from maternity leave, it appears Wilson's mannequin-like former assistant has been demoted. I spot the deposed "Watson" amid a "supporting cast" of plain-clothes officers and notice he doesn't seem *that* unhappy. Working closely with Wilson can't be good for anyone's nerves…

I've never quite understood why the police insist on leaving bodies in situ until a senior police officer has gawked at them. Surely a photo would do? My worry now is *when* Wilson will give the go-ahead to move Mr Fortescue's remains.

From the restaurant, there are only two ways out—through the kitchen, or the residents lounge. Louis has already publicly stated that nobody is taking a corpse out through his kitchen, citing Health & Safety regulations I suspect he made up. But I'd *really* rather not have a body bag carted through the residents lounge until our guests are all back in their rooms. Unfortunately, with free brandy on tap, there's no telling when that'll be.

Wilson has requisitioned our snooker room (which Murder-Meals use as a dressing room and general HQ on performance nights) to do interviews in. Which is another reason the guests won't be back in their rooms anytime soon—Wilson wants statements from every one of them first.

(Did I mention tonight was a sellout?)

I intercept Inspector Wilson on his way to the snooker room and vocalise my concerns about exposing innocent guests to further angst. He shrugs. 'I can't leave bodies lying around for the sake of your hotel's public relations, Miss Chessington.'

'Could you at least tell me *when* you expect to move him?'

'About five minutes—the meat wagon's on its way.'

Charming turn of phrase he has

I smile sweetly before spinning on my heel. (Figuratively speaking—I'd fall flat on my face trying to do that for real.) 'Thanks for nothing,' I mutter, but not until there's no danger of him hearing.

Jodie appears at my shoulder and she *does* hear—*and* notices. 'What's he done now? And I thought you'd stopped being a wimp.'

'That was tactical—no point in riling him when he's made up his mind. And I'm *not* a wimp.' (Which latter has become a standing joke between me and Jodie.)

I explain the problem and she thinks for a moment. 'You know, Louis *is* pretty shaken up. Might be a nice gesture if you take him through to the residents bar for a dose of that brandy Logan's pouring down everyone's throats.'

She's right—and now I feel guilty. 'Poor Louis. He's obviously in shock—I should have checked on him before. Yes, good idea, Jodie. I'll do that straight away.'

Jodie winks. (Is *everyone* able to do that except me?) 'Or you could send Daisy to fetch Louis. Then, while she's feeding him brandy in the residents lounge, there'll be nothing to stop you sending the body out through the kitchen.'

4

It worked.

Louis was reluctant to join what's become a rugby scrum at the residents bar, but Daisy promised to fast-track him. Naturally, she was careful to make him wait just long enough to allow the undertakers a clear run. Wilson's "meat wagon" turned out to be driven by a local funeral director I know from dealing with Aunt Claire's untimely passing, who was happy to do things my way. Of course, Louis *will* cotton on later, but I'll deal with that when it arises.

Maybe it'd be easier to avoid him for a day or two...

With Mr Fortescue discreetly dispatched, I join Daisy in the residents lounge and give her a secret nod whilst flopping into an armchair. Meanwhile, with the rush dying down, Logan has brought a drink over and sat himself on Daisy's other side. He's relinquished command of the bar to Colin since hotel receptionist Hazel came through to help.

Poor Louis is sitting at the bar, and his glass already looks like it needs topping up.

Daisy puts down her pint. 'Get you something, Sam?'

Reluctantly, I decline. 'Not right now—I need to keep a clear head.'

Logan leans forward to meet my eyes. 'What are we going to do—about the mid-week and next weekend's murder mysteries?'

Good old Logan—ever practical. Suppose somebody has to be

'We cancel Wednesday's performance,' I state firmly. 'And put Hazel onto contacting everyone who's booked—we'll have to refund their deposits.'

Logan winces, but agrees.

'As for the weekend show—and going forward—who knows if Murder-Meals will be able to carry on after tonight? If they can't, then ultimately it's a case of finding another company—but specialist operations like Murder-Meals aren't exactly thick on the ground.'

I turn to Daisy. 'Remember, before we found Murder-Meals, you made up a plan for putting on our own productions. Do you think we could revert to that—on a temporary basis?'

She nods. 'Yeah—I've still got the file, including a list of locals who fancy themselves at amateur dramatics. It'd be great if Ricky would let us use Murder-Meals' scripts and props... except the knives...' nobody laughs '... and I don't see why he shouldn't. It's no skin off his nose and keeps us sweet while we wait for Murder-Meals to figure out what they're doing.'

Although Daisy knows Ricky Malvern better than I do, he's always struck me as a reasonable sort. But that was before witnessing him stab somebody. Ricky may well be otherwise occupied for the foreseeable future, leaving Murder-Meals "headless"—and us in shtuck.

Logan covers his eyes. 'This is a disaster,' he blurts, then adds hurriedly: 'I mean, it's also a tragedy, but the adverse publicity could bankrupt us.'

He squirms under Daisy's glare. 'Don't be stupid,' she retorts. 'There's no such thing as bad publicity.'

We both manage to keep a straight face as Logan draws himself upright and tries to remain authoritative. 'But someone was murdered. Who's going to stay in a hotel where that happens?'

Daisy holds up a palm and lays her index finger across it. '*One*—it wasn't a customer who got topped. I grant you *that* would scare people off, but happily we haven't lost a guest yet. *Two...*' her middle finger joins the first as she ignores Logan's answering bluster '... it was Sam's Aunt Claire's murder that put this place on the map. Never mind visiting a former crime scene—after tonight's drama, all the murder-buffs out there are going to think they're in with a chance of seeing the real thing. It might actually drive business *up*. '

'That's a bit callous...' Logan retorts, and Daisy dips her head.

'I know—only saying. I'd obviously rather it hadn't happened.'

'Do we have any idea *what* happened?' I put in. 'I mean, we saw Ricky stab that poor guy, but why?'

Daisy points. 'There's the man to ask. Ghostface himself.'

Ricky Malvern just exited Wilson's impromptu interview room. He slopes toward the bar and Daisy springs up. 'Ricky, over here.'

To Logan, she says: 'Go get him a brandy.'

'Why me?'

'Because I want to hear what he says. Hi, Ricky. Sit down—Logan's getting you a drink.'

Logan accepts defeat (although, if looks could kill, the one he gives Daisy would be more lethal than Ghostface's knife) and stomps off to the bar while Ricky collapses in the last remaining chair.

Daisy leans towards him. 'What happened to Mr Fortescue, Ricky?'

Ricky closes his eyes for a moment, then forces them open. 'His name's Joe—it was Joe Booth who was playing Mr Fortescue. And I didn't *know* it was a real knife. Some absolute swine must have switched it.'

'Switched it?' I repeat, but Daisy's face lights up.

'Cor, that's a new one—flippin' brilliant, though. Fooling some sap into offing the victim for you—it's sheer genius. Oh, sorry Ricky.'

'Don't worry—I *feel* like a sap. The maddening thing is, that policeman says it was a hundred-to-one shot the knife wasn't blocked by Joe's spine or ribs. Slipped right into his heart, they reckon.'

'So Wilson believes you, then?' I put in.

Ricky screws up his face. 'Not sure if I'd go that far. I've not to leave the building until he's spoken to everybody—and it was pointed out there are guards on all the exits in case I think about doing a bunk. But, yeah—he considered what I said to be a *possibility.* His word, not mine.'

Daisy mock-punches Ricky's shoulder. 'Cheer up, Ricky. We believe you—isn't that right, Sam?'

Although I nod, we don't actually know Ricky that well. At least, *I* don't. Daisy took to do with most of the setting up for our murder mystery nights—it *was* her idea in the first place—so has worked closely with Ricky. And she seems to be accepting he's innocent, which is probably good enough for me. But I can't get Inspector Wilson's "hundred-to-one" reference out of my mind. If someone *did* plant the knife in order to "murder by proxy", surely they'd also have realised those odds—and not fancied them?

Daisy shrugs when I voice that last. 'A lot of murderers are idiots.'

'Ricky?' I ask, leaning towards him. 'Were you out with those roaming ghouls earlier, scaring people?'

He shakes his head. 'No, that was four other actors. Why?'

'One of them gave Sam a fright,' Daisy tells him while the besom rolls her eyes.

Ricky looks curiously at me. 'That's what they're being paid to do.'

Before I can explain further, Daisy laughs and jumps back in. 'Of course it is. Listen, Ricky. I thought you said nobody could crack tonight's mystery without solving some puzzles first? But if Ghostface killed Fortescue, that only left one valid suspect. Unless I'm missing something.'

Despite himself, Ricky can't help a little smile. 'Aha. Thing is, I wasn't really Ghostface—Fortescue was.'

Daisy stares. 'Huh?'

Ricky settles back, looking more like himself. 'I... that is, my character... lost a family member to Ghostface, then discovered his identity. So "I" was avenging my sister's murder, and the solution was that Fortescue was Ghostface—with bonus points for figuring out who killed *him*.'

'Wow.' Daisy looks impressed. 'Didn't see that coming—nice one, Ricky. Well, it would have been...'

I'm hardly listening because something doesn't add up here. 'Hang on, Ricky. Ghostface had already stabbed three other people—how come they weren't hurt?'

'That was Joe. I only played Ghostface at the end—my character was trying to pin Fortescue's murder on him, seeing as no one else knew who Ghostface really was.'

'Did you have separate "Ghostface-kits",' Daisy demands, and Ricky nods.

'His costume wouldn't have fitted me properly—and vice versa. We didn't want to make the solution *too* obvious.'

Daisy swallows. 'Listen Ricky, don't take this the wrong way—I'm sure the police have asked too—but did you have any motive for murdering Joe? Not saying you did. Just trying to get the full picture.'

For Daisy, that was quite tactful

'Absolutely not. Like I told Wilson, Joe was an employee and nothing more. Never saw him outside work and got on fine with the bloke. Anyway, I'm not convinced Joe *was* the real target. My own theory is it's somebody wanting to put me out of business.'

"Who?" is the obvious question—so I ask it.

'Deadly Dinners' he replies instantly.

'Who?' I sound like a parrot.

Ricky frowns. 'A rival murder-mystery company that hasn't been operating long. They'd just love to pick up all my contracts.'

'Did you tell Wilson?' Daisy asks.

'Yeah—hard to say how seriously he took it, though. But Ronnie Richards—he's the guy behind "Deadly Dinners"—is a bad lot. I don't know him personally, but if you believe the stories…'

'Stories?' Daisy echoes.

Now SHE's doing it

'… word is, Richards will stop at nothing to get what he wants. He's been done for GBH in the past—of business rivals. He was in a different line, then—had a catering service that went bust.'

Daisy looks thoughtful. 'Sounds a viable suspect. I'm sure Wilson…'

'I'm not,' Ricky breaks in. 'Wilson has a nice easy patsy lined up in me—why should he look further? Daisy, how would you feel about looking into this? On my dime. Find out if Richards *was* responsible for Joe's death.'

I lean forward. 'Ricky, you're jumping the gun. Give Wilson a chance to…'

He shakes his head and interrupts. 'No, I'm square in the frame for this. I mean, okay—I'm not denying it was me who stabbed Joe. I know it beggars belief, me not realising the knife was real, but honestly—I had no idea. C'mon, girls—I need your help.'

Daisy looks at me with raised eyebrows. I can see she's champing at the bit—might as well give in gracefully. 'Alright, no harm in taking a look. Come in tomorrow morning and we'll get the paperwork done...' I break off as Daisy whips a sheet of A4 from inside her jacket and slams it in front of Ricky.

'I just happen to have a contract handy. Sign on the dotted line Ricky, if you please... Oh, and may we use your stuff to put together our own murder mysteries in the meantime...?'

A COUPLE OF HOURS LATER, AFTER SUFFERING THROUGH our own grillings by Wilson, we're walking back to the cottage and I can finally ask her. 'Do you *always* carry a retainer agreement?'

'Course—pays to be prepared. Hey, wasn't that good of Ricky to say we could use Murder Meals' scripts and props until he gets on his feet again?'

'You made it plain we wouldn't take his case if he didn't.'

'I might have hinted...' her head snaps sideways '... what the dickens is that?'

We're almost at the hotel gates and I'm hearing the same thing. A weird moaning coming from somewhere to our left. Jerking round, I peer across the moonlit lawn and wonder "what now?". I don't know if my heart can stand any more excitement tonight. 'Look,' I say, pointing.

Daisy follows my finger to a far corner where three shadowy figures are... dancing? 'Okay,' I tell her, firmly. 'Let's go and fetch Wilson...'

Too late—she's off at a sprint. Leaving me with a difficult question—whether to hobble after her or head back to the hotel for reinforcements.

'Daisy, one of these days you'll be the death of me,' I mutter, stepping onto the lawn.

As I get closer the moaning changes to lilting howls, then metamorphoses into words I immediately recognise.

"For a charm of powerful trouble, like a hell-broth boil and bubble. Double, double toil and trouble; fire burn and caldron bubble."

That's from "Macbeth"

'Oi,' Daisy challenges, and the... witches? ... stop dead. Yes, they *look* like witches. Pointy hats and cloaks—definitely witches.

All three are middle-aged, with not a wart between them. In fact, they'd seem quite normal—if it weren't for their headgear and flapping capes. The tallest one glares. 'What?'

Daisy does a double-take. 'What d'you mean, "what?". That's *my* question—why are you out here playing at witches?'

The tall woman is obviously their leader. She struts right up to Daisy and tries to stare her down.

Good luck with that

'We are *not* playing—and *are* witches. From the Paisley coven, on our annual outing. As such we are obliged, this being Allhallows Eve, to perform certain rituals.'

Daisy cocks her head. 'Rituals? That was Macbeth you were quoting.'

'We were just warming up.'

I bend to Daisy's ear. 'They aren't doing any harm.'

'S'pose not,' she agrees. 'Right, you lot—em—behave yourselves, alright?'

One of the other two women, both of whom took several steps back during Daisy and Agatha's exchange, pipes up: 'Put a spell on them, Agatha.'

Agatha waves a long-taloned hand. 'Be quiet, Bertha. Anyway, they're going now.'

'C'mon.' I start walking, hoping Daisy will follow. She does—and giggles softly.

'Talk about loonies.'

I grab her arm and hustle Foghorn Freda along. 'Ssh, they'll hear you. Um, do you think we should go back and tell Wilson about them?'

'What for? They're just a bunch of weirdos. There again, if I thought they might Wilson into a frog...'

To my relief, we make it to the cottage without meeting any hobgoblins or vampires. 'Flip,' Daisy says. 'They were quick.'

We phoned for a Chinese before leaving, and the delivery van is here already. It reaches our front gate at the same moment we do, and the driver jumps out. He hands Daisy a plastic bag that smells heavenly. 'Wait a minute,' I call, stepping up to Daisy and rummaging under the cartons.

'Take these back with you,' I tell the driver, handing over two packets of complimentary chopsticks they persist in sending.

Poor man gives me a puzzled look, but does as he's told—perhaps seeing in my expression the sort of evening I've had.

'Sam,' Daisy wails. 'You're rotten. How will I ever learn to use them if you won't...?'

'Do it on your own time,' I mutter, opening the gate.

I just want my Chinese, a couple of drinks, then bed

5

The Chinese is delish, as usual, and with Daisy using a fork I don't have to worry about ducking airborne chopsticks. Afterwards, we leave the kitchen table littered with foil cartons and cardboard lids (for me to clear away before I make breakfast?), and retire to the living room with a bottle of red.

I had expected to head straight upstairs after we'd eaten, but feel too exhausted to sleep. What a crazy thing to say, yet it makes sense. My weary mind isn't up to processing the angsty thoughts flitting around it like clouds of angry mosquitoes—which leaves the little beggars free to keep me awake.

We both sink onto the couch with sighs of relief. Daisy expertly opens a bottle of Rioja (although screw-tops don't take *that* much skill) and passes me a glass. She pours her own, then turns back. 'What?'

'What d'you mean, "what?"'

'You've thought of something new to obsess on—I can tell. C'mon—out with it.'

She knows me too well

'The knife that killed Joe—do you think it was the same one somebody attacked *me* with?'

'Oh, not that again. Sam, that was only an actor—with a *plastic* knife.'

'You almost convinced me before—but knowing now there *was* a real knife, *and* someone was murdered with it, I may have had a lucky escape.'

'Rubbish. Nobody was trying to kill *you*, Sam. Why would they?'

I shrug. 'No idea, but… brr… it's just, my gut's telling me…'

'That's the Chinese food,' she breaks in, making us both laugh.

'How are we going to go about investigating Deadly Dinners for Ricky?' I wonder, pushing away thoughts of my brush with death for the moment—because I'm increasingly convinced that's what it was.

Daisy's gaze slips to the ceiling—a sure sign she's thinking. 'First off, we need a word with this Ronnie Richards guy.'

'Deadly Dinners' owner?' I confirm.

'Yeah, we'll see if he's got an alibi for tonight. Course, he could have hired somebody to do his dirty work...'

'Seems a bit unlikely to me—the whole concept of murdering an innocent bystander to put your rival out of business.'

'Effective, though. The entire cast's in shock—who knows how many will leave as a result? Not to mention Wilson could lock Ricky up at any moment. Plus, Murder-Meals can expect a bunch of cancellations when their other clients hear about this.'

'I thought you told Logan there was no such thing as bad publicity?'

'Yeah, so far as the public's concerned—but other hotel owners may not feel the same. Especially if they're anything like Logan,' she adds meaningfully.

'Which most of them are,' I admit. 'But I think Ricky's main concern is going down for a murder he didn't commit. We are *sure* he's innocent, aren't we?'

'Course we are...' she breaks off for a gulp of wine '... well, I only know him through the murder mystery evenings, but according to Ricky he had no motive and you can bet Wilson will check that out big style. Anyway, who would knowingly murder somebody in front of an audience?'

'Double bluff?' I suggest.

'Maybe theoretically a possibility, but surely there are better ways—like dark alleys? No—no way did Ricky know it was a real knife. Which brings us to another avenue worth looking down—how did that knife get into the snooker room, *AKA* the cast's dressing room? We need to make a list of everyone who had access, then try and plot their movements...'

'Um... what if it was a guest who planted the knife? Good luck plotting *their* movements.'

'Mm, that's a point. Okay, it looks like Dinner Death and Ronnie Richards are our best bet. First thing tomorrow.'

On which note, and by mutual consent, we slug back what's left of our drinks and head for the stairs.

Halfway up, Daisy chortles. 'Hey, what d'you make of the witches?'

'Harmless old biddy's, I reckon.'

'Yeah, you're probably right. I noticed them before the production started—they were still scoffing spider web cookies and eyeballs. What *were* the eyeballs made of, anyway?'

'Boiled eggs. He used edible dyes to ink in the details.'

'Yeeugh. Okay, see you in the morning.'

She vanishes into her room before I can clarify who's cooking breakfast. Wouldn't have been much point—why ask a question when you already know the answer?

DAISY DASHES STRAIGHT OUT AFTER WOLFING HER breakfast. She often does that, to avoid clearing up—which is supposed to be the job of whoever *doesn't* cook breakfast. 'Sorry, Sam. I want to get started gathering some gen on Ronnie Richards.'

Yeah, yeah... there's always an excuse

After scraping the plates, loading them in the dishwasher, tidying up (am I labouring the point?) I pop into the hotel to check how things are going. To my surprise, none of the guests have checked out prematurely. (The Halloween mystery was a two-night package.) Hazel tells me the police forensic team finished up early this morning—so on the surface at least, everything's back to normal.

Then Hazel inclines her head at the residents lounge, eyebrows raised. I hear him before I turn. 'Miss Chessington—I need to 'ave vords vith you.'

Louis

On second thoughts, I don't turn—not yet. 'Hazel,' I hiss urgently. 'On a scale of 1-10, how upset is he?'

'10,' she whispers.

No—not in the mood for this

Pretending not to notice Louis' increasingly urgent attempts to attract my attention, I crab sideways and dive into the stairwell. Already fumbling in my bag, I find the Last Chance Saloon's key and let myself in—locking the door behind me. We strictly restrict access from here into the main hotel, to protect our guests from the sometimes crass (if good-hearted) Cairncroft Cowboys. There's no reason for Louis to have a copy of the key I just used—so I'm betting he doesn't.

Letting myself out through the bar's public entrance, I reckon by the time Louis backtracks through his kitchen I'll be out of sight.

Especially if I go through the shrubbery.

I'D PLANNED ANYWAY TO CHECK IN WITH DAISY AT THE detective agency and see what progress she's making. My intention was to tie up a few routine loose ends at the hotel first, but there's nothing that can't wait.

Halfway there, I sense movement in the bushes ahead. For a moment, my heart stutters as I expect Ghostface to leap out with his knife held high. To my relief, it's only Agatha who emerges. 'Hi... what are you doing here?'

'Oh, it's you. From last night. Are you the manager?'

Smiling sweetly, I tell her: 'I'm the owner.'

'Ah.'

She looks taken aback but recovers quickly. 'Well, I trust you've no objection to my friends and I doing a little foraging.'

Somebody shouts from behind a patch of lupins: 'I've found some lovely wisteria.'

'None whatsoever,' I say in answer to Agatha's question. 'It's still a bit wild back here—our gardener has grand plans for it, but he's had other stuff keeping him busy. What are you looking for?'

'Ingredients for our spells,' Agatha tells me, straight-faced.

Daisy was right—nutty as a fruitcake

'So what sort of spell would you make from wisteria?'

She looks at me like a certain maths master used to. 'Love potions, of course.'

No offence dear, but I think you'd need more than that—magic mushrooms at a minimum

'Well, I hope you find plenty of... everything you're looking for,' I murmur, trying to sidle past her.

She blocks my way and fixes me with an intense stare. 'I see... energy all around you. Do you have the gift, my child?'

Gifts—with Davy as a boyfriend? I'm lucky if he remembers Christmas

'Um, no. Not that I know of.'

One of Agatha's companions emerges from the shrubbery. This one's short and round, and it was her voice sounding excited about finding wisteria. 'You again? What do you want now?'

Agatha flaps a hand, which makes her nails flash in the morning light. 'Hush, Gertha. I think this lady may have the fire in her blood.'

Gertha's eyes saucer and she regards me with new respect. I can't help myself. 'So... you're Agatha, Gertha, and... Bertha, if I remember correctly from last night? Are those your real names?' I finish on a note of disbelief.

Agatha looks faintly offended. 'Of course they are. Well, our craft names—which mean more to us than those inflicted at random by our unfortunately mortal parents.'

'So, the "tha"—is that something to do with your coven? Does *it* have a name that ends in "tha", too...?'

Gertha appears confused and Agatha shakes her head. 'They're simply traditional names, my dear.'

'Traditional *witch* names, you mean? Oh, I see—like Terry Pratchett's Gytha Ogg?'

'Is this "Terry Pratchett" a warlock?' Gertha asks innocently.

Agatha rounds on her. 'Don't show your ignorance, Gertha.'

She turns back to me. 'I'm going out on a limb here but, tell me, what is *your* name?'

'Um—Samantha.'

Nodding, Agatha says "figures" while Bertha squeals 'Saman*tha*—she *must* be one of us.'

Oh, cripes

'Listen, ladies—I have to go now.' So saying, I hobble past them at a speed that makes my left leg throb in protest.

Agatha's crackly voice races to catch up. 'We'll see you soon, dear. In fact, we're having a cookout during witching hour tonight—same place as before. Do come along—we can help you discover what power lurks within that mortal shell.'

6

Liz's shrieks bring Daisy and Rebecca out of the office. 'What's so funny?' Daisy asks.

Still giggling, Liz drags a sleeve over her eyes. Then points at me. 'Seems Sam's secretly a witch who hasn't come out of the closet yet.'

Daisy puts a hand on my shoulder. 'I wondered about that broomstick she keeps in the garage.'

Rebecca's jaw drops. 'Somebody said you were a *witch?*'

When I explain, Rebecca nods knowingly. 'Oh, I've seen *them* a few times. Graham chased them yesterday for trying to build a campfire.' She stoops to pick up Hector, her cat, who promptly swipes a paw at Daisy.

Daisy ducks back and returns Hector's snarl with one of her own. 'Do they need a cat?' she snaps.

Rebecca giggles and tickles under Hector's chin. 'How about that, Hector? Would you fancy being a witch's familiar?'

'I was thinking more they could boil it in their cauldron. Listen, Sam. I've located Ronnie Richards—he lives in Glasgow and his business premises are there too. Feel like a drive?'

'You bet,' I respond too quickly. Daisy stares at me, then the penny drops.

'Ah—right. You're planning to drop in on Davy while we're there.'

'Exactly—give me five minutes to find out where he'll be today, then I'm all yours.'

Rebecca coughs. 'Actually, it was *me* who found those addresses for Ronnie Richards.'

Daisy wrinkles her nose. (Which probably isn't smart when you wear a nose ring.) 'Yeah... but it was *me* who showed you how to work the database services.'

TWENTY MINUTES LATER, WE'RE HALFWAY TO ABERDEEN AND the M90 south. 'You *do* know this is a six-hour round trip? Interviewing this Richards bloke will use up a whole day.'

Daisy shrugs. 'He's our best lead.'

I blast the horn at a grouse who wisely decides crossing in front of me isn't such a good idea after all. 'If Richards *was* involved, I don't see him admitting to it.'

'Course he won't—but we need to hear his story. And whether he has an alibi—then verify it.'

'What if Richards hired somebody to kill Joe?'

'Sam, one step at a time—let's talk to him first. It's amazing what comes out when you ask the right questions. Hey, this is a stroke of luck for you—getting in a sly visit to lover boy. Did you manage to reach him on the phone?'

'Yep—I've to ring back when we finish with Richards and he'll meet us somewhere.'

'*You*, Sam… he'll meet *you* somewhere. I've no desire to play gooseberry, thank you very much.'

'Now I feel bad if it means leaving you hanging for an hour.'

'An *hour?* I was thinking more… Oh, never mind. I'll find something to amuse myself.' She winds down the window and sticks her head out.

'What are you doing?'

Daisy cranes around, stares at the sky, and her response is drowned by engine noise. When she finally finishes up whatever that was and closes her window, I repeat my question.

'There's a drone up there. Thought that was what I heard.'

'What's it doing?'

'Duh—flying? I don't know—maybe it's taking aerial photographs.'

'Out here?' I murmur, glancing around endless arrays of fields beyond stone dykes on both sides. 'Hardly postcard views.'

'Some sort of agricultural thing maybe...' Daisy starts to say before she's interrupted by a loud bang that makes us both jump.

'What was that?'

'Dunno.'

She turns to check through the rear window. 'Don't see anything, but it seemed to come from under the car.'

'It *felt* more as though a bit broke *off* the car,' I tell her, my pulse racing. If we get stuck out here, it means walking miles just to find a phone signal.

'Better pull over and take a look,' Daisy suggests. 'Before it overheats or something.'

She's right—so I tap the brakes.

And nothing happens.

'Sam—you drove straight past an ideal stopping place.'

'The brakes aren't working.'

I'm pumping the brake pedal, which anyway feels spongy, and it's having no effect whatsoever. I'm forced to take the next bend far too fast, making our tyres squeal as we slingshot around it. And, oh boy—now we're on a steep hill.

Going down.

'What about the handbrake?'

Of course. While some people call them a "parking brake", they aren't *only* for parking. Grabbing the lever, I jerk it up—and again, *nothing happens*. 'IT isn't working either.'

Grim-faced, Daisy reaches up to grip the grab handle over her door. 'You'll just have to keep us on the road until we get back on flat ground,' she mutters.

My gaze drifts to the speedometer—fifty, and climbing. 'We're in trouble if there are any steep bends,' I grate.

'Um. Hate to tell you, but...'

I see it too. At the bottom of this hill, the road turns at an acute angle. I'll never manage around that—we're going far too fast. And there's still a stone wall either side, cutting us off from the fields. If I could only get into one of them, it would be a simple case of turning the engine off and circling to let our momentum expend itself.

'Sam.'

Daisy points, her voice full of excitement. 'Look, see that gate down there? It's open.'

I follow her finger to a huge five-bar gate that's been opened all the way, presumably by the farmer driving his tractor around stacks of hay bales. Unfortunately, there's no chance of *turning* in there—not at this speed—but field gates are wide to allow for agricultural machinery and if I can angle us precisely enough, we might slip through at forty-five-degrees.

No time to think—we're almost on it. I heave at the steering wheel and hear Daisy swallow hard as the wall rushes towards us. Just when collision (and probable extinction) seems inevitable, the gap appears directly in front of us and Panda's nose plunges through. I *nearly* got it right—but a horrible scream of ripping metal tells me our back passenger side didn't quite make it. The impact sends us spinning across the field until a loud "whump" precedes the windscreen's disintegration into a shower of hailstones as we're both thrown forward against our seatbelts. Two rude-sounding "pops" later, we collide with twin airbags that don't feel any softer than the dashboard they burst from.

For long moments, I'm too stunned to figure out what stopped us. I blink as sparks dance in my vision and reflexively claw at the airbag, crumpling it sufficiently to see over.

'Oi.'

A florid face appears where my windscreen used to be. 'Best turn that engine off, lass—I smell petrol.'

THE FARMER'S YOUNGER THAN HIS STOCKY APPEARANCE AND ruddy complexion suggest. Turns out he's old Struthers' son. 'Ee, ye's were lucky, lasses. Yon could have been nasty.'

Looking at my battered Panda, I wonder where the "could" comes into it. The stone dyke left an ugly mass of scrapes and dents on my back nearside bodywork. Then one of Struthers' hay bales *sort* of cushioned the impact that finally brought us to a halt—but also caved in the front end of my poor car. Even if the damage is fixable, which doesn't look promising, could I ever again drive Panda with confidence after her brakes failing like that?

Daisy wanders around the car, humming and hawing. 'Think it's mainly bodywork,' she comments.

'What does that mean?' I snap, irritated—since she knows as much about cars as I do.

'Well... all the wheels stayed on...'

'Here,' the farmer says, thrusting a huge flask at us. 'That's some hot tea for while you're waiting. I'll go back to the farm and organise a breakdown truck.'

For a moment, I'm puzzled. Oh, of course—there's no phone signal out here. Daisy's quicker on the uptake. 'Cheers, mate,' she says, taking the flask.

Farmer Struthers nods, then strolls to the field entrance. He bends and scrutinises the stone dyke intently. Finally, he straightens, turns, and gives us a thumbs-up. 'S'allright, you haven't damaged my wall.'

Daisy looks at me in disbelief. 'Easy to see he's old Struther's son.'

After the tractor rolls away, Daisy demands: 'What happened?'

'The brakes failed.'

'Yeah, got that, but... why?'

'How should I know? It's not even due a service... right, hand that flask over.'

Farmer Struther's tea is boiling hot, but we're in no rush because it takes *two hours* for Ian from Donstable motors to arrive. 'You again?' he jokes. 'Getting to be regular customers, you pair are.'

Ian attended the wreckage of my last car when a woman (who was Daisy's prospective mother-in-law back then) rammed us off the road.

Daisy sure knows how to pick 'em

'What do you think?' I ask cautiously. 'Another write-off?'

Ian fingers his chin and walks around my Panda—a bit the same as Daisy did, except I have more confidence in Ian's assessment. 'Maybe—maybe not. Hard to say—need to see her up on the ramp.'

A part of me hopes it *is* a write-off—I don't want a car that can't be relied on for basic safety issues.

Like stopping, for example

'Any chance of a courtesy car this time?'

'You'd have to ask Roy.'

Roy? Oh, Arthur—the salesman we first met when he sold Daisy her motorbike. (And will forever in my mind be Arthur Daley.)

Today just gets better and better

'COURSE I CAN DO YOU A COURTESY CAR, MISS Chessington,' Arthur assures me after Ian brings us back to Donstable in the cab of his breakdown truck.

Arthur still has a trilby cocked on his head at the same jaunty angle, and that cigar he's never without doesn't smell any better.

'What do you fancy? Got a Fiesta going spare, or I think there's a nice Volkswagen knocking about somewhere if you'd like something bigger? Oh, no, wait—you need an automatic. Which, it just so happens, the Fiesta *is*.'

'A Fiesta sounds fine,' I say immediately. 'I actually prefer a smaller car.'

Ten minutes later, we're driving back to Cairncroft in a green Ford Fiesta and I'm already enjoying the way it handles. The steering is light as a feather and its accelerator responds to the slightest touch—the ideal compromise to a

Formula 1 for people who don't like high-powered cars.

The garage wouldn't commit themselves on Panda's chances—I'm still wrestling with what I want the verdict to be. I love my Panda—but if it's going to start this sort of nonsense, maybe I'd be better off without it. 'Nippy, isn't it?' I can't help saying.

Daisy sweeps her eyes around disparagingly. 'Thing probably only weighs a few pounds—*course* it's nippy. Why aren't you getting a *proper* hire car through your insurance, like last time?'

'Because Arthur could give me this straight away. Last time I spent hours arranging something with a big car hire company in Aberdeen, because my insurance wouldn't deal with Arthur...'

'I wonder why,' Daisy puts in.

'... so it's more convenient,' I finish flatly.

She pretends to look puzzled. 'I thought the "courtesy" in "courtesy car" meant you got it for free?'

'Arthur says it *is*—because he's only charging me depreciation and insurance.'

'Twenty quid a day? At that rate of depreciation, it'll need scrapping by Easter. And by the way, it's

"Roy"—not Arthur. Don't think he appreciated it when you slipped up and called him "Arthur". Twice.'

'Didn't, did he? But I reckoned, at twenty quid a day, I was entitled to call him whatever I wanted... so, have we given up on getting to Glasgow today?'

She nods. 'It's too late now and after what happened, who's in the mood? Well, I'm certainly not—what *did* happen, anyway?'

'Don't know—I assume some vital part of the braking system failed. Arthur looked a bit puzzled, though—so it isn't something he sees often.'

'Mm.'

Daisy looks thoughtful, then shakes her head. 'Let's wait and see what the mechanic says when he phones. Later today or tomorrow, wasn't it?'

'That's what Arthur said.'

As we pass the Cuppa Tea, I ask: 'Hotel or cottage?'

'Hotel. I need a word with Colin.'

'What about?'

'Our drinks order. What are you having? Just to speed things up when we get there.'

Something wet, long, and alcoholic—but before I can say that, Daisy's phone chirps. She holds it up to her ear and listens, presumably to a voicemail from our time out of signal on the way back from Donstable. Then groans. 'Oh, flip. They've arrested Ricky.'

'Hardly surprising—he did stab Joe.'

'Yeah, but... arrgh, that's Wilson all over. The man's got no imagination. Hasn't it penetrated his thick skull there's more to this?'

'He'd look a right Charlie if Ricky disappeared, though. I agree something's not kosher about it, and Wilson must see that too, but what else could he do?'

I pull into a space outside the main door and we get out with Daisy still huffing. At the residents bar, Colin watches us hoist ourselves onto adjacent stools. 'What are you having, ladies?'

'Pint, please,' Daisy says urgently. 'Oh, and a soda lime for Sam.'

She half-turns, hands rising defensively as I reach for her throat. 'Ricky wants us to go and see him. You can't drink *and* drive.'

7

On our way out, we meet Rebecca and Liz coming in. 'Who stole your sweetie?' Liz asks.

'Sorry, can't stop,' I explain. 'I'm off to get measured for my chauffeur's uniform.'

'Not fair,' Daisy chimes in. 'I offered to drive.'

'You only have a motorbike licence and I am *not* riding pillion on that two-wheeled death trap.'

'Hah. After this morning, *you* can talk.'

Rebecca's game attempt to follow all that put her in danger of pulling a neck muscle. 'What happened this morning?'

I tell her and both girls squeal. 'Oh, that's terrible,' Rebecca breathes. 'Do you think it was sabotage?'

'Sabotage?'

'You know—somebody trying to do away with you. Maybe it's one of the people we're investigating who's taken umbrage...'

Daisy blows out her cheeks. 'Apart from Ricky, all we've got on just now are cheating spouses. Who anyway aren't aware we're watching them...'

'Well, we don't think they are,' Rebecca puts in sagely.

'Rubbish,' Daisy dismisses, but suddenly I'm not so sure.

'Maybe she's onto something, Daisy. This is a big coincidence, after me getting attacked by Ghostface...'

Rebecca slaps her cheeks—it sounded sore. 'Ricky attacked *you*, too...?'

Daisy snorts. 'That wasn't Ricky and neither was it an attack. Sam's got it in her head that a roving ghoul last night was carrying a real knife, but you know what she's like...'

'Excuse me,' I begin, but Rebecca's already gabbling.

'There *was* a real knife—the one Ricky killed Joe with. Maybe Sam was the target all along. Then, when he struck out with Sam, the killer went back to Murder Meal's dressing room, got out of costume, and left the knife lying—where Ricky picked it up. Thinking it was a prop.'

I turn to Daisy, who's glaring at Rebecca. 'That fits. It explains everything.'

'No, it doesn't,' Daisy says, but without her previous conviction. 'Because who would want to kill Sam?'

Liz has been standing quietly, listening. 'Is life always this exciting around here?'

Daisy's right—there's absolutely no way anyone is out to murder me. Try as I might, nobody with that sort of grudge comes to mind. And yet—like I said, it *does* fit.

WE LEAVE THE GIRLS TO IT (I THINK THEY'RE HOPING TO TALK Louis into rustling them up a snack—and might have more luck if I'm not around) and make our way out to the "courtesy" car. 'Will Wilson let us see Ricky?'

Daisy shakes her head. 'Not a chance—but I texted Jodie, who says greetin' face is out for a couple of hours and left her in charge. Happily, *she* doesn't think there's any harm in us speaking to Ricky.'

The trip to Donstable passes in near silence. I'm still thinking about Rebecca's off-the-wall theory—and have a feeling Daisy is, too.

Either the usual desk sergeant has changed his sex since our last visit, or he's on a day off. The policewoman who greets us is polite—pleasant even—which raises grave doubts regarding her professional future. 'Sure thing. I'll give Jodie a buzz and she'll be right down. Do you want to take a wee seat?'

Disappointingly, the chairs aren't due any holiday days. The wood must be specially imported—normal chairs are nowhere near this hard. Happily, it's only a minute or so before the inner door swings open and Jodie pokes her head out. 'In you come,' she calls—so we do. But instead of leading us to the cells, Jodie takes a deep breath. 'Look, I'm sorry guys, you can't see Ricky—it's out of my hands.'

Daisy squares up to her. 'But you said...'

'Wilson phoned just five minutes ago. His exact words were: "Don't let those loonies from the Cairncroft Detective Agency talk to my prisoner".'

'How did he find out...?' I start, but Jodie holds up a hand.

'I certainly didn't tell him—actually, I doubt he *knew,* per se. But you two...' she nods at Daisy '... especially *her,* are never far from Wilson's mind when you're involved with one of his cases.'

Daisy relaxes her posture into something less threatening. 'What he doesn't know won't hurt him.'

'Uh-uh. Absolutely not—there are no secrets in a police station. Agreed, he's being an... silly about this... but it's more than my job's worth to go against an imperial command.'

I pull Daisy away from an increasingly flustered Jodie. 'That's okay. We're grateful you tried—c'mon, Daisy. *C'mon*...'

Reluctantly, she allows me to drag her through the door as Jodie opens it. The desk sergeant calls "bye," cheerfully, then recoils at Daisy's answering expression. Once we're in the car park, I let go of Little Miss Angry.

'It's not fair,' Daisy bleats. 'Wilson's an...'

Holding up a hand, I advise: 'Don't say it—that's how people got arrested in Nazi Germany and the same rules probably apply in Wilson's nick. Anyway, what does it matter? Ricky's told us everything he could.'

'You're missing the point, Sam,' she hisses. 'Ricky said in his message he wanted us to come and see him—so he must have remembered something.'

'We should have got Jodie to ask him, then she could have passed it on,' I muse, and Daisy looks at me disbelievingly.

'You're right,' she says. (I wasn't impressed by the surprise in her tone.)

She gives herself a shake. 'But I'd still rather we heard it for ourselves—with the opportunity to question Ricky about whatever it is.'

Then her head snaps sideways. 'Look.'

A blue Polo is reversing into the space next to my (borrowed) Fiesta. When the driver's door swings open, Kat gets out. Daisy opens her mouth wide and yells: 'KAT!'

Kat is a very grounded and terribly confident lass, so it's surprising (disturbing, even) to see her jump nearly a foot into the air. She lands in a defensive crouch.

'It's just me,' Daisy expands amiably, ambling over.

Kat breathes out. 'I might have known—the human megaphone.'

Showing no regard for the poor girl's personal space, Daisy asks the tip of Kat's nose: 'What are *you* here for?'

'Why?'

'Look, I already know Mr M's representing Ricky Malvern. Is it him you've come to see?'

Kat nods warily as she steps backwards. 'Yes, as it happens. Dad asked me to go over a few things with Ricky.'

'Great. Can I tag along?'

'No.'

'Why not?'

'Because a solicitor's meetings with her clients are confidential.'

'S'okay, he's our client too. You could tell the flatfoots I'm your assistant.'

Pursing her lips, Kat makes a show of looking Daisy up and down. 'I assume you've just been turned away. Somehow, I can't see them believing that between then and now you've magically transformed into my assistant. They aren't stupid, Daisy.'

With a flourish, Daisy produces a Covid face-mask and puts it on. 'There, that better?'

Kat looks at me and we both giggle. 'What?' Daisy demands.

'Two things,' Kat tells her. 'First—that skunk-streak across the top of your head's pretty distinctive. Also, you've got a certain... overall presence... that wearing a mask does nothing to hide.'

With a sigh, Daisy rips off the face-mask. 'You're right,' she grumbles. 'Give me your coat.'

Kat jerks back. 'What... no. It's freezing today. Anyway, my coat's far too big for you.'

'It's not *for* me—if Sam wears the mask and your coat, they won't recognise *her*. *She* hasn't got a presence—or a skunk-streak. Afterwards, she can tell me what Ricky said.'

Still smarting from her "no-presence" remark, I glare at Daisy. 'No way am I doing that.'

Daisy nods at Kat. 'Give her your coat.'

Kat shakes her head firmly. 'Not a chance.'

BACK IN DONSTABLE POLICE STATION'S WAITING AREA, KAT squirms on the chair alongside mine—she's probably worried about getting haemorrhoids. (Well, they say sitting on rocks can cause them, plus I've got her coat.) She turns her head and hisses: 'How does she do that?'

I shrug. 'No idea, but somehow Daisy always gets her way.'

The desk sergeant rang through and told them Ricky's solicitor is here. Now we're waiting for someone to come and fetch us. I'm wearing a face-mask, am drowning in Kat's bearskin-like coat, and Daisy also insisted on gathering my hair at the back in a rubber band. Having a "not exactly long" style, it feels as though my ears are edging closer together every minute. I nudge Kat. 'What if it's Jodie who comes? She'll recognise me straightaway.'

'No, Jodie's too senior. It'll be somebody with nothing better to do.'

Then the connecting door opens and Wilson's estranged "Stepford sergeant" steps through. His eyes linger on me and I can almost hear him thinking: "Where do I know her from?" But he's too dim-witted (or too lazy) to follow up on the thought, and leads us along several corridors until we're outside a row of steel doors. After sliding its metal cover aside and peering through a little square window, thus ensuring Ricky has neither hung himself nor is lying in wait, Wilson's former sidekick unlocks the door with a key so big it wouldn't look out of place on Hagrid's belt.

Ricky's eyes fasten on me and he does a double-take, then opens his mouth to speak. Kat gets in first. 'I'm Ms Dougall from Dougall and MacLachlan and this is my assistant... um... Mildred?'

Mildred? Oh, thanks very much, Kat

'I'll leave you to it,' Wilson's former sidekick mutters. Which, thankfully, he does.

Ricky points at me. 'What's all this about, then?'

'They wouldn't let Daisy and me in,' I explain. 'So Kat kindly agreed I could accompany her to find out what you've got for us. Daisy said it sounded important.'

Ricky squints, then shakes his head. 'Um... no, I haven't come up with anything new. This was more about hearing how *you're* getting on with proving my innocence.'

I stare at him. 'You moron. Do you know how much trouble we went to—to hear that? Not to mention the wasted time...'

'Hey, it's driving me crazy being shut in here. I was hoping you'd have made some progress by now.'

'Well, we haven't. The only lead you've given us is Ronnie Richards—Daisy and I are going to see him tomorrow.'

'Why not today?' Ricky demands?

'We were,' I blurt. 'Except… oh, long story. Look, are you sure there's nothing else? We could use some help here.'

He shakes his head again.

'Didn't notice anybody wandering around who had no right to be?' I prompt.

'Sam, it's a hotel full of guests. How do I know who should and shouldn't be there?'

He's got a point. But what if we narrow the parameters down…? 'Okay, but *only* Murder-Meals personnel should have been in the snooker room—um, dressing room. Which is where you picked up the knife. Think hard, Ricky—did you see anyone *in there* who shouldn't have been?'

He looks thoughtful all of a sudden. 'I went into the dressing room a little before seven and some blonde lass was hanging up a Ghostface gown—she'd obviously just taken it off. So presumably one of the "wandering ghouls" but… she didn't look like anybody I know.'

'Great. Now concentrate, Ricky—I need a description.'

'I only ever saw the back of her head. She turned away as I passed, then left straightaway.'

'Details, please. Height? What was she wearing?'

He screws his eyes tightly closed. 'She was about your height, but shorter. Had on a sweater and jeans. Oh, and a beanie.'

Kat's eyebrows soar and she can't restrain herself. '"About your height but shorter"? Are you kidding? How *much* shorter?'

Ricky squeezes his temples. 'Taller than Daisy, but shorter than Sam. Somewhere in between.'

'Didn't you challenge her?' I ask.

'C'mon, Sam—a lot of our players are students, and they change all the time. Sorry—her not being familiar means nothing.'

I breathe out in exasperation. 'Give it some thought, Ricky—this could be important. If you remember any more about her—the *colour* of her sweater, for example—tell Kat or Mr M and they'll pass it on.'

He nods glumly. 'I wasn't taking a lot of notice.'

'Oh, one more thing.'

I said it casually, but Daisy would kill me if I forgot to ask. (Luckily, I remembered in the nick of time.) 'Where was the knife you used on Mr Fortescue? Like, was it lying out by itself...'

'No, there was a big box of them. We had lots of Ghostface's on the prowl, remember. I just grabbed one out of the box. Why?'

'Because it implies Mr Fortescue—Joe—wasn't the target, and it was simply bad luck you picked out the wrong knife.'

AND adds weight to the theory that I WAS attacked—and what Ricky saw was my assailant dumping (her?) weapon

'Right.' Kat slams her briefcase on the bed and announces: 'Lawyer time. Sam, this *is* confidential—do me a favour and stick a finger in both ears, would you?'

8

'The man's an idiot,' Daisy fumes. 'All that palaver for him to tell us he's got nothing new?'

We're standing in the car park behind Donstable police station. I take a quick look around—but no one else is within earshot. Kat clears her throat. 'This blonde bimbo sounds interesting.'

Daisy shakes her head. 'And he didn't think to bring that up himself?'

She breathes heavily for a moment. 'But, yes—it is. Interesting. Especially since the way he tells it suggests she tried to keep her face hidden.'

I shrug. 'It isn't really a lot of help. He can't even remember the colour of her clothes.'

'Still—doesn't sound like any of the Murder-Meals mob. Don't recall any of them being blonde. So, who was this woman? And why was she wearing a Ghostface outfit?'

Which is when I fill Kat in on my own fright last night. 'I think it's safe to say Ricky's mysterious blonde was the Ghostface who attacked me. Which adds weight to my observation she was carrying a real knife.'

Daisy's jaw drops. 'Yeah... sorry, Sam. Maybe I should have given more credit to what you said.'

'Maybe you should,' I growl, nonetheless feeling extremely smug.

Kat coughs. 'Anyway—it's becoming plain that poor Joe's death was an unfortunate accident.'

I explain to Daisy what Ricky said about taking the knife from a box full of them and she nods at the Fiesta. 'Let's go back to the hotel—see if anyone else saw her.'

'Keep me in the loop,' Kat calls. 'Corroboration that this girl was there might help get Ricky released on bail.'

We discuss this fresh development on the way to Cairncroft, but neither of us has a scooby who the blonde woman could be. At the hotel, we're disheartened to discover nobody else on our staff saw her. We retire to my "office"—a cubby-hole entered from the residents lounge and comprising some partitioned-off space in the snooker room—with two Americanos. 'Not looking hopeful for Kat's "corroboration",' I comment.

'So, what do we think? Blondie sneaked in, suited up, went out on the prowl, then came back to dump her costume? Sam, I hate to say this, but it does look like you were the target.'

A shiver runs through me. 'But why? Who'd want to kill *me*?'

Daisy spreads her palms. 'No idea. But we need to find out, and quick—before she tries again.'

I feel the blood drain from my face. 'Could Panda's brakes failing have had anything to do with her?'

Daisy looks at her feet. 'Maybe. Sam, until we sort this out, don't go anywhere by yourself. And stay alert.' She stands, reaching for her coffee.

'Where are you going?'

'Back to the detective agency. I'll track down the Murder-Meals cast by phone—see if any of them saw Blondie. Meanwhile, give some thought to who might have it in for you.'

She steps through the door and I hear her say: 'Oh. Hello, ladies.'

Following my nose, I find her chatting to the witches' coven. Of course—*they* were out and about last night.

Agatha listens solemnly when Daisy asks, then nods. 'Yes, we saw her. We were scoping out the front lawns for a suitable location to harness the power of Allhallows Eve—standing in the same place we met you later.'

'What time did you see her?' Daisy asks excitedly.

'Um...' Agatha looks at Bertha and Gertha. 'Do either of you have any idea?'

Bertha raises her hand. 'Just after seven—I remember looking at my watch and thinking it was only half an hour until we missed Coronation Street.'

'That must have been her.' I feel my heart thump. 'What can you tell us about her?'

'Well...' Agatha strokes her chin. 'Let's see. She came out the main door, walked down the drive, and left through the gates.'

Daisy leans in, right up to Agatha's face. 'What – did – she – look - like?' She enunciates each word, the way some people do when talking to foreigners with a poor grasp of English.

'She was blonde...'

'We *know* that. *I* told *you* that.'

'Yes, but I thought you'd appreciate having it confirmed. I do remember she was wearing a woollen hat. Let me see—what else? Jeans, a heavy sweater—think it was navy—and trainers.

Oh, and glasses—with thick, plastic frames. She was in her twenties, I'd say—very pretty girl.'

Daisy looks at me. 'Now we're getting somewhere. Any distinguishing features? Fat—thin—did she limp?'

Agatha shakes her head. 'She wasn't fat, or thin—had a really nice figure, as it happens. But there was nothing out of the ordinary about her—other than a troubling aura.'

'*Aura?*'

'Yes, very angry it was. Too many colours—and all the wrong ones.'

'Okay. Going back to her *corporeal* form—if I get a sketch artist in, will you work with him? Try and build up a picture of her face?'

Agatha looks at the other two in turn. 'Between the three of us, I should think we'd manage,' she says, her eyes betraying a gleam of excitement. 'But we go home tomorrow.'

'Where's home?' I ask, then remember. 'Wait a minute, you said. Paisley, yes?'

They all nod and Daisy asks: 'What time are you leaving?'

'After lunch.'

'Okay—could you come by the detective agency tomorrow morning at nine? I'll arrange to have an artist waiting.'

Agatha says they will and Daisy skips off looking happier than she did. As I turn to go back into my office, Agatha calls over. 'I have something for you, dear.'

She presses a small glass bottle into my hand. 'What's this?'

Agatha peers into my eyes and I'm shaken by the intensity of her scrutiny. 'You have difficulties in your love life, is that not so? A man is mucking you about?'

How could she know that?

But I say nothing and instead stare mutely. She smiles. 'If you would only allow the self within to emerge—you could concoct your own love potion. But since that hidden incarnation is yet to manifest, I took the liberty of mixing one for you. Just pour it into something he's drinking and you will have no further problems with this man.'

'Ah… wisteria,' I say weakly.

'That—and other things,' Agatha murmurs ominously. 'Now—I hope to see you at midnight.'

'Midnight? Oh, the... cookout? Em... sorry, don't think I can make it. Maybe catch you tomorrow, though, at the detective agency?'

All three "tut" in unison. 'Very well,' Agatha concedes. 'But if you have a change of heart—tonight would be an excellent time to draw out your inner witch. Allhallows' energy is the ideal medium with which to initiate rebirth...'

Daisy doesn't reappear that afternoon and I get caught up in the inevitable mini-crises that form a routine part of every hotel's day.

A little after six o'clock, I arrive back at the cottage—and ten minutes later, Daisy walks in. Having had a liquid lunch (non-alcoholic, in my case), we decide to order pizza. 'After a drink,' Daisy says, and having waited six hours for mine I'm quick to agree.

Daisy makes my usual and isn't shy with the vodka. 'There you go—and well done today, by the way. Nice piece of driving.'

'Thanks.'

I take a big sip and feel myself relax for the first time since my brakes failed. 'Did you track down the other cast members?'

'Yeah, most of them, but nothing came of it. None of them saw Blondie. Rebecca's going to chase down the rest tomorrow.'

'I didn't know we had a sketch artist on call.' I've been puzzling over that all afternoon.

Daisy grins. 'Wilf does it.'

'Wilf? He's an artist?'

'Naw—guy can't draw a straight line to save himself. Wilf's a computer whiz, though, and has this app—same one the police use. He works through a checklist of questions with the witness, then inputs their answers to his computer and the program comes up with a likeness. Then he shows them it and makes adjustments according to what they say isn't right.'

There's obviously more to Wilf than meets the eye

'Okay... oh, wait till you hear this.' I tell her about the love potion Agatha gave me, and Daisy chuckles.

'Do you think it'll work?'

'Of course it wouldn't—and I certainly *won't* be Mickey-Finning Davy with it.'

'Let's have a look.'

She holds the bottle up and scrutinises it. 'Looks like water.'

'Doubt it's any more effective.'

'You never know. There are loads of old remedies gaining credibility these days. Maybe Agatha's onto something. If it was me... I'd give it a shot.'

'Don't be ridiculous,' I snap, snatching the bottle back and slamming it down on the coffee table. 'Anyway, that's not an issue—we already *love* each other. The problem's his stupid job.'

'But if Davy loved you *more,* he wouldn't let the job come between you...'

I know when she's winding me up and answer by tossing the pizza menu at her.

'Alright... just saying. You up for Glasgow tomorrow—confident enough driving the Fiesta?'

'Sure, but I thought that'd be off? Now we've established this blonde girl's the likeliest culprit.'

'Blondie might still turn out to be someone with a perfectly reasonable excuse for being there. Or maybe this Richards character *sent* her. I know what you're going to say—the knife that killed Joe was in a box full of harmless props, so nobody could bank on Ricky pulling out the real one. But what if Blondie panicked and decided to play the odds? "Worth a try" sort of thing. If she'd run out of options, there was nothing to lose—and everything to gain.'

'Kinda high odds when you add in what Wilson said about how it was just bad luck Ricky's knife thrust was lethal?'

'Wouldn't have mattered if it hadn't been, though—not if the objective was to damage Murder Meals' reputation. Any old flesh wound would have done.'

'Okay. It could have happened that way.'

But I'm still sceptical

'Of course it could—I doubt Richards or his cronies are master criminals. *If* he's involved, an amateurish stunt like this makes sense. Hey, going to Glasgow means you can meet up with lover boy. Better remember to take your potion.'

Grabbing back the menu, I scan it while muttering: 'Right, what do I want on my margherita… oh, bother. They don't *do* wisteria.'

9

I hate driving in Glasgow.

Granted, London's worse—I discovered that way back while visiting the capital to play in a tennis tournament. Not Wimbledon, unfortunately, although I *did* qualify for the "All England" a year later—but life intervened before my first match.

The Weegies give Londoners a run for their money, though.

It isn't just other motorists—pre-school children flinging paint around could have made a better job of designing Glasgow's road system. Doesn't matter where you try to go, it inevitably involves a circuitous route through one-way systems twistier than the paths in Hazlehead maze.

'Why don't you get a satnav?' Daisy suggests helpfully.

'It isn't my car,' I reply through gritted teeth.

'Yeah, but—you didn't have satnav in the Panda, either.'

'I don't *need* a satnav to drive around Cairncroft and Donstable—or even Aberdeen.'

'Mm… but if Davy sticks with his new job, you'll be coming to Glasgow regularly—might even end up living here.'

'That's what trains and buses are for.'

And anyway, if he does, then I'm not sure there's a future for us. I *couldn't* move here—Edinburgh was bad enough, but at least it's laid out logically. Glasgow's one endless trudge through a sprawling jungle of urban nightmare.

But I don't intend to get into my "Davy problem" with Daisy—not at this precise moment. 'I thought you'd want to be there while they're doing the identikit picture.'

She shakes her head. 'Honestly, I'm having my doubts about whether Blondie *was* involved. She doesn't exactly sound like a hired killer—it's more likely one of Ricky's regulars took sick and got her to fill in without telling him. His people love Ricky's laid-back attitude—so long as the show goes on, he's the sort of boss who isn't interested in details.'

'So where'd the knife come from?'

'Maybe Richards sent somebody else we don't know about yet, and *they* planted it.'

'Sorry, but I still can't see it—one of Ricky's competitors framing him for murder.'

She snorts. 'Granted, it's a bit out of the box—but I checked up on what Ricky told us, and this Richards guy's arrest sheet is longer than "War and Peace". Ronnie's favourite business tactic is putting the opposition in hospital—and anyone else who gets in his way.'

A shiver runs through me. 'I hope he isn't another Dougie Dobson—or Jack the sack.'

I still have nightmares about the man who came close to killing us—in a horrific manner—only a few months back. Before him, it was Jack the Sack...

'In fact,' I add, 'It's time we started avoiding gangster-types altogether. Otherwise, our luck's due to run out...'

'Don't fret,' she snaps, looking annoyed. 'Dobson and Jack were the exceptions that prove the rule—Richards won't come after us, even if we do find evidence to hang Joe's murder on him.'

'*Dobson* did—for precisely that reason,' I point out.

'Yeah, but... look at Wilson. Incompetent as the man is, he's put loads of villains away and you don't see *them* queuing outside his nick to duff him up.'

'That's completely different...' I start to say. She interrupts, pointing to a lamppost and the nameplate screwed to it. 'Forest Street—isn't that ours?'

It is. We're now on the other side of Glasgow, in an area dominated by industrial estates. I turn onto Forest Street and follow a sign that says (inaccurately) "*Central* Business Park" before stopping by a giant map mounted at the roadside. Having found "Unit 8" on it *and* worked out how to get there, I move off again. 'Isn't this a strange place to house what's in essence a theatrical company?'

'Not really. They want cheap premises with plenty of space for the actors to rehearse—so it ticks all the boxes. You've never been to Ricky's HQ, have you?'

I shake my head. She dealt with all that.

'He's based in a converted barn out in the middle of nowhere. It's so isolated, Ricky sends the minibus to bring his people in for rehearsals. Look, there it is...'

"It" is a four-foot number "8", resplendent in purple paint. Either we've arrived, or the local graffiti artists have a strange sense of humour. Pulling up at the kerb right outside, I hope that's alright. There's nothing to say I shouldn't, but it somehow feels cheeky.

'You worry too much,' Daisy belittles my concern.

She jumps out of the car and I follow her across an extra-wide stretch of pavement to a wooden door which has seen better days. It opens into a small anteroom staffed by a woman in her twenties—who looks more dilapidated than the door did. She's lounging behind a chrome and glass desk—and going by the cosmetics case lying open in front of her, bored senseless.

'Yes—help you?'

Daisy flashes her bus pass and gets away with it because the receptionist doesn't even look up. 'Cairncroft Detective Agency—we're here to talk with Ronnie Richards.'

'You haven't got an appointment.'

'Don't need one.'

'That's what you think. I can tell you now, he won't see you today.'

'Why not?'

Having exhausted her welcoming skills, Miss PR lifts an emery board and starts shaping her nails.

Realising we're still here, she grudgingly informs us: 'He's busy.'

Daisy lunges at the desk and smacks her hands on its glass top. 'I don't care if he's having heart surgery—let him know we're here.'

'He's auditioning,' she says, without looking up from her manicure. 'More than my job's worth to interrupt Ronnie when he's auditioning.'

Daisy stares at her for a long moment, then her eyes twinkle. 'Alright, sorry to have bothered you,' she trills, and leads me outside. I'm not surprised when, instead of making for the car, Daisy turns left and takes off at a fast pace. I lose sight of her as she rounds a corner, then catch up halfway down the side alley. 'We'll go around back,' Daisy explains over her shoulder. 'Try and sneak in.'

'But he's *auditioning*,' I parrot, unable to keep a straight face.

'Yeah—exactly. It's given me an idea—you can get a lot more out of somebody when they don't know you're doing it.'

I HAVE GRAVE MISGIVINGS ABOUT THIS PLAN—WHATEVER IT is—considering Richards' reputation, but there's no arguing with Daisy when she sets her mind to something.

When we emerge at the building's rear, it's immediately apparent this is where the business park's inadequate signage *should* have brought us. The tarmacked yard contains loads of marked-out parking spaces, one of which is occupied by a minibus which is currently disgorging men and women of various ages, shapes, and fashion sense. Worryingly, they all have a similar blank expression to the helpful lady around front.

Daisy approaches a lad with geeky specs that dwarf his face and whose nose ring is at least twice the size of hers. 'What's this all about, then?'

Rather than asking who she is, or why she wants to know, he simply mutters: 'Auditions.' And keeps walking.

Daisy scratches her head. 'Bet this is Richards taking on more staff for the Murder-Meals contracts he intends hoovering up from Ricky. C'mon, Sam...'

She tags on to a crocodile that's formed to file through the back entrance. Makes me think of school, after playtime.

Inside, we find ourselves in a large space which is empty but for a line of rickety camping chairs along one wall. A man slightly older than us with what *has* to be permed hair stands at an inner door, waving a clipboard around and waiting for everyone to sit down. In a whispered aside, Daisy christens him "Curly" while he clears his throat. 'All right, couple of questions. If selected, can you start straight away?'

Every hand goes up, even mine—after Daisy's elbow lands in my ribs.

'Anyone got experience working in hotel murder mysteries.'

This time only two hands go up. My ribs can't take much more of this.

Curly points at us. 'We'll have you pair first, then.'

He marches off and we scurry after him, ignoring death glares from the other hopefuls. At the end of a corridor, we follow Curly into an office dominated by a massive hexagonal glass and chrome table that vaguely reminds me of the Tardis' control panel. Curly waves us towards two tubular chairs which sway alarmingly when we sit down opposite a rough-looking individual sporting a face that never recovered from a bad case of teenage acne and who has an obvious obsession with denim. Closing the door on his way out, Curly leaves us alone with—I'm guessing—Ronnie Richards. Especially since *he*'s sitting in an executive-style wheelie chair with padded armrests.

'I'm Ronnie Richards,' he confirms, tapping a pen on the table while craning forward to inspect us. 'So you've got experience, huh? Which hotel—or hotels? And who with?'

He's looking at me but before I melt into a puddle on the floor Daisy changes position, narrowly avoids falling off her chair, then crosses a leg over its fellow and tells him nonchalantly: 'Cairncroft—with Murder-Meals.'

Richards throws his head back and howls with laughter. 'Oh, bad luck. Poor old Ricky—I'm hearing he injected a tad too much realism into Monday night's performance. And the silly sod's got no chance of anybody believing that stupid story about not knowing the knife was real.'

'You reckoning to mop up all his contracts, then? Now he's out of the way.'

Richards nods. 'Yep. Matter of fact, had that hotel in Cairncroft on the phone this morning begging me to take over their gigs.'

I can't help myself. 'Who'd you speak to?'

Richards glances at me curiously. 'The one-legged lassie that owns it. Know them well, do you?'

Daisy delivers a warning tap to my knee and holds up a hand with her index and middle fingers intertwined. 'Like that, we are. With Sam *and* Logan—her co-owner.'

'Are you now?' Richards murmurs, and it's nauseatingly obvious his salivary glands are working themselves into a frenzy. 'Actually, I'm remembering wrong—it was another hotel with a similar name I was meaning. Which puts us in a position to help each other out, eh? If I give you jobs—you could put in a good word with the Cairncroft management.'

I really *really* want to ask more about the "similarly named hotel" with its "one-legged owner". But Daisy will kill me if I blow our cover.

Richards' eyes widen as a new thought strikes him. 'Were you there? On Monday night?'

'Yep,' Daisy confirms smugly. 'Saw it happen.'

'You *saw* that actor being stabbed—by Ricky?'

She shakes her head. 'Naw, the police put that story out—they always fuzz up any important details. It's so they can weed out false confessions, or trip people up in the interview room. The guy who died was actually *shot*.'

Now Richards looks baffled. 'Shot? But I thought Ricky was playing Ghostface—Ghostface doesn't use a gun.'

Daisy leans forward and unconsciously Richards does the same. 'It was the other actor—the one Ghostface was about to stab—who had the gun. The script has him pull a gun and make Ghostface drop his knife—but then Ghostface jumps him, takes away his gun, and shoots him.'

A frown appears on Richards' troll-like face. 'That isn't so straightforward as Ricky stabbing him. Ricky not realising the gun was real—is *much* more believable. Oh heck, d'you think he might walk on this?'

Daisy nods happily. 'Probably—in fact, almost definitely. As you say, how was he to know somebody had switched the prop for a real gun?'

I start when Richards' fist crashes into the table, and my springy tubular chair nearly catapults me onto it. 'I've doubled my staff on the back of this—given the new folk contracts—and you're telling me Ricky will probably get off? This is going to cost me a fortune.'

Daisy stands and I follow suit. She shrugs. 'Sorry to be the bearer of bad news—guess you won't be needing us after all?'

Richards shakes his head, lips working silently as he calculates how much money he's about to lose. Then jerks upright. 'Why'd you bother coming today—if your jobs are safe?'

'Murder-Meals will still be out of action for a few weeks. We were hoping for some temporary work to fill the gap.'

'Look somewhere else. I'm fully staffed—oh, and tell that mob out there to go home.'

Soon as Daisy closes the door behind us, I round on her. 'You're a sneaky besom—know that?'

She beams. 'Yeah—gets results, though. Let's find Curly—think sending the other hopefuls away would come better from him.'

BACK IN THE CAR, DAISY STOPS SNIGGERING LONG ENOUGH to say: 'Right—so Richards is out of the frame. He didn't even know what the murder weapon was.'

Then her face sobers. 'Why am I laughing? He was our prime suspect.'

'Still got Blondie,' I remind her.

She scowls. 'S'pose. What a waste of time *this* was, though.'

'It wasn't,' I placate. 'Eliminating a suspect is equally important to incriminating one—and I seem to remember it was *you* who told me that.'

'You're learning,' she mutters grudgingly. 'Right, get on the phone to Davy and arrange to meet up in a coffee bar. Promise I'll make myself scarce after a quick double-shot—oh, and a sanny, of course.'

10

Davy can't get free for an hour, which is just as well because finding the centre of Glasgow again takes thirty minutes—I'm sure somebody moved it while we were in with Richards—plus another ten to locate parking. From the multi-storey we end up in, it's only a five-minute walk to the Cowcaddens café Davy and I agreed to meet in. That leaves fifteen minutes to feed Daisy in return for making herself scarce when Davy arrives.

Perfect timing

Davy walks in as Daisy swallows her last bite of chocolate biscuit and adds the wrapper to a pile of empty sandwich packets. She immediately jumps up, declaring her intention to fetch my fiancé a drink—uncommonly tactful I can't help thinking, but it allows Davy and I to "say hello" properly.

I'm a little worried about losing some of our precious hour if Daisy succumbs to the temptation of "just one more" at the counter, but my fears prove unfounded. She slams Davy's latte in front of him and wiggles her fingers at me. 'See you back at the car in an hour—*don't* be late.'

'I won't,' I shout after her as the café door crashes shut.

Davy laughs. 'Daisy never changes, does she?'

'No danger of that. Listen, I'm glad of a chance to talk. I've been worried about you after that last phone call. These "teething problems" at work seem to be getting out of hand.'

He huffs. 'Tell me about it. They sent me out to another site yesterday and yet again I was out of my depth.'

'Why does that keep happening?' I demand and he blushes.

'Um… think I know, but you won't like it.'

Surely Daisy wasn't right? 'Does this have something to do with Leslie?'

The answer's written all over his face. 'I didn't want to say anything without being sure, but after confronting her on Sunday…'

'You were at work on Sunday?'

He goes bright red. 'No, I… uh… took Leslie out for a drink, just so we could have a private chat. Rather delicate, asking someone if they talked you up for a job because of... um... some kind of misguided crush...'

Okay. See that. I think...

'So what did you find out?'

He takes a long sip of coffee and peers over his paper cup. 'Is your coffee alright? Mine's got a funny aftertaste.'

'Stop stalling,' I snap.

He exhales heavily. 'Leslie admitted to overstating my qualifications. Being in human resources, it was easy for her to...'

'Why would she do that?' I interrupt. Of course, I know damn well—but want to hear him say it.

'Look, you were right all along—she *does* have a thing for me. And before you ask, it *isn't* reciprocated. Especially after Sunday.'

'What happened on Sunday?'

'She got very... emotional. Said I was her first love and a lot of claptrap like that. Sam, I've been asking around. Everybody—except me—knows Leslie's a bunny-boiler. She develops unhealthy obsessions about new boyfriends, which of course scares them off—and that just reinforces her insecurity.'

'Quite the Doctor Freud, aren't we?'

He reaches back to rub a hand over the nape of his neck. 'She was the same when we were together in uni—in fact, it's the main reason I broke up with her. Too clingy. Now, all these years and however many men later, Leslie's got it into her head that because of our history—"we" were "meant to be".

'She sounds bonkers—I hope you set her straight.'

'Oh, I did—and made it plain you're the love of my life. You can imagine how that went down—suffice to say the poor girl didn't turn up for work on Monday. Leslie *says* it was a tummy bug, but I reckon she was cracking up over being rejected—again.'

Doesn't sound like the confident blonde-bombshell I assaulted only a few months ago, but that was before Davy burst her bubble. 'Davy, you have to tell the bosses what she did—it's not fair you're left carrying the can for her delusions.'

He sits back with a sigh. 'Something of a Hobson's choice, that. See, the reason they offered me such a brilliant package was because Leslie made out I was the building trade's equivalent of David Beckam. If I let them know who they really got, it means kissing the job goodbye.'

'Do you still want it?'

'Not any more. Sam, I've been an idiot—letting myself be lured here when everything was going so well in Donstable.'

My heart lightens and a warm glow spreads inside. His hand turns over to receive mine and I squeeze gently. 'Don't be too hard on yourself—who wouldn't have been tempted by what they offered? Not least because it said a prestigious company thought you were worth paying over the odds for. And you *are*—it's Leslie's fault they expected too much. But I can't tell you what a relief this is—not having to think about leaving Cairncroft.'

'Would you?' he asks, cocking his head curiously. 'Have left?'

'I don't know,' is my honest answer. 'Just glad I won't have to make that decision. Right—how long until you're out of here? Will they insist you finish up the trial period?'

'I'm contracted to, but after having a word with my line manager—i.e. telling him I'm not staying—and considering how things have gone, with any luck they'll release me straight away.'

'It's lucky the estate agent didn't manage to rent out your house.'

He grins. 'Sure is. I can't tell you how good it'll be to get out of that crummy B&B and back home.'

BIT OF A PANIC WHEN I REACH THE MULTI-STOREY CAR PARK and forget what floor we left the car on. It takes me ten minutes to find it on the fifth.

'Where have you been? We said an hour.'

Sitting in the Fiesta's passenger seat, flicking through her phone, she looks for all the world like a disgruntled teenager. If I ever have one, handling it will be a breeze after Daisy. In fact, after the time I've spent with Jodie's baby, neither end of the dependent-progeny life cycle is a mystery any more.

Why am I thinking about children? Messy little gremlins that disrupt your lifestyle... still, maybe it's something Davy and I should talk about...

'Oi. Bad enough turning up fifteen minutes late, but what's with the soppy grin?'

Dragging myself back to the present, I start to explain. 'See, what happened was...'

'You forgot where we parked, didn't you?' Daisy asserts smugly.

'Of course not—what makes you think that?'

'Been like a ruddy disco up here—I take it you've been pressing that radio-control thingummy, hoping to spot the lights flashing?'

Busted

'Don't know why you're moaning. Presumably that's how you got into the car.'

She shakes her head and holds up a small plastic box with buttons on it. 'I arrived before your firework show started. So I used this—a frequency analyser. It read what wavelength your key-doofer was on when you locked up earlier, and now it can broadcast a duplicate signal. Good as having a spare key, it is.'

'Wouldn't it have been simpler to *ask* me for the spare key?'

'That's not why I got it. I've been thinking about buying one of these for a while. You've seen me opening car doors with a jemmy and some stiff wire, but most vehicles these days have central locking. *They* don't *have* lock-knobs to pull up—hence my need to move with the times.'

'How much did it cost?'

She ignores that. 'Come on, then—what's with the happy-face? Can't see Davy luring you into a cleaning cupboard—and there wasn't time to get a room.'

Mock-glaring, I let it out. 'He's chucking that stupid job, Daisy—and coming home to Cairncroft.'

She rolls her eyes. 'Lucky you!'

Then her expression softens and she squeezes my arm. 'Hey, I'm pleased for you. Really, I am—especially since it means my landlady won't be running off to Glasgow.'

Screwing up my face, I finally admit to myself as much as Daisy: 'There was never any chance of that. But I *do* love him...'

'I know,' she says quietly. Then punches my shoulder. 'Right, let's go. Get this thing moving and don't stop until Cairncroft 'cos we've got work to do. Unless we're chasing unicorns and Ricky simply went temporarily bananas.'

'Maybe it's that simple,' I observe drily, wondering for a moment if it could be. Then I reverse the Fiesta out of its space.

Daisy looks slightly (if minimally) embarrassed. 'Oh, what I said about "not stopping". Liz phoned to tell me how Wilf's "sketch artist" session went, and it seems she's got a thing about some niche baker's macaroni pies. Wants us to bring some back.'

'Macaroni pies?'

'Yeah. Liz says she used to work around here and by all accounts practically lived on the things. When she realised we were in the area…'

'Alright, fine. Did she tell you where it is? Hope there's parking nearby.'

'Gave me a full set of directions, insists it's on the way—and you can stop right outside.'
She looks thoughtful. 'Don't care much for macaroni pies myself, but I could murder a pasty.'

'Did Wilf manage to produce a likeness of our mystery woman from the witches' description?'

Stony-faced, she mutters: ' Don't ask.'

11

It's another twenty minutes before we reach "The Pastry Palace". My heart always sinks when I see these new-fangled "4-way" traffic controls at roadworks. They take longer to get through than an Aldi checkout on Friday night.

At last, we're allowed to weave around barriers protecting what looks like a resurgent interest in coal mining, and from there it's only a short distance to the row of shops Liz described. Daisy's nose twitches—ring and all. 'Mm... smell that?'

Okay—maybe this wasn't such a bad idea. We were up early and it's been a long time since breakfast. The buttery-yeasty aroma Daisy's detecting is topped with sharper tangs of strong cheddar. Somehow, it manages to resist the efforts of less savoury odours (such as exhaust fumes and clogged drains) to mask its charms.

My taste buds tingle.

As promised, there's a stopping area adjacent and I swing into it. Another car, a black Merc with tinted windows, pulls up behind. Daisy glances back and sniggers. 'Look—Ronnie Richards sent the mafia after us.'

'Don't joke about things like that.'

Exiting the Fiesta, we check out the baker's window. Daisy points excitedly. 'They've got bacon pasties. I'm having one of those.'

A sugared apple turnover clearly labelled "hot out of the oven" catches my eye. 'Mm. D'you think they do takeout coffee? We could have a picnic in the car.'

'Let's find out.'

Daisy steps sideways to the door and pushes it open. Just as I start to follow, a sharp "crack" inches from my ear makes me freeze. Simultaneously, spider webs of radial fractures erupt around a newly formed, marble-sized hole in the glass. Belatedly, from a nearby tower block, the sort of sound you normally associate with Guy Fawkes night reaches my ears. With the 5th of November only three days away, it *could* be somebody setting off squibs early... but that doesn't explain the window cracking.

Daisy screams: 'We're being shot at. Get down.'

She flies at me, flinging us both to the pavement in a mess of tangled limbs. My heart almost stops when part of the wooden window frame erupts in a flurry of splinters—because that's where my head was before Daisy bulldozed into me.

She springs to her feet and pulls me upright. 'C'mon, we need to get out of sight behind the car.'

My brain struggles to grasp what just happened while an annoyingly detached part says if the interval between those... bullets...? stays constant, then there's no way we'll reach cover before the shooter picks one of us off. The realisation turns my muscles to water as Daisy tugs desperately at my hand. With a numbing sense of fatalism, I start a mental countdown—will I even know when the fatal shot comes? Then my fragmented mind registers a car revving like it's about to pass the chequered flag at Le Mans.

The Merc I last saw parked behind the Fiesta skids to a stop beside us, two wheels mounting the kerb so it's only feet away. Daisy drags me down into its shadow, shielding us from further incoming fire.

The door facing us flies open, an inch shy of taking Daisy's head off, and a voice yells: 'Get in!'

Daisy hoists me up again and manhandles both of us into the Merc's rear. Whoever's sitting in the front passenger seat must have long arms because he reaches back, grabs the door handle, and pulls it shut with a slam. Then the car's moving—and fast, going by a nerve-jangling screech and the cloying smell of burning rubber.

Daisy ended up on top of me. When she shuffles off, I drag myself upright and try to make sense of what just happened.

The important and glorious thing is, we're safe… then something smashes into the rear window with an ear-splitting CRACK and I scream.

'Don't worry, this car's bulletproof.'

With so much to process, it hadn't occurred to me we may have jumped from the frying pan into an even more hellish situation. But I recognise that voice…

Turning towards the face keeking around his headrest, I find myself face to face with Rebecca's boyfriend. Alan.

Who (and in view of the last few minutes, this is probably significant) happens to be a detective inspector with the National Crime Agency.

THE DRIVER HASN'T SAID ANYTHING YET, WHICH I'M GLAD about considering his driving style. And I thought the Weegies were bad? It's definitely in all our interests that this Nigel Mansell wannabee concentrates on the road.

Even Daisy swallows noisily after we zip past a hulking HGV and only avoid colliding with the oncoming bus because it brakes sharply. 'Don't you have blues and twos on this thing?' she snaps.

Alan shrugs. 'Yeah, but we're trying to stay inconspicuous.'

Rolling her eyes at me, Daisy demands: 'What's going on? Who was shooting at us?'

Alan holds up a hand. 'Look, hold the questions for just a few minutes and I'll answer them over a strong cup of coffee. Meantime...' he tosses a silver wand on Daisy's lap '... I'm sure you know how to use one of those. Check yourself and Sam for tracking devices.'

Tight-lipped, Daisy examines the wand. Then flicks a switch on its side and waves it up and down the length of me. It beeps in a series of urgent squawks and Daisy holds out her hand. 'Give me your phone.'

Obediently, I rummage in a pocket for my battered old mobile—then pass it over. My mind feels like it's short-circuited—if she told me to hang out the window and sing "Yankee Doodle", I probably would. "Shock", the ever diminishing still-functioning part of my brain informs me.

With my phone in her other hand, Daisy does another impression of Harry Potter—and this time the wand stays silent. She hands it to me, together with both my phone and her own, then instructs me to "check her". I wave the wand around like she did, without being exactly sure what I'm doing, and she nods at Alan. 'We're clean. Why'd you think we might not be?'

He shrugs. 'Somebody knew where to find you.'

The driver turns sharply at a new-looking block of flats and takes us down a ramp to its underground car park. Only half the spaces are taken, and we stop adjacent to a lift. Alan jumps out, reaches under his jacket, and draws a pistol. When the driver opens my door, I see he's carrying its twin. 'Quickly,' we're urged.

Alan and the driver hustle us to the lift, guns poised and ready, both their heads swinging back and forth as they scan for… what? I know some areas of Glasgow are rough, but…

The lift is waiting with its doors open, which I assume has something to do with the doofer our driver clicked in this direction when he got out. Once inside, Alan taps at a keyboard mounted below the floor buttons. There's a *whoosh* of closing doors and we ascend. It seems to take a long time—are we headed for the penthouse?

When we arrive, the driver leaps out and waves his gun around. 'All clear,' he snaps at Alan, who pushes us across a small square foyer with a single door on each of its other three walls. We end up outside the farthest away one, opposite the lift, where Alan slaps his palm against a metal plate on the adjoining wall. It beeps, and he throws open the door.

Daisy swings to face Alan when he puts a hand on her back. 'Push me again and I'll deck you.'

Alan withdraws the hand with a grin, but his voice is urgent when he says: 'Fine—just get inside, wilya?'

He ushers us down a hallway and into the flat's bright, spacious living room. With a sigh, I slump on a couch. Daisy, though, stays standing. 'Where are *you* going?' she barks at Alan, who's turned back to the door.

'To fetch some coffee?' he throws over his shoulder. 'I thought you'd need it.'

Alan pauses in the doorway. 'If you don't, take it from me—you soon will.'

12

Daisy drops onto the couch and we wait for Alan to return. 'Dais', what's going on?'

'No idea—but I don't like it much.'

When Alan reappears, it's with three mugs of coffee on a tray—nose twitches at the realisation we're talking bistro standard here. 'Our machine's one of those fancy bean-to-cup jobs,' Alan explains, as he sets down the tray and seats himself in an armchair opposite. 'Sorry about them, though,' he adds, waving his hand at a plate of dried-out biscuits sharing space with the coffees. 'Nobody's been in residence for a while, meaning everything in the cupboards is getting to its sell-by.'

'Nobody's been...'

Daisy's brows crinkle as she works that out. 'Aha. This is a "safe house", isn't it?'

Alan nods and I say: 'Glad to hear it.'

Daisy shakes her head. 'No—it *is* safe, obviously, but—a "safe house" is where spook types like the NCA stash people at risk. They're "safe" because the underworld doesn't know about them.'

Alan claps. 'Spot on—as usual. It's so much easier dealing with someone who…'

'Cut the flannel and explain what's going on,' Daisy interrupts grumpily. 'You can start by telling us how you "happened" to be around when some nutcase started shooting at us.'

'Okay.'

He gulps at his coffee, then leans forward. 'A few days ago, our street snitches reported whispers that the Glasgow Mob had put contracts out on two witnesses. Right now there are quite a few people waiting to testify on mob-related crimes, so it wasn't immediately apparent who the actual targets were. But then I spoke to Rebecca, and she told me about your brakes failing—which, all things considered, struck me as suspicious—so I stuck a protection detail on you. Rebecca also let slip you were coming to Glasgow, which was a convenient opportunity for me to have a wee chat—I was here anyway for something else—so I substituted myself into your security team this morning. But before I could approach you, all hell broke loose…'

'Wait a minute.'

Daisy's hand shoots up. 'No way have your people been tailing us—I'd have spotted them.'

Alan coughs, then fixes his gaze on something across the room. 'No—you wouldn't. Daisy, you're good—honestly, you are—but totally out of your depth in this scenario. If my guys don't want to be seen—they aren't.'

'Alan,' I ask hesitantly, scared of what the answer will be. 'Are you saying there's a "contract" out on Daisy and me?'

He nods sadly. 'It's because of Dougie Dobson, the fairground fellow. His murder trial comes up in a couple of months, and you two are the star witnesses. See, although we can't prove it, the NCA knows Dobson was laundering money for the Glasgow mob—and obviously they'd prefer he kept doing that instead of going to jail.'

'But Alan, surely the case against Dobson doesn't depend on us? What about Paul's sister, Tina? I assume *she*'s testifying as well. If only to prove her dad's murder was down to Dobson, rather than her.'

'Sorry—Tina refused to rat Dobson out. She must have appreciated the potential risk—and suffered a sudden attack of amnesia. Which means it's all down to you two. Dobson confessed to you—because he thought you'd both die on that fairground ride. Nobody saw him slip Mr McNab poison in the Cuppa Tea, and he was gone before the police arrived at his place in Stonehaven. As for the incident at your detective agency—while Rebecca *could* testify to *that*— it doesn't speak to the wider issues. Small change, in other words. Without *your* eyewitness testimony, the principal case against Dobson crumbles and he walks—especially considering the high-powered briefs Gilmartin hired to represent him.'

'Who's Gilmartin?' Daisy demands.

'Gregory Gilmartin—head honcho of the Glasgow mob. He's a nasty beggar—and powerful with it.'

'So the shooting today—and my brakes failing—are down to him?' I ask weakly.

'Afraid so. I sent a tech guy over to look at your Panda this morning—and he says there were traces of plastic explosive in the brake system. Somebody must have followed you, waited for a downhill slope, then detonated the charges by remote control.'

I shake my head. 'No, that's not right—the road was deserted when we heard that bang. There was definitely nobody behind us.'

'Duh.'

Daisy slaps her forehead. 'The drone—remember? Just before our brakes failed, I spotted a drone overhead. They were watching through that.'

Alan nods. 'Makes sense.'

Daisy squeals when I drive my elbow into her side. 'Puts my being attacked by Ghostface in a different light, eh? All you could say was "Sam's got it in her head" and "you know what she's like."'

'Sorry,' Daisy mutters, and Alan sits up straight. 'GHOSTFACE?'

We tell him what happened and he strokes his chin. 'Sounds as though that was the first attempt on your lives.'

'But that was only me,' I remind him.

'Yeah, but Daisy was due along the same path. The assassin probably reckoned it would be easier to take you out individually—until that masterful display of self-defence.'

'Her shoelace came undone,' Daisy says—gleefully.

'I was being sarcastic,' Alan replies, straight-faced. 'Hmm… I'd better have a word with Wilson about letting Ricky out on bail. It's looking like he was just unlucky—wrong place at the wrong time. Poor guy can't be blamed because your contract killer left a real knife lying around the dressing room.'

Daisy leans forward and catches Alan's eye. 'So what happens now—do we get protection until the trial?'

'Of course—and what I really want is for you both to move in here meantime.'

'What?'

Alan bites his lip, but I have to make him see this isn't on. 'The trial won't be for months—we can't just disappear to Glasgow. I've got a hotel to manage and Daisy…' I catch her eye '… as well as having the detective agency, you need to brief Logan about putting on the murder mysteries.'

Daisy rounds on Alan. 'Sam's right. She and I can't simply vamoose without time to prepare. No offense, but Rebecca could run my business into the ground if I don't set everything up for her. And those murder mysteries Sam's talking about are the hotel's lifeblood.'

'Girls, you have professional assassins after you. Look what happened today. How are we supposed to protect you against those sorts of tactics? Your only chance is letting us hide you away.'

Remembering the terror-filled minutes when I was sure we were about to die—maybe he has a point. 'How about a compromise—what if we go back to Cairncroft for a day or two, stay indoors, and do what we have to so the hotel and detective agency can function without us? *Then* come and hide out here.'

Daisy nods approvingly, but Alan looks dubious. 'Well, I can't keep you here by force. Alright, and we'll do our best to protect you in Cairncroft, but—the sooner you're out of there, the better.'

'Got it,' Daisy tells him, springing to her feet. 'Okay, how does this work? Do we ride with you, or drive in convoy?'

'We'll follow you,' Alan decides. 'Gives us more options if anything happens on the way. And let's be clear, I don't like this one bit—although it will be nice getting to spend time with Rebecca.'

'Um.'

I wait until he looks at me. 'Any chance somebody could fetch my Fiesta over? Only, the thought of going back there...'

'Sure, I'll arrange it,' Alan says, standing and holding out a hand for my keys. I drop them in his palm and he moves towards the door.

'Oh, Alan,' Daisy calls after him. 'Could you ask whoever goes for the Fiesta to pick up four macaroni pies, two bacon pasties, and a couple of apple turnovers?'

13

The trip home passes without incident (if you don't count Alan losing us at Perth, but I'd been trying to drive with my legs crossed since Stirling and almost didn't see the retail park turnoff in time—anyway, he got back on our tail just before Dundee) and we go straight to the detective agency.

Rebecca, predictably, is one happy bunny when she sees her boyfriend. (The "Playboy" version of "bunny" being a fairly accurate description of her latest outfit.) When they finally put each other down, Alan goes to find his sidekick (who we now know is called Ralf) and Rebecca swoons into a client chair in front of Liz's desk.

Liz giggles. 'He's pretty fit, your fella.'

'Oh, he is—Alan spends an hour in the gym every day,' Rebecca confides.

Liz looks momentarily confused and Daisy uses the pause to ask: 'Has Alan transferred to some kind of spook unit? The guy's starting to remind me of Rowan Atkinson in "Johnny English".'

Rebecca nods. 'Alan's very tight-lipped about his work, but they moved him to "special duties" a couple of months ago. That's all he'll say about it, though. Trouble is, ever since, they've been sending him off all over the country at a moment's notice. Sam, how are *you* coping with a long-distance relationship? Because *I'm* finding it stressful.'

I smile. 'Good news is Davy's coming home. No more weekend trips to Glasgow...' My words tail off as the irony of our new situation hits me. Davy's returning from Glasgow—and I'm off to hide out there for the next few months. We'll probably pass each other halfway... talk about bad timing.

Daisy clears her throat. 'How'd that identikit session with Wilf and the witches pan out? Liz sounded a bit dubious when she phoned.'

Rebecca giggles and Liz holds up a printout. Daisy takes it from her and squints. 'That could be anybody.'

Liz is having trouble keeping a straight face. 'Yes, Wilf got quite frustrated with Agatha and her crew. They kept going on about the woman's aura, and her psychic energies—but gave him precious little to work with regarding actual physical appearance.'

'Probably doesn't matter,' Daisy says, dropping the picture on Liz's desk. 'We think she's a contract killer, so it's Alan's problem now.'

'Contract killer?'

We fill the girls in and I see mixed feelings in Rebecca's eyes. 'Gosh, I wish this wasn't happening—but, em, will I be in charge while you're away?'

Daisy snorts loudly. 'S'pose so—but I'm leaving a strict list of "dos and don'ts" *and* I'll be at the end of the phone anytime you need advice. Also, there'll be a mandatory conference call with Sam and me every day.'

Rebecca claps her hands. 'Oh, wonderful. Well, not... you know? But Liz and I can hold the fort—can't we?'

Liz nods, smiling. (But it doesn't reach her eyes—is she *quite* so enthusiastic about this as Rebecca?) 'Course we can. Will you leave me your new address in case I need to send something over? For signing, or whatever.'

Daisy shakes her head. 'Nope, it's a secret. Anything like that, give it to Rebecca. She'll pass it to Alan and he'll see we get it. But you should be able to put most stuff in an E-mail. What do I ever sign since they invented the internet?'

Liz waves her biro about. 'Right enough. I was just anxious to cover all the bases.'

She is trying—reassuring me it WAS a good idea taking her on

Rebecca grins suddenly. 'Agatha said she gave you a love potion to use on Davy. Is that why he's coming home?'

'Don't be ridiculous. I didn't even take it with...'

When Daisy averts her eyes, it speaks volumes. And also explains the text that was waiting on my phone when we arrived back. 'Daisy, did you...?'

She tries to cover her giggles with a fit of coughing. 'Why would you think...'

'You *did*. You slipped that garbage Agatha gave me in Davy's coffee before leaving the café—didn't you?'

She shrugs. 'How'd you know?'

'He just texted me. Poor love's had to go home from work because of acute diarrhoea.'

'Oh. Oops, sorry. Anyway, isn't my fault. Blame Agatha.'

It's nearly five o'clock. Daisy and I both need a drink and decide on the Last Chance Saloon, where we can also get a bar snack. Not that Daisy should be hungry after polishing off two bacon pasties and one of my apple turnovers on the road back.

Additionally, The Last Chance Saloon is a better venue than Colin's more-staid residents bar for the haranguing she's due after poisoning my fiancé.

As we exit the detective agency, Ralf appears behind us. 'Where'd you come from?' Daisy snaps.

'I was waiting for you.'

'Why?'

Ralf wilts slightly but ploughs on. 'I'm your protection detail. Everywhere you go, I go.'

The disbelief must show in my face because he nods firmly. 'Surely we're safe in the hotel?' I protest.

Ralf shakes his head slowly. 'You aren't safe anywhere, and especially not here. Until we have you stashed away at a secret address—better get used to having me around.'

Daisy harrumphs but starts walking without saying anything more. I hurry to catch up and Ralf follows a few feet behind. 'This feels weird,' I tell her.

She glances over her shoulder. 'More than weird—but he's right. It's not like they can lock the place down with new guests arriving all the time. And any one of *them* could be another hit man.'

'Brrr.'

We walk on in silence and enter The Last Chance Saloon through its public entrance. 'You want a drink?' Daisy shouts to Ralf, who's settling himself at a table by the door—which, conveniently, has a panoramic view of the entire area.

'Diet coke would be nice,' he calls back.

Logan waves from the bar's far end, but I'm relieved when Jeff serves us. I'm not looking forward to telling my co-owner he's on his own for the next few months. After the events of today, I could do with putting that off until tomorrow.

Jeff offers us the bar menu, but I'm not hungry yet and Daisy's still digesting half the Pastry Palace's stock. We take our drinks to a table three down from Ralf's after dropping off his coke. It's relatively quiet at this time—there are too few Cairncroft Cowboys to get a good brawl going (which is just as well with Ralf around, the bulge under his left arm apparent) so the early birds are shovelling coins into one-armed-bandits and playing table-football tournaments. Daisy sinks half her pint in a oner, then looks straight at me. 'What a day.'

'Yeah, Davy thinks the same.'

She dips her head. 'Sorryyy. Just trying to help...'

'I wish you wouldn't. Oh, he'll live.'

I hold up my vodka tonic. 'Cheers. And you're right—it's been a terrible day. I can't believe we're being targeted by the underworld—again.'

For once, she looks serious. 'This is bigger than any of our past messes. Still, in a few months' time, we'll look back and...'

Daisy stops mid-sentence and I wonder what popped into her head to cause that worried expression. 'C'mon, out with it.'

'Just thinking, is all.'

'What about?'

'Well, we're saying a few months—then our evidence will send Dobson to Barlinnie for the foreseeable.'

'Yup—what am I missing?'

'Thing is, Dobson isn't the one who's after us—it's this Gregor Gilmartin character. Grand don of the Glasgow mafia by all accounts. And *he* won't be going to prison.'

She necks what's left of her pint. Draws a sleeve over her mouth. 'You don't think Gilmartin's the sort to hold a grudge—do you?'

'What are you saying? That—after the trial—Gilmartin will *still* want us dead? For revenge?'

She shrugs. 'That's how it happens in all the movies I've seen...'

I tip back half my vodka tonic in one gulp, then stand. Feel light-headed. 'Daisy, we need to find Alan and ask him about this.'

Daisy sneers. 'Five gets you ten the beggar already knows.'

RATHER THAN GO AND "FIND" ALAN, DAISY HAS RALF CALL him on his mobile—no point in having a dog and barking yourself—and arranges to meet in here.

Alan arrives five minutes later, with Rebecca in tow. Honestly—all she lacks is bunny-ears and a fluffy cottontail. Has nobody told her it's winter?

Alan goes to fetch drinks and Rebecca flops down beside us. 'Thanks for asking Alan and me to join you. Poor thing's been working *so* hard—maybe a night out will help him relax.'

Oh dear

'Um, Rebecca,' I start, wondering how to break it. I needn't have worried. Not with Daisy on the job.

'Listen, spongehead. His *work* at the moment is keeping us alive, which is what we want to talk about. And it's private.'

Luckily, Rebecca knows Daisy well enough not to take offence. 'Fine, you should have said...'

'I just did.'

'Okay, I'll... go and play the fruit machines. Um... don't suppose you have any change...?'

After pooling our resources, we ladle about a fiver's worth of coins into Rebecca's waiting hands and she flounces off to try her luck. Alan puts her drink down beside the machine as he passes. He sits next to us and swings a thumb. 'Rebecca's just done telling me how nice it'll be to relax together over a few drinks—then she takes off to play the bandits?'

'Yeah—we asked her to give us some space. You're holding something back, Alan—aren't you?'

Alan raises both palms. 'What d'you mean.'

'She means,' I interject, 'that we need to know what happens *after* the trial if Dobson goes down. We're sort of worried Gregor Gilmartin might still want to kill us.'

'Ah.'

Alan takes a long swig of lager, then puts down his glass. 'Alright, I wanted to lead up to that gently.'

'To what?' Daisy demands.

Rubbing his chin, Alan looks at the ceiling. 'Assuming Dobson *is* found guilty—I'm afraid you're right. Gilmartin won't just let it go.'

'He'll carry on gunning for us, won't he?' Daisy says in a tired voice.

Alan nods. 'He will. It's a matter of "face"—taking it lying down would look too much like weakness on his part.'

'So what do we do?' I squeal. (I didn't *mean* to squeal—but that's how it came out.) 'You can't protect us indefinitely.'

'No, I can't. Your only answer, really, is the witness protection programme.'

'What's that?' I know full well, but need to hear him spell it out.

'We'll relocate you somewhere far away. Give you new identities and assist in finding suitable employment...'

Daisy slams her glass down so hard I'm amazed it stays intact. 'C'mon, Alan. You can't be serious.'

She looks at me. 'It also means cutting off all contact with everyone we know—forever. Leaving our whole lives behind and starting afresh as new people.'

And I was worried about moving to Glasgow with Davy

Rebecca glances over and calls: 'Everything okay?'

'Fine, doll,' Alan shouts back. It's getting noisier in here, but Rebecca must have heard because she sticks up a thumb then carries on feeding our change into the bandit. Her expression, however, says she's unconvinced.

Despite the clatter of pool balls and hoots of triumph (and derision) every time someone scores at table-football, when Alan releases a huge breath it makes several cowboys look around. 'I don't like it either, but this is your only chance. It's that, or get yourselves some funeral insurance quick.'

'There has to be another way,' Daisy mutters, her eyes boring into him.

He shakes his head. 'Sorry, love. There isn't.'

'Then we won't testify,' I state firmly. 'They can't make us.'

'Afraid they can,' Alan tells me. 'They'll just subpoena you. Once you're in the witness box, refusing to answer questions is only allowed under certain circumstances.'

'Shouldn't fear for our lives qualify?' I demand.

He shrugs. 'You could argue something along the lines of human rights on that basis, but then every question counsel asked would turn into a legal debate—and you'd likely have your objection overruled often enough to bring out sufficient facts for a conviction. Think about it—human rights are all very well, but if witnesses were allowed to excuse themselves willy-nilly, the whole justice system would break down. And the other alternative—staying schtum regardless—will result in *you* going to jail. Where Gilmartin has the reach to get at you easily—which he would—on the assumption you would cave eventually, and testify rather than stay locked up.'

'How come Tina gets a free pass?' Daisy demands.

'Tina didn't give the police a statement about Dobson, so she can't be impeached. You did—so can.'

'So *she* just walks away?' I shout. 'While we …'

Alan shrugs again. 'I don't make the rules,' he mutters.

A tear runs down my cheek. 'Our lives—as we know them—are over, then? For the rest of our naturals, we're going to be working in some call centre or factory… where? The south of England?'

'To be safe—probably. South of England, I mean,' he adds hurriedly. 'We can help with liquidating your assets, though—maybe you could open a bed-and-breakfast?'

'In Bournemouth,' Daisy says flatly.

'Better than being dead,' Alan counters quietly, then gets up and goes to join Rebecca.

I'm gripping Daisy's hand and didn't even realise—until she squawks. 'Ouch.'

'Sorry…'

I let go and she throws an arm around my shoulders. 'S'allright. Look, maybe it won't be so bad. Doesn't have to be a B&B—we could start a burger chain.'

I'm not sure if the sounds coming out of me are laughter or sobs. 'It's not fair, Daisy.'

Her mouth tightens. 'It isn't. But... listen. I'll think of something. Okay?'

'Okay,' I agree, swigging back my vodka. After all, she always has in the past.

But deep inside, I know even Daisy will be hard pushed to get us out of this one.

14

The Last Chance Saloon isn't for the faint-hearted—but in essence it's a happy place. Which, right now, makes *us* feel *out* of place—so we decide to nurse our wounds at home, and make do with a sandwich. Ralf jumps up and insists on going out first. Just as he reaches the door, it opens, and Wilf swaggers in with another man.

Wilf's a rotund, jolly figure (if you ignore the knuckle-art) but his companion couldn't be more of a contrast. The newcomer's face is craggier than the Cairngorms and he's got a sinewy look, but what comes over most is a sense of something primeval which seems to ooze from every pore. One thing's for sure—I wouldn't fancy meeting this man in a dark alley.

Heck—am I seeing auras now? Thank goodness Agatha isn't here

Ralf's assessment must match mine. (Maybe he can see auras too?) His arm rises to create a barrier, resting lightly against Craggy-Face's chest.

Craggy-Face stops, but there's something almost derisory in the movement. Like he *chose* to obey but could just as easily not have. His flinty gaze locks with Ralf's, and our bodyguard flinches. For a fleeting moment, I saw fear flicker in Ralf's eyes.

Wilf tilts his head at Daisy and points to Ralf. 'Is he with you?'

She nods, looking amused.

'For his own sake, I'd call him off sharpish.'

Daisy steps forward and smacks Ralf's shoulder, then indicates Wilf. 'This is a mate of mine, Ralf.'

Ralf scowls. 'And the other one?'

'A mate of my mate—which makes *him* my mate, too.'

'Alright.'

Ralf takes a step back, then his eyes bulge. He yells: 'Beggar's carrying' and launches himself at the little craggy-faced man. What happens next is too fast for the eye to follow. Suddenly, Ralf's sprawled amidst the splintered remains of a table five feet away, looking dazed.

Daisy nudges me. 'Ogoshi,' she says in my ear, which translates to "floating hip throw". (She insists on dragging me along to her judo gradings and I've picked up some of the lingo.) Then she fixes Wilf with a glare before flicking her eyes at his friend. 'Please tell me I don't have to worry about *him*.'

Wilf shakes his head, but before he can say anything Alan leaps in front of Craggy-Face with his pistol drawn. 'Freeze.'

An excited murmur fills the sudden silence. Cairncroft cowboys love a fight. Daisy turns and bellows: 'BACK OFF, YOU LOT.'

The murmurs change to grumbles, but they do as she says—to the Cairncroft Cowboys, Daisy's word is law. Wilf waves frantically at Alan. 'Angus has ID.'

'Have you?' Alan snaps. Behind him, Rebecca's face is the colour of alabaster.

'Finger and thumb?' Angus growls—and at a brief nod from Alan uses the aforementioned digits to extract a leather wallet and toss it over.

Alan stoops to retrieve it—his eyes never leaving Angus. When he flips open the wallet and glances quickly at its contents, Alan's expression turns to stone—but he holsters his gun. 'Sorry,' he mutters. 'You should have announced yourself.'

'Didn't know I had tae,' Angus retorts.

He studies Alan for a moment, then barks: 'NCA?'

Alan nods, just before Ralf noisily extracts himself from the table's remains and advances threateningly. His boss holds up a hand. 'ICE,' Alan tells him.

Ralf stops dead in his tracks. Alan tosses the wallet back to Angus, who snatches it from the air. Alan frowns. 'I did notice it's a temporary ID, though. What's that about?'

Angus smiles, but there's no humour in it. 'Above your pay grade, son.'

He turns to Wilf. 'So—we havin' that pint, or no?'

Daisy buys the pints—three of them. And another vodka-lime for me. Nosiness is a wonderful antidote to discovering "life as you know it" is about to end.

'Who's your friend?' Daisy asks Wilf once we're settled at a table. 'Or, *what* is he?'

Not one for beating about the bush, our Daisy

Wilf stares into the foam on top of his pint. 'We was in Special Forces together.'

Daisy's mouth drops open. Then she leans in and eyeballs Wilf. '*YOU*—served in Special Forces? That's the SAS, isn't it?'

Wilf smiles, and his eyes glaze as he looks back through the years. 'Aye, Lass. I didn't always have a beer belly. The army was what saved me, after prison. But Afghanistan finished me. Nasty lot, them Al Quaeda.' He points at Angus. 'No like him—he thrived on it.'

Angus shrugs. 'I wouldnae say "thrived"—but the experience stood me in good stead.'

'So what are you now?' Daisy asks, her tongue practically hanging out. 'Some sort of secret agent? Whatever that ID was, it shut Alan down quick enough.'

Angus shakes his head. 'No, I'm the same as you, lass—Wilf's told me a bit about you two, ye see. I'm a private detective tae. Down in London, though.'

Daisy looks puzzled and I ask: 'So why are you here?' Suddenly wondering if it could be anything to do with our current problem.

'My mother lives in Aberdeen. She won't move down South—stubborn old besom—so I'm forever trekking up here tae check on her. Which is when, often as not, I remember it's Wilf's round and pop over to remind him.'

'It's been my round for twenty years,' Wilf mutters, smiling.

Daisy's not interested in whose round it is. 'So what's this ICE stuff about?' she demands.

Angus sighs. 'I was in Inverness helpin' out a friend of mine a while back when he was called away tae Edinburgh—kind of an emergency, it was. Problem being, we were in the middle of an almighty ruckus because terrorists had just blown up a wee plane. So he left me to sort it out—and I needed the authority of that ID tae do it.'

He laughs shortly. 'Knowing Mr Roger, it's probably no even genuine.'

Daisy puffs. 'So, same question—what *is* ICE? Is it some kind of law-enforcement agency? Only, I've never heard of it.'

'No, ye wouldn't—ICE stands for "investigation of criminal exploitation". They're on the little people's side—folk who through no fault of their own get caught up in the mayhem wreaked by bad uns like terrorists and mobsters. ICE is an international organisation, bit off the books, very powerful—but my connection is all down tae that friend and his sister.'

Daisy's gaze fixes on Angus' shoulder. 'If you're a private detective—most of the time—how come you carry a gun?'

I find myself casting around for a handy electrical socket—she'll need it for when the Anglepoise comes out.

Angus pats his shoulder. 'I occasionally have tae deal wi' dangerous people—sometimes in my own work, but more often because of them two I mentioned. I am *licenced* tae carry, though.'

'Cor—how d'you get one of them?'

Angus laughs. 'Ye don't. I've got—let's say special permission. From friends in high places—and that's all I'm saying, seeing as I've already tellt ye more than I should.'

Angus tips back the last of his pint, then checks his watch. 'Are ye forgetting what Harriet said she'd do tae us if we were late for that vegan meatloaf she's concocting?' he asks Wilf. 'Although how ye make meatloaf without mince beats me.'

Wilf laughs. 'Quorn do mince—lovely, it is.'

He looks at his own watch, then jumps up. 'You're right—this was supposed to be a quick one. We need to go.'

Daisy watches them leave with wistful eyes. 'If only Angus were twenty years younger,' she sighs.

'More like thirty,' I point out. 'Daisy, that's a dangerous man—I knew no good would come of you getting in tow with an ex-con.'

'Don't be daft. Angus is lovely—maybe a wee bit sinister, I'll grant you, but there's something grandfatherly about him.'

My Grandfather didn't carry an automatic weapon under his arm

Her eyes shine suddenly. 'Do you think we should ask Angus if he could help with—you know?'

'What are you expecting him to do—go and shoot up the Glasgow mob for us? Oh, I'm sure he could fit that in on his way back to London.'

She flaps a hand. 'Don't be sarcastic—it doesn't suit you. No, seriously—he obviously knows some powerful people. Maybe…'

'Daisy, we've got the NCA on our side. If they can't stop Gilmartin, how is Wilf's old army mate—or his questionable-sounding, so-called *powerful* "friends"—going to wave a wand and make everything come right?'

She isn't listening. It's like she's speaking to herself now. 'I might have a wee chat with Wilf—get his take on it.'

15

Next morning, Daisy heads straight to the detective agency (where she has a series of training sessions planned for Rebecca and Liz) accompanied by one of Ralf's colleagues. Alan's taking no chances—he's brought in reinforcements. (Or maybe just considers himself too senior now for "grunt" work?)

Ralf spent last night on our couch and is shadowing me as I make for the hotel to face Logan. I can't put this off any longer.

Things have changed, of course—instead of telling him I need a leave of absence, it's looking more like a permanent goodbye. A tear slithers out as I wonder whether Logan can raise enough capital to buy my share of the hotel. If not, I'll have to become a "sleeping partner."

Will the witness protection people *allow* me to be a sleeping partner? Maybe they'll say the paper trail thus generated would jeopardise Daisy's and my security.

So deep in thought am I that Jodie takes me by surprise when she grips my arm and hustles us both into the residents lounge, which—possibly fortuitously, if her expression's anything to go by—is empty. 'You okay, Jodie?'

She stares at me for a long moment. 'Sam, I'm aware of what's going on—Alan gave me a full rundown.'

I'm taken aback. 'Why'd he do that?'

'Because I'm a police officer—it was basic professional courtesy. Look, I need to know what your plans are.'

'Oh, right. Actually, I was just on my way to find Logan and have a chat about...'

'*Not* about the hotel. That's your and Logan's concern. What I'm worried about is my daughter's safety. Sorry, Sam. I don't mean to come across uncaring about your problems—I really feel for you and Daisy—but has it occurred to either of you that swanning around here with targets painted on your backs puts everybody else slap in the middle of any crossfire?'

I smack my forehead so hard it hurts. No, I hadn't given a thought to the danger we've put our friends in. Suddenly, I'm *so* ashamed of myself. 'Jodie—sorry, sorry, sorry. You're right, of course. Daisy and I need to leave straight away.'

Her eyes glisten and she grips my shoulder. '*I'm sorry, Sam. I hated doing that, but as a mother...*'

'Jodie, I understand. Our coming back at all was unforgivable—we should have stayed in Glasgow. Listen, I'll go and find Daisy, then Alan—and promise we'll be gone before you can blink. Today, if possible. The businesses will just have to get sorted over the phone.'

She nods, and I think she's about to cry, so I gently remove her hand—then reach out to cup a cheek. 'Jodie, it's fine—I'm glad you were brave enough to point out what we should have seen for ourselves.'

As I turn away, her fingers close around my wrist. 'Sam,' she whispers. 'Good luck. I hope somehow...'

I can't speak through the lump in my throat, so force a smile and hurry off.

Ralf stayed in reception. I don't know if he heard what Jodie said, but if so, gives no sign. He simply follows me out and down the steps.

I'm going to the detective agency the long way, walking around the building instead of through it, because I need some air and a few minutes to think. As I reach the bottom step, car doors click open on either side. From a battered old Honda, Wilf emerges and calls a cheery "Good morning." The passenger door also opens as Angus gets out.

Behind me, a much newer Alfa Romeo disgorges a woman who brings to mind a young Joanna Lumley. I sneak another quick backward glance, confirming my first impression that everything about the newcomer screams money. Leather trousers, angora top, the car—especially the car—Logan *will* be pleased. He's always on about attracting "a better class of guest"—which generates endless "Fawlty Towers" jokes from Daisy.

Returning my attention to Wilf and Angus, I try to seem composed—cheerful, even—despite the harsh reality dragging me down after speaking to Jodie. 'Back already, gents? I know our beer's good, but...'

Wilf laughs. 'Bit early for that. Naw, lost my phone—thought I might have dropped it last night.'

Angus saunters over to join us, then, without warning, grabs my shoulders and flings me roughly to the tarmac. I land with a bone-rattling "thump", roll over once and, dazed, jerk my head up to yell at him. The words die in my throat as Angus draws his gun—but it's not me he's targeting. The blonde woman from the Alfa Romeo (my mind insists on thinking of her as "Joanna") strides towards us and she, too, has a pistol in her hand.

Angus barely has his own gun clear of its holster when Joanna's booms. The little man staggers backwards and, horror-stricken, I watch blood blossom on his chest. Snapping my head back to the stylish woman, I'm in time to see her spin and shoot Ralf. Like Angus, his weapon is only half-drawn when he crashes to the ground.

Wilf starts towards Joanna, then stops dead when the gun swivels his way. He raises both hands to his shoulders and the woman sneers. As she moves closer her gun swings from Wilf to me.

It all happened so fast—I'm about to die, but haven't even had the chance to work up a decent degree of terror. There's not a thing I can do—squeezing shut my eyes, I wait for the explosion that will end everything.

Then a familiar voice screams: 'ARMED POLICE—DROP YOUR WEAPON.'

It's Jodie—my eyes snap open and I see her, crouched in a two-handed shooting stance on the top step. Holding a gun that's bigger than Joanna's.

Joanna whirls and Jodie fires a warning shot over her head. The woman freezes. 'You're police?' she shouts.

Jodie nods grimly. 'That's right. Now drop it.'

'Certainly, officer.' Joanna lets go of the gun and it's still mid-air when she launches herself at her car and dives through its open driver's door. Moments later, engine roaring, the Alfa Romeo's tyres screech as the beggar takes off like an Exocet missile.

Jodie pounds down the steps two at a time, then drops to one knee. She fires three times, presumably at Joanna's tyres, but must miss because the car only speeds up as it disappears down the drive.

Yanking out her phone, Jodie yells into it. 'Shots fired. Two officers down. I need ambulance and armed backup—NOW.'

IT'S CHAOS IN THE CAIRNCROFT HOTEL. (*MURDER HOTEL*, I mean—oh, I hate that name. I wish we'd never changed it—there again, does that matter any more?)

I'm slumped on a chair in the residents lounge, which the carloads of police officers who responded to Jodie's call have taken over as their command post. Daisy's sat alongside me and looks defeated as I feel.

Inspector Wilson sidles up and waves a hand through my blank stare. 'Beginning to look like I should book myself a room here—save all this travelling back and forth. Do you give police discounts?'

Being a Thursday, and since we cancelled the Mid-Week Mystery, there are hardly any guests in residence—which isn't a bad thing because the black-clad, crash-helmeted storm troopers strutting about with machine guns slung from their shoulders would terrify the wits out of them.

Well, they are me

I haven't answered Wilson, barely registering what he said, but Daisy glances up. 'Ha. For you, we've got a "plus 50%" deal.'

Wilson frowns. 'Oh, come on—don't be so hostile. I know we bicker, but when push comes to shove… I could have locked you up a dozen times if the fancy took me. Didn't, though—did I?'

Daisy narrows her eyes. 'Why not?'

'Because we're basically on the same side. I might not approve of your approach to law and order, but that doesn't detract from the results it's achieved.'

While Daisy gapes disbelievingly I ask: 'Any word on Angus?'

Wilson nods. 'He'll be fine. Wasn't so bad as it looked—the bullet missed all his major organs. Lucky so-and-so got away with little more than a cracked rib from falling awkwardly on tarmac. It's a sore thing that, mind.'

'What about Ralf?' I'm dreading his answer.

Wilson's face clouds. 'Straight through the heart. Died instantly. At least the poor beggar didn't suffer,' he adds almost plaintively.

I've had enough—can't take any more. Seizing Daisy's hand, I yank her upright. 'Come on—this has gone far enough.'

She doesn't resist—Daisy's shell-shocked as I am. The gunfire was clearly audible even from the detective agency and, rushing over here, I think she expected to find me dead. Then the wee darling burst into tears and hugged me so hard I thought *my* ribs would snap.

I drag her through a mass of official bodies, some in police uniform, others wearing white "scene of crime" PPE. A good proportion of them are queuing at the bar where Logan's dispensing coffee by the bucketful.

Which is where I'm headed, because that's where Alan is. Beside an ashen-faced Rebecca and nursing a huge mug with steam coming off it.

'Alan,' I shout, drawing glances from the throng. When I get close enough, a punch to the shoulder hard enough to jar my wrist ensures his attention. 'Enough is enough—it's time Daisy and I weren't here.'

He looks older—defeated. 'Sam, you're perfectly safe—look around. Nobody's getting through all these armed police.'

'It's not us I'm worried about—we're putting our friends in danger. We'll go to Glasgow with you—I don't care anymore. Just get us out of here before anyone else is hurt.'

Rebecca steps forward and wraps me in her arms. 'C'mon, Sam—calm down. Everything's under control.'

Thrusting her away, I shout: 'NO. It isn't. Ralf's dead—and Angus is wounded. Who'll be next?'

Daisy throws *her* arms around me from behind and whispers in my ear. 'Take it easy, Sam. None of this is our fault—but yeah, I see where you're coming from. I'm with you—we'll go to the safe house and work forward from there.'

I suck in a long, noisy breath and muster my most threatening glare. 'So—how quick can you organise that?'

Alan grimaces. 'Look, this isn't my idea—but you'll have to hang fire a little longer. Seems Angus has influential friends—and I've been told to keep you here until they arrive.'

'Arrive?' I spit. 'Who's *arriving*?'

'Couple of bigwigs is all I know—sounds like they've taken Angus' shooting personally. Sorry girls, but my hands are tied.'

'Okay—so when do you expect these "bigwigs"?'

Alan holds out his palms, looking more helpless than I've ever seen him. 'Coupla hours? They're flying down from London.'

I step forward, going nose to nose with him. 'Let's hope nobody *else* dies meantime.'

16

Alan assigns Daisy and I a firearms officer called Hugh, in Ralf's place.

Hugh is in full "battledress"—a bulky Kevlar tunic makes him look even bigger than he is, and the sub-machine gun dangling from his shoulder sets my stomach churning. He follows us through to reception, where I just spotted Kat come in.

She does a double-take on seeing Hugh, then pretends to ignore him. 'You alright? Hazel's been telling me what happened.'

Hazel... that reminds me

Holding up my palm, I lean across the reception desk. 'Hazel—would you cancel the weekend guests, please?'

'And return their deposits...?'

'Afraid so. Or rebook them if they want. Let's assume things will be back to some sort of normality from the beginning of next week.'

She nods. 'I've kept a list of the people who tried to book since... you know? Spun them a line about our computer being down and took their phone numbers.'

'Good thinking. Ring round and offer them bookings for anytime from Monday on. If they ask, tell them the murder mysteries *are* going ahead as usual.'

Daisy rolls her eyes. 'Talk about optimism. Do you really think Logan is capable of having everything up and running by next week?'

'That's his problem.'

It's not that I don't share her scepticism, but Logan will have to pull up his big-boy trousers and do whatever needs doing—because Daisy and I won't be here to help him after tonight.

'If there's anything I can do...?'

Oh, Kat—I forgot she was there. Shock—and a sudden inability to comprehend all that's happened—makes my head swim and I grab the desk to stay upright. Both Daisy and Kat lunge for me, but I wave them off with my other hand. 'It's alright—*I'm* alright. Just came over dizzy for a sec. Thanks, Kat. Can't think of anything right now, but if I do...'

'We might need a lawyer,' Daisy tells her, grim-faced. 'Not sure whether witness protection involves legal contracts—but if it does, maybe you could advise us on whatever they offer.'

'Witness protection?' Kat blurts, and I nod.

'We're being targeted to stop us testifying at Dobson's trial. Listen, sorry Kat—I haven't asked why you're here. Is there something *I* can help *you* with?'

She looks at her feet. 'Um… came to give Jodie a hand with moving out. She and Alanna are coming to stay with Dad and me for a while…'

The guilt comes rushing back. Poor Jodie—she's decided decanting with her baby is the only way to keep Alanna safe.

Right on cue, the lift doors slide open and Jodie strides out. She's carrying a suitcase and has Alanna hanging from her neck in a baby sling. Daisy dashes forwards to take her case as Jodie stops to glare at the lift. She swings around and jerks the thumb of her free hand at its closing doors. 'Better steer clear of that thing, girls. I think it's heard about the bounty on your heads and saw me as a practice run. With Alanna in her sling, I couldn't deliver its usual kicking.'

'Should have threatened it with your gun,' Daisy says, deadpan. 'What was all that about, anyway? You aren't normally armed.'

'I'm fully firearms-certified. Wilson signed a special permit for me in view of the current situation. Just as well he did.'

'Jodie, I'm so sorry about all this.'

It's hard hugging somebody when there's a baby between you, but I give it my best shot. 'And I didn't get to thank you properly. You saved my life. Jodie, I feel terrible about...'

Jodie smiles tightly. 'None of this is your fault, Sam—I know that. And I'm glad I was there earlier. Just wish the shooter hadn't gotten away.'

Memories of that nightmare incident flash before my eyes. 'Why did she ask if you were a police officer?'

Jodie's teeth show when she snarls her reply. 'Besom knew a police officer wouldn't shoot if she dropped her gun and legged it. She was right—but I've never been more tempted to ignore procedure.'

My gaze drops to the case in her hand. 'Jodie, I understand why you're moving out and promise Daisy and I will make ourselves scarce soon as Alan lets us. But he says we've to stick around until some "bigwigs" arrive—I assume they want to hear what happened today from the horses' mouths. Then we're offski—and it'll be safe for you to come back.'

I dip my head at Alanna, who's gurgling happily and trying to unbutton her mum's cardigan. 'Where's Rosemary?'

'It's my day off—which means it's hers, too.' (Rosemary is Alanna's nanny, who looks after the baby while Jodie's working.)

A lightning bolt of inspiration zings out of nowhere. 'Wait a minute, Jodie. Instead of going to Mr M and Kat's, why don't you move into our cottage while we're away? Then Logan can go with you. I know his hours here are all over the place, but the cottage is only two minutes down the road—it won't be much different from working out of the owners flat.'

She thinks, then grins. 'That would be ideal. If you're sure...?'

'Of course I'm sure. Listen, if the "bigwigs" don't let us away tonight, can Daisy and I bunk in your flat?'

'No problem. Fair exchange and all that. Thanks, Sam—Logan didn't feel he could be too far from the hotel just now, but your cottage is a brilliant compromise. I wasn't looking forward to leaving him here on his own.'

'Great—we'll help with moving your stuff over. Okay, Daisy?'

Daisy nods, but Hugh steps up and shakes his head. 'I've not to let either of you leave the building—sorry.'

Daisy prods his chest. 'What a load of cobblers. Listen, mate, if we want to...'

Squeezing her arm, I smile apologetically at Hugh. 'Daisy, he's right. Look at what just happened. And remember, it's not only about us any more—Angus is already in hospital. And Ralf...'

Daisy dips her head. 'Yeah, okay...'

Kat flounces over and takes Jodie's case from Daisy. 'Don't worry, I'll help Jodie.'

Jodie steps towards the residents lounge. 'Give me two minutes and I'll fill Logan in on the new plan.'

As Jodie disappears through the archway, I throw Kat a nervous smile. 'Hope your dad isn't too disappointed. He dotes on Alanna—*and* Jodie. Poor soul's probably dead excited about them coming to stay.'

Kat "harrumph"s. 'He knows nothing about it—beggar took off first thing this morning. It's either a golf match, or another secret assignation.'

That grabs Daisy's attention. 'You still got no idea who the new woman is?'

'None, but Dad's out of the office more than he's in just now. Miss Dobie's almost as bad—but I'll stomach running the place on my own meantime, because Dad's agreed to let me hire my own secretary.'

'Does Miss Dobie know?' I ask, grinning.

'No—and he can blooming well tell her himself. It's not that I'm scared of the woman, but...'

Daisy nods sagely. 'Yeah, best leave that to Mr M. What's happening to Miss Dobie, then? Is he going to give her the push?'

'Of course not. She'll still be Dad's assistant, but I'll have my own. I've drummed up a lot of new business, so it makes sense.'

Jodie re-appears and I hand her the cottage keys. 'I feel terrible we can't prepare it properly—just bung our stuff in the attic room if it's in your way. And make use of any food—and booze—you find.'

Daisy scowls. 'Not like *we'll* be needing it.'

'Thanks, Sam.' Jodie hands me the owners flat keys in return. 'Same goes for you, upstairs—move anything you want, and help yourselves from the fridge and pantry.'

Since the various law enforcement agencies seem to have run out of questions for us, and with precious little else to do while waiting for Alan's "bigwigs" to arrive, we retire to the owners flat. Hugh insists he doesn't mind carrying a chair out to the landing and sitting guard there. I feel terrible about letting him do that, but grit my teeth on the impulse to protest. We need some time to unwind—and looking at an armoured gorilla with a sub-machine gun is *not* conducive to de-stressing.

Daisy and I started our life at Cairncroft up here, on the hotel's top floor. The owners flat is a spacious, airy, two-bedroomed abode that has housed Jodie and Logan since we flitted to our cottage. Gazing around, I wonder why we ever wanted to move.

Alright, why *I* wanted to move.

I suppose it felt like work was taking over and I had this misguided idea that living off-site would broaden Daisy's and my horizons. I had visions of finding new hobbies and getting more involved in village life—but the truth of the matter is it made not one iota of difference. The flaw in my thinking was the notion we needed to "get away" from work—while the reality is neither of us could be happier than when solving a case or organising a hotel function. (Okay, maybe that last's more me.)

'Funny being back,' Daisy comments.

'We're here all the time, visiting Jodie—especially since Alanna came along. In a sense, we never left.'

'Yeah, but—it's different *staying* here.'

'Only for one night at most,' I remind her, and something goes cold in my chest.

Daisy gives me a hug. 'We'll find a way through this, Sam—when have we not? Look, why don't I knock us up some bacon rolls while you phone your fiancé? Speaking to Bob the Builder always cheers you up.'

Usually it does—but not with news like this to share

She's right, though—Davy and I need to talk.

Daisy heads for the door. 'Come through to the kitchen when you're done,' she chirrups, the thought of food obviously sufficient to cheer *her* up.

'Um... do you want to wait until I've finished? Then I could cook the bacon...'

'Naw, it'll be fine—I'm a dab hand at frying.'

I'VE JUST HUNG UP MY CALL WITH DAVY WHEN A PIERCING siren splits the air. Either there's been another incident downstairs, or Daisy's set the smoke alarm off.

I race to the kitchen and sure enough find her flapping wildly at the saucepan with a dishtowel— while an overhead alarm unit wails, flashes, and practically crawls across the ceiling.

'What happened?' I gasp.

She stops mid-swipe. 'Dunno. Think the oil must have been too hot—bacon's nice and crispy, though. Any idea where Jodie keeps her buns...?'

Smoke alarms are wired in these days so we end up turning it off at the mains box, then Daisy produces two bottles of lager. 'Sorry, it's own brand stuff from the supermarket. How can Logan work in a bar and drink this rubbish?'

'If it's wet and alcoholic,' I tell her, 'it'll do.'

My blood sugar must be desperately low because I actually enjoy Daisy's bacon butties. There were no rolls to be found, only bread, so we had to settle for bacon *sandwiches*. Daisy toasted the bread (so it matched the bacon?) and somehow managed to avoid burning *it*... Maybe it's just having some quiet time to let everything sink in that blinds me to Daisy's unique take on cookery, but suddenly even Logan's lager tastes like nectar.

'So—how's Bob?' she asks.

'Don't call him that—and his stomach still hasn't settled.'

'Oops. Sorryyy. Might not have been the potion, though. Builders eat in some right dives.... Em, what'd he say about witness protection?'

I sigh. 'Couldn't bring myself to tell him. I've barely got my own head around this, Daisy.'

'Hmpff—he can hardly complain. Not after expecting *you* to trot off across the country after *him*.'

'It isn't that simple, as you well know. He didn't ask me to change my identity and go into hiding.'

'No, but...'

'Oh, Daisy,' I cry, my eyes tearing up. 'What's going to become of us?'

She shakes her head. 'It'll be fine. I still think there has to be a way out of this, but if worst happens—we'll get used to it. New friends—a fresh start—it won't be *that* bad.'

'I don't *want* a fresh start—this is the happiest I've ever been.'

She goes silent then and we sit for a while in companionable silence—each thinking our own thoughts. After a while, Daisy gets up and fetches two more bottles of Logan's bargain lager. She pops the caps and sets one in front of me. 'You've been through worse, Sam. Losing both parents—and your leg—you came back from that. Your entire life went up in smoke, but look how everything worked out. You can do it again.'

'I suppose. You too—it's obvious you don't enjoy talking about it, but I've gathered your childhood wasn't pretty—and kind of inferred things still weren't a bed of roses after you left home.'

She looks thoughtful, staring through the years. 'Yeah, I've been in some bad places too. Same as you, though, my time here has been the best ever—not that there was much competition. But—life goes on. We have to adapt—I'd rather start anew somewhere else than end up six feet under.'

She's right. I hate what's happening, but at least we're still alive—and lucky to be.

A loud bang at the door jerks us out of our newfound pragmatism. Daisy leaps up and grabs a kitchen knife from the worktop, then Hugh's voice echoes down the hall: 'It's just me. Alan says those people from London are due any time and he wants you there when they arrive.'

'Coming,' I shout back, relief flooding through me. I nod at the butcher's knife as Daisy lays it down. 'Lot of good that would be against a gun.'

She sniffs. 'Worked for Ghostface.'

Then she pats her pocket. 'And I've got my taser, too. C'mon, let's go see what these "bigwigs" want.'

17

Hugh escorts us to the residents lounge. I see through the archway that Alan has set up shop in there. He's pulled two tables together and laid out his laptop, iPad, and mobile phone neatly alongside each other. There are still a few uniformed officers drifting about, but the main caucus has dispersed. Turning back, to Hugh's obvious annoyance, I approach the reception desk. 'Hazel—have we *any* guests staying right now?'

Hazel shakes her head. 'The last of them left this morning. After...'

I nod, grimly, and she goes on: '... I've cancelled all the weekend bookings. A few weren't happy and refused to be re-booked. Most of them agreed to alternative dates, though. Logan came by while it was going on and told me to offer a 25% discount for their inconvenience—that helped.'

Good thinking, Logan

'So we've nobody new arriving until—when?'

'Tuesday.'
That's 5 days away—should be long enough
'Fine—well done.'

Hugh shuffles impatiently, so I give Hazel a thumbs up and follow him through to Alan's improvised nerve centre. It's quietened down a lot in here—the local police have cleared out now, leaving only a handful of Alan's NCA men. Daisy's already there, standing beside his chair. Absently, she picks up Alan's iPad and he snatches it back with a glare. For a moment I think he's about to smack her hand, but (luckily for him) thinks better of it. I drag another seat over and Daisy does the same. When we're sat facing Alan, I ask: 'Where are they, then?'

Alan purses his lips. 'Sorry, I might have been a little premature. I got a report their plane had landed but just received an update saying they went on to the hospital. Checking on Angus, presumably.'

A ripple of annoyance goes through me after Hugh rushing us down like that. But more importantly: 'How *is* Angus? Have you heard any more about his condition?'

Alan dismisses my concern with a casual flap of his hand. 'Broken rib and a hole in his chest.

They've sown up the hole—all he can do now is wait for the rib to mend. Sore things, ribs,' he adds as an afterthought.

'That's what Wilson said.'

I look down to see my hands clasped so tightly all the knuckles are white. 'If it hadn't been for Angus and Jodie...'

I let the thought hang, not wanting to finish. 'It feels like I should send Angus flowers or something. Just so he knows I'm grateful.'

Alan picks up a ballpoint and chews its end. 'Hospitals don't allow flowers these days. I've a better idea—if you ask Colin to look me out a nice bottle of malt, I'll arrange for somebody to smuggle it in. With a broken rib, I think Angus would appreciate that more.'

'Brilliant, Alan—tell Colin I said he was to give you something good. At least ten years old.'

Alan nods and makes a note on the pad beside his laptop. Obviously a very organised person. Daisy shifts in her chair and leans forward. 'So, what? You want us to hang around here like lemmings until these pen-pushers deign to arrive? Who are they, anyway?'

Alan smiles tightly. 'What they *aren't* is pen-pushers. No, sounds as though they'll be awhile yet. I'll let Hugh know when they appear.'

We get up and wander into reception. 'Okay, having impressed Alan with how valuable our time is, what do you propose we do with it?'

She shrugs. 'Dunno. No, I do. Let's go over to the detective agency and indoctrinate Rebecca some more. If we do somehow turn this around, I don't want to come back and find my business in tatters.'

Optimistic as ever. I've all but accepted we *won't* be coming back, which thought makes my chest tighten as I drink in the hotel's familiar ambience—while I still can. Although, without guests, the atmosphere is unusually flat. But anything that keeps us busy and diverts our minds from what we stand to lose is fine by me.

Daisy crooks a finger at Hugh and he sidles over. She tells him where we're off to and adds: 'We'll go around the outside, if that's okay.'

Hugh looks dubious. 'My orders say you're to stay inside, but I suppose since it's onsite—I'd rather we use the back door, though. To limit your exposure.'

Daisy shakes her head. 'I need some air,' she retorts, face set in a stubborn scowl. 'Want to make an issue of it?'

Exhaling heavily, Hugh dips his head. 'Alright, but if I tell you to do something—do it. Like throwing yourselves flat on the ground to clear my line of fire.'

'They won't try the same stunt twice,' Daisy snaps back, taking off towards the exit so suddenly I scurry to keep up.

Outside, it's a typical November day. A light breeze plucks at the last dead leaves and cold sunlight makes a layer of moisture over the lawns sparkle like low-flying fireflies. I blink away a tear and find myself committing the scene to memory, hoping I can remember in the sort of detail time tries to erode.

We descend the steps and Daisy stops abruptly. She points. 'Look at that.'

I follow her finger to a bright red sports car hurtling up the driveway. 'You're right. That idiot's going far too fast.'

Daisy screws up her face and I try to ignore the nose ring's resultant acrobatics. 'Sam, that's a Porsche Cayenne. They don't *go* slow.'

'Since when do you know anything about cars?'

She huffs. 'Since Richard on Top Gear raced one of them against a Red Devils parachutist who was free-falling in a flying suit. Don't you remember? You were there when it was on.'

'No... wasn't watching. Who won?'

Her face falls. 'The parachutist—but he had the wind behind him.'

'Right, inside... NOW.' Hugh hustles us back into reception while a radio on his shoulder jabbers incomprehensibly. Meantime, Alan races past with three other "suits" hot on his heels. We watch through the glass door (despite Hugh's efforts to shoo us away) as the Porsche draws into a space next to the entrance. Instead of Richard Hammond, it's a woman who unfolds from the driving seat. Her passenger's a man in his mid-twenties, possibly a few years younger, and they both exit simultaneously.

The woman holds up a leather wallet, and from the way Alan practically prostrates himself at her feet I'm guessing it isn't a bus pass. He turns and beckons frantically in our direction.

I look to our bodyguard for permission and he shrugs. 'If the boss says it's okay...'

Daisy leaps ahead and scuttles down the steps. Following at a pace more appropriate to negotiating steps with a partial prosthetic, I feel the woman's eyes bore into me.

About my height, her ease of movement getting out of the car suggested lifelong training with The Royal Ballet. Flaxen hair, almost shoulder length and cut in a bobbed, simple-to-keep style, suggests regular hairstyling sessions aren't a priority. That Arran-knit jumper must have cost a few bob and those tight black jeans are obviously designer. It'd be easy to label her "loaded" but she has a mean-leanness about her, of the sort you don't expect in wealthy people.

It's the eyes that tell you who she is, though. Blue as the Mediterranean, studded with shards of jade, they burn like twin lasers. This is *not* a woman I'd care to cross.

Her gaze snaps to Alan and he wilts visibly. 'Are those the targets?' she demands, with a wave of her hand.

Alan nods. 'I thought you'd want to...'

Behind the woman, her male companion sniggers. Alan takes an involuntary step back when she advances on him. 'You moron. WHAT are they doing out here? Get them inside—NOW.'

Alan and Hugh march us back up the steps. Daisy squints around at Alan. 'Gonna let her talk to you like that?'

He shrugs. 'I don't have a lot of choice.'

'But you're a detective inspector.'

'Yeah, and she's... let's just say she outranks me.'

We watch as bossy-woman's passenger helps Angus from the Porsche's rear seat. I frown and turn to Alan. 'They've got Angus with them—should he be out of hospital?'

'Probably not—but *I'm* not telling them.'

Angus comes up the steps with one of *them* on each side, supporting him. 'Angus,' I shout, wanting to hug the little man but knowing someone with a broken rib wouldn't appreciate it. 'It's so good to see you—and thanks. A million times over.'

The woman shakes her head. 'Silly beggar should still be in hospital, but he signed himself out. Stubborn as a mule, aren't you?'

Angus tilts his head. 'And you aren't, Miss Dawn?'

She tuts, but with unmistakable affection. Then her death-stare reboots and fastens on me. 'Where's your bar?'

I raise a hand to the archway. 'Through there—in the residents lounge.'

Alan and Hugh stop inside the archway where they stand rigid, like two sentries outside Buckingham Palace. Daisy and I follow the others to a table and watch as *they* help Angus into an armchair. Poor guy grunts all the way down—obviously in pain, but trying (unsuccessfully) not to show it. Dawn—as I now know she's called—catches Colin's eye and yanks a thumb at Angus. 'He'll have one of those disgusting malt whiskies. The best you've got. How are you at making martinis?'

Colin looks offended. 'Pretty good, actually.'

'Bone dry—with two olives?'

Colin's expression falters. 'Yes... I can do that.'

'Well, what are you waiting for? Oh, hang on. Have you any red wine with a decent vintage?'

Colin draws himself straight. 'A Cabalié 2021. It might not sound much, but...'

Dawn's male companion suddenly perks up. 'That'll do nicely.'

'My brother approves—praise indeed. Alright, get on with it—before we die of thirst.'

Colin—grins? *I'd* have taken offence at Dawn's attitude, but my barman positively preens and rummages for a bottle from the case he talked me into ordering several months ago. Finding one, he twirls a corkscrew over it like a seasoned drum majorette.

No need to show off, Colin

Daisy's still standing, as am I—it's almost as though we're waiting for an invitation to sit.

In MY hotel?

Defiantly, I throw myself onto the armchair nearest Angus—and Daisy crashes down opposite. Raising a hand (and realising too late that smacks of primary school) I catch Colin's eye. 'We'll have our usual.' He nods absently—intent on building Dawn's martini.

There's a sudden silence until Daisy breaks it. 'Nice car,' she says, looking between the siblings.

Dawn slips languorously into the seat on Angus' other side and her brother sits opposite, beside Daisy. 'It's only a rental—best we could get on a short-term hire. I prefer my Lamborghini.'

'Dawn likes the Lambo so much she has two,' the brother interjects.

'You have two Lamborghinis?' Daisy practically mouths. I'm starting to worry. The woman is obnoxious—what's with this hero worship she seems to garner so effortlessly?

Colin brings the drinks and Dawn waits until he's put them in front of their owners, and retreated to the bar. 'I like smart cars,' she says ruminatively. 'And nice hotels. Which reminds me—we'll need three rooms. Roger and I have no special requirements, but he...' she tilts her head at Angus '... needs everything doing for him. Can you oblige?'

Her gaze roams the empty tables. 'You don't exactly seem rushed off your feet.'

She's getting on my... nerves. 'I'll organise something. Whatever Angus wants—he only has to ring down.'

Dawn looks around with a scornful expression. 'This isn't what I'm used to, but we have to sleep. Do you have a charge-point for my car?'

'There's one in Donstable,' Daisy mutters. 'Behind the Co-op.'

I feel my cheeks burn. 'We've been meaning to... I mean, electric cars are getting more popular, so I suppose we should... but haven't yet...'

Dawn sniffs. 'Luckily, it's a hybrid—so we won't stick. I presume there's somewhere around here sells petrol?'

'Behind the Co-op in Donstable,' Daisy repeats tonelessly. 'Same place that has the charge-point.'

That gets a glower before Dawn says: 'Alright, Roger and I had better go and have a recce.'

She snatches a quick sip from her martini. Colin's been watching intently since delivering the drinks, and Dawn catches his eye. When she gives him a thumbs up, the silly beggar turns bright red.

Then she springs to her feet, which makes me stiffen. 'I thought you wanted to interview us?'

'All in good time.'

Daisy's lip curls. She's obviously had enough. 'Now just hold on a minute, you supercilious cow. We've already wasted hours waiting for you—and want to be out of here tonight.'

Dawn regards her stonily. 'That won't be possible, I'm afraid. Until the Scorpion's dealt with, moving you would be too risky.'

'The Scorpion?' I repeat weakly.

'She's a contract killer,' the brother—Roger?—murmurs before taking a big swallow of his wine, smacking his lips, and standing. 'A good one.

Believe me—while she's on the loose, you're safer here with us.'

He nods at Angus. 'Not many people could take Angus down.'

Dawn's face turns livid and suddenly she doesn't sound so controlled. 'And in doing so, she made this personal. Don't worry about the Scorpion—I'm just itching to get my hands on her.'

She catches herself, takes a deep breath, then barks: 'Roger—with me. Alan—keep an eye on *them* while we look this dump over.'

'DUMP?'

Dawn's already disappeared under the archway, passing Alan on his way over. Roger ambles across to our side of the table and slips between Angus' and my chairs, then bends to give me a sympathetic smile. 'Ignore her—she's upset. Your hotel's quite... quaint, really.'

Then he dashes after his sister and I turn on Alan. 'Who *are* these people?'

It's Angus who answers. 'Right now, I'd say they're your and Daisy's best hope.'

18

"Dump?" Who the HELL does she think she is, driving up in her fancy Porsche and calling MY hotel a DUMP?

Daisy, who was ready to blow just a moment ago, pats the back of my hand. 'Calm down, Sam. Don't take this "not being a wimp" thing too far—I liked it better when you were scared of your own shadow.'

'I was NEVER...'

Having sat down in Roger's chair, Alan stands abruptly. 'At the risk of disobeying "orders", I think Hugh's quite capable of "keeping an eye on them". Meantime, I have work to do.'

He stalks off, obviously as incensed by Wonder Woman as I am. Angus laughs softly. 'She's something else, isn't she? Miss Dawn?'

Daisy ignores him and turns to me. 'You do see what's happening here? Joan of Arc's got it in for this "Scorpion" person and she plans to use us as bait.'

'Bait?'

'Yeah, it's obvious. She knows the Scorpion won't give up trying to eliminate us. We're the cheese in Dawn's mousetrap.'

Angus claps his hands—three times—then nods. He's grinning. 'I was right about the two of ye.'

He waves a hand then uses it to pick up his (rather full—I need to have a word with Colin) glass of Lagavulin. After a sip, his gaze settles on me. 'Yer friend's spot on—Miss Dawn won't rest until she's dealt with the Scorpion. Neither is she likely to balk at using unconventional tactics. Then her and Mr Roger will fly away again—which would be a pity.'

He's lost me. '*What* would be a pity?'

Angus sucks in a huge breath, then grabs at his chest and gasps. 'Ae my life—I must remember *no* tae dae that. Aye… going by what Wilf told me, it's my impression all four of ye are cut from the same cloth. By that, I mean ye've all got a nicely developed sense of right and wrong. Now, I'll be honest—my friends are no' themselves at the moment. Recently, they lost somebody and it's knocked them off kilter—particularly poor Mr Roger. They need a worthwhile challenge tae help them get back on track.'

Daisy rocks her head. 'Protecting us, you mean?'

Angus scowls. 'Aw, they'll protect the two of ye from the Scorpion, that goes without sayin'. Nay, I'm talkin' about yer other problem with this Glasgow gang boss. What's his name—Gilmartin?'

Daisy stares at him incredulously, despite her own thoughts last night in the same vein. 'What can *they* do about *him*? And why would they want to?'

Angus huffs and takes another (somewhat unappreciative, I can't help thinking) swig of the most expensive whisky we stock. 'Were ye no listenin', lassie, tae what I said about right and wrong? When Miss Dawn and Mr Roger realise what's at stake for the two of ye, there'll be no stoppin' them. And believe me, if them two decide tae sort Gilmartin—sorted he will be.'

Angus waves a beckoning hand (not the one holding his Lagavulin) and we both lean closer. 'They're furious with this "Scorpion" wifey for shooting me—but it was yon Gilmartin fella who sent her. I'll remind them of that—and subtly suggest that after neutralising the Scorpion, Gilmartin deserves their attention tae. Just tae fan the flame.'

He grins. 'Win-win. My friends need takin' out of themselves and you two want yer lives back. Now—if ye don't mind, I'd best go and lie down. It's been a while since anybody shot me...'

WE'RE OBVIOUSLY GOING NOWHERE TONIGHT, SO DAISY and I decide to sort out our sleeping arrangements in the owners flat. Hugh insists we use the stairs "because it would be safer".

'Why are we safer on the stairs?' I ask, puzzled.

'I was in your lift earlier—it's mental.'

Ah—right

'Take it you're camping out in our living room,' I check. Hugh nods and then, as we approach the top floor, he stiffens when someone appears at the landing door.

'There you are.'

It's Roger. *Her* brother. Hugh relaxes visibly and Roger moves back to let us through. He holds out what looks like two silver pens. 'These are emergency signallers. Any trouble, twist the barrel...' he demonstrates with a third pen from inside his jacket '... then press the button on top and we'll know you're in danger. And activated or not, it constantly transmits your precise location—which is a refinement I only added recently. Bitter experience,' he adds, winking. (WHY does everybody feel a need to do that?)

Daisy stuffs hers in a pocket and I drop mine in my bag. 'Thanks. Is that all?'

Roger hangs his head in response to the hostility I'm making no effort to conceal, while Daisy takes her chance to give him a good once-over—and seems impressed with what she sees.

He *is* handsome—lean and lithe, with deep wells of intelligence bubbling in those hazel eyes. Also, in complete contrast to his sister, Roger has an air of humility about him. He's obviously fit (and I don't mean in the way Daisy's thinking), probably a trained killer, but nonetheless gives off a strange sense of vulnerability. Just occasionally, that confident swagger melts into the scared look of a little boy.

Angus told us they're grieving for someone and said "particularly Roger." Is he saying Roger was closer to whoever died—or that Dawn's brother is made of less stern stuff?

'Listen,' Roger says. 'We don't mean to be... Angus getting hurt on top of other things that have happened recently, well—it's thrown us somewhat. Dawn *can* come over a bit strong sometimes, but when you get to know her better...'

'If we survive that long,' Daisy snaps, squaring up to him. Her "pie-eyed" look's a memory. 'I see what's going on here—the pair of you are counting on this assassin coming back to finish Sam and me. My worry is how close you'll let the Scorpion get—to us—just so you can take her down.'

Roger's unruly chestnut hair is thick and wavy. He runs his fingers through it, slowly, and Daisy softens visibly. 'Your safety is our priority,' he insists. 'We won't put you at risk. But the Scorpion *has* to be stopped.'

He stops and thinks for a moment—hard, from the looks of it—glances at Hugh, then breathes out noisily. 'The Scorpion killed one of our fellow ICE agents a month ago. There's been an entire task force after her ever since, and they've come up with squat. It's very important to us, *and* our organisation—not to mention her future victims—that we put a stop to the woman.'

'Especially because she shot Angus?' I suggest, because it seems to me that's what this is *really* about.

He nods. 'Yep, you're right. When we heard Angus had been shot… after… that *does* make it personal. But we're also pros—don't worry about being in danger, because we'll keep you safe. Losing a pair of innocents like you—that would finish us. And we're a long way from being finished.'

I'm pretty sure he silently mouthed those last words again. Is Roger trying to convince himself? Then he pushes past and goes down the steps two at a time.

'That guy's well screwed up about something,' Daisy comments, although I notice her eyes stay with Roger until he disappears.

'Something's shaken them both badly,' I agree. 'But if this is about proving they're still capable, it could work in our favour. Might make them try harder.'

'Hopefully', she says with an eyeroll, then I follow her to the owners flat.

Hugh diplomatically withdraws to the kitchen, ostensibly to brew himself a cuppa, and Daisy cracks open a bottle of wine. Before pouring, she reads the label. 'What would Roger have said if Colin had given him this?' She pulls a face and turns the bottle so I can read it too.

Laughing, I wonder out loud: 'Why does Logan buy such rubbish when there's decent stuff downstairs—which he'd get at cost?'

Daisy sniffs the bottle's neck suspiciously. 'Because even at cost, this crap's probably still cheaper.'

She pours a little into her glass and tastes it tentatively. 'Ugh.'

After stomping out of the room, she returns a moment later carrying a box of supermarket lager. 'At least this was drinkable,' she says, handing me a bottle.

I slump on the sofa and Daisy puts her box down between us before following suit. She tosses a bottle opener in my lap. 'You'll need that.'

'Thanks.'

After snapping the bottle's crimped cap, I hand back the opener and sigh. 'Daisy, what was Angus trying to tell us?'

'He seems to think Dawn and Roger could do something about Gilmartin—if he motivates them enough.'

'That was my take on it, too. But what can they do the NCA can't?'

'Nothing. They're obviously Angus' blue-eyed substitute grandchildren—well, brown in Roger's case—'

'Oh, you noticed the colour of his eyes?'

She ignores that. '—and Angus has an overrated opinion of their capabilities. Let's just hope Dawn and Roger are good enough to catch this "Scorpion" tout suite—then we can get out of here before more of Gilmartin's stooges arrive to shoot the place up.'

'Amen to that,' I say, holding my bottle up in a toast. Daisy clinks hers against it, takes a swallow, then holds it in front of her face. She stares balefully at the label.

'Well, I *remembered* this being drinkable,' she mutters. 'Oh, blow it... I'm knackered. Think I'll go to bed.'

I stare in disbelief. 'It's barely six o'clock.'

Then I yawn, hugely, and Daisy giggles. 'Maybe everything's catching up with us? Either that, or Logan's lager is stronger than we realised.'

I laugh shortly. 'It *isn't* the lager—you'd get more kick from a glass of tap water. But we have been through a lot the past few days... did you check whether there's a bed in the second bedroom? And not just Alanna's cot.'

'Oh cripes.'

She dashes off, then reappears—looking relieved. 'Naw, there *is* a proper bed as well. Only a single, but who cares so long as it's soft and flat. Right, I'm going to lie down before I fall down.'

I stand, and a wave of dizziness makes me sway.

'You okay there, Sam?'

'Fine—look, I'll probably see you later. I'm sure a couple of hours' shuteye to recharge is all we need.'

She grins. 'Maybe meet up for a midnight snack?'

I sigh. 'Don't start without me—better if I cook the bacon this time.'

Popping my head in the kitchen, I tell Hugh what we're doing and that he can make free with the living room. Then it's through to Jodie and Logan's bedroom where I flop on their bed fully clothed. Perhaps I only need a ten-minute lie-down to revive me.

My thoughts zing like angry bees—I don't see me getting to sleep anytime soon. Imagination drags me back to the runaway Panda, re-creates my terror at finding myself a duck in that sniper's shooting gallery, and simultaneously—is this some weird form of mental 3D vision?—dumps me on the drive outside where I once again look down the muzzle of Scorpion's pistol. Then everything goes grey and...

19

gosh, must have dozed off after all. Swinging both legs off the bed, I grab at my skull—which feels like there's a cannonball rattling around inside. Sitting very still, I try to get my bearings. I came through here to lie-down, catnapped for a few minutes, then woke up with the world's worst hangover.

One thing's for sure—it wasn't Logan's lager.

Then my eyes stray to the digital display on Jodie's alarm clock. Which isn't helpful because it's miles out. 9.00am? My best guess is seven—*pm*. There's no need really, but habit makes me check my wristwatch. Strange—it's wrong too.

Exactly the same "wrong" as Jodie's clock.

The bedroom door crashes open and Daisy staggers in, head clasped in her hands. 'Sam, did we tie one on last night? 'Cos I honestly don't remember doing that…'

She collapses on the bed next to me and we stare at each other. 'Let's take this slowly,' I suggest. 'We both suddenly felt incredibly weary and headed for our kips—just before six—and now it's nine the following morning. We must have fallen into a deep sleep—and no, we didn't "tie one on", although I feel the same as you look. Daisy, what's going on?'

She moans and puts both hands to her crown. 'Ow. My head's sorer than Angus' rib. Sam, we've been Mickey-Finned. There's no other explanation.'

'Mickey-Finned?'

At first I'm incredulous but, as with most of her epiphanies—it fits. 'How?'

'Dunno—somehow, those siblings from hell must have spiked our drinks.'

'Why, though?'

'Again—dunno.'

She stands, then grabs my hand to pull me upright. 'C'mon—I need coffee. A *lot* of coffee.'

Her expression darkens. 'After which, Dawn and Roger have some explaining to do.'

Four Americano pods later, Daisy and I feel much better. We thought maybe Hugh could shed some light on our lost hours, but he's nowhere to be seen. Which is very odd, after the way he's stuck to us like flypaper. Daisy's first reaction when we found him missing was to lock and bolt the front door, just in case...

She gets up from the breakfast bar and tosses another pod into Jodie's machine, then raises her eyebrows.

'Yep,' I confirm. 'Keep 'em comin'.'

I gesture towards the living room where Hugh *isn't.* 'Surely, if there was anything untoward about his disappearance, we'd have heard by now.'

She shrugs helplessly. 'Who knows? I'll phone down to Hazel before we leave the flat—make sure they haven't got another war raging down there.'

Then her expression darkens. 'It *was* them,' she says—yet again. 'They doped us.'

'How, though?' I counter.

'*How*—they must have done it in the residents lounge. Beyond that, I'm baffled—despite being a trained pickpocket who should have picked up on any sleight-of-hand tricks.'

I close my eyes, remembering. 'Okay, *if* that's what happened—Roger was next to you. It would have been easy enough for him to slip something into your drink—assuming he has the same dubious skills you do.'

She nods—and from the wince it incites, wishes she hadn't. 'Yeah, but *you* were sitting opposite—with Angus between *her* and you. And Angus wouldn't have managed to pull off anything like that. He couldn't move without grunting—you'd have heard him coming a mile off.'

Slowly, more memories from last night return. 'Remember, after *she* mouthed off about our hotel being a "dump", Roger ambled across to reassure me his sister was just stressed?'

Her eyes widen. 'That's it. Yes—that besom knew exactly what she was doing, slagging off the hotel. She was setting up an opportunity for her traitorous brother to go over and spike your drink.'

'Traitorous—c'mon, Daisy. I know you fancy him, but he doesn't owe you anything.'

She rears, fixing me with a pair of bleary eyes. 'Okay, let's keep it simple. If that beggar put something in my drink last night, he's dead.'

When Daisy rings down using the owners flat extension, Hazel not only confirms everything's quiet—she adds that all the NCA personnel (except Alan and Hugh) cleared out early this morning.

We go down in the lift for speed. 'All we need is some numbered ping-pong balls,' Daisy suggests. 'Then we could run our own lottery.'

Being "shaken, not stirred" does nothing for either of our sore heads—or moods. In reception, before Hazel can speak, Louis flies through the archway. 'Miz Chessington—zees ees ze final straw. I vill not vork under zese conditions.'

Obviously, the milkman delivered skimmed milk again

Daisy doesn't help when she mutters: 'What "vork"? We've no guests.'

Patting Louis on the shoulder, I try to placate our angry chef. 'Whatever it is, Louis, I'll fix it.'

'You say zis before, ze last time.'

'I'll get onto the dairy straight away…'

He looks blank for a moment. 'Dairy? What 'ave zey to do with all zese dead bodies people keep carrying through my kitchen?'

'Dead bodies?'

Looking equally puzzled, Daisy pipes up: 'What dead bodies?'

'Ze first vas on Halloween—zis morning I come in to find another body bag in my kitchen. Zey were planning to put eet een ze valk-in freezer, but I refused to give zem ze key.'

Zey? I mean—they?

'Who?'

'Zat voman and her brother.'

Coincidentally (?) Dawn and Roger saunter out from the residents lounge at precisely that moment. Roger grins. 'Is he still on about that? The cleanup team took it away an hour ago.'

The cleanup team?

'You got rid of a body?' I clarify as Louis stomps off in disgust while Roger nods casually, as though we're talking about a council uplift.

'*Whose* body?'.

Dawn's been watching with a sly smile. Now she speaks for the first time, in a voice that drips satisfaction. 'Why, the Scorpion's, of course.'

Daisy and I blurt it in unison. 'The Scorpion?'

Roger looks smug as his sister. 'Yep, we reckoned—for a second attempt—she was most likely to come after you during the night. It's well-known people are at their most vulnerable between 3 and 6am, which is why law enforcement favours dawn raids. Anyway, we were right. She made her move at 5am—and found us waiting for her.'

Daisy turns pink. 'You moron.'

Dawn blinks and Roger takes a step back. 'You're welcome—you know, for keeping you safe and all.'

Daisy's in his face now. 'Keeping us safe? You drugged us last night—call that keeping us safe? What if the Scorpion had got past you? We'd have been helpless.'

'You'd have been just as helpless awake,' Dawn points out dismissively, but her eyes stay on Daisy. Then she adds, grudgingly: 'Alright. Maybe not *you*...'

Charming

'... but we didn't want the pair of you getting in our way while...'

Roger steps forward and slips his arm through Daisy's. 'Why don't we all sit down? I'll sweet talk Hazel into bringing more of that delicious coffee she's been magicking up from somewhere and we'll explain everything. You were never at any risk—I promise.'

―⁂―

THE COFFEE *IS* GOOD—I SUSPECT HAZEL POACHED IT FROM The Last Chance Saloon, since her chances of getting into Louis' kitchen would have been zero. He's probably barricaded the door by now.

Hazel beats a fast retreat after delivering the tray and Daisy fixes Roger with her most ferocious glare. Meantime, Dawn makes a show of adding precisely the right amount of cream to a huge mug of coffee, then swigs it back like Daisy at her best.

In a clipped tone, Daisy says: 'You said we weren't at risk? How come?'

Dawn answers, after patting her mouth with a linen napkin. 'Because the Scorpion never got inside the building. We took her down outside.'

Daisy stares disbelievingly. 'So our safety depended on you spotting this assassin in the dark? Oh, great. That makes me feel *really* safe—I hope you at least had night-vision goggles.'

'We had better than that,' Roger tells her. 'I had a drone up, equipped with infra-red sensors. It detected the Scorpion's body heat and told us exactly where she was.'

Daisy's silent for a moment. Then she turns to Roger with fresh interest. 'You've got a drone that does *that*? Can I see it?'

Huffing impatiently, I flap a hand to get their attention—because I'm worried about precisely what "took her down" means. 'Never mind the drone—Dawn, did one of you shoot the Scorpion in cold blood? Was this an execution?'

To my surprise, Dawn looks shocked. 'Absolutely not—we aren't killers. In fact, it was an NCA man who pulled the trigger. A head shot—because he assumed, rightly as it turned out, she'd be wearing a bullet-proof vest. The Scorpion died instantly.'

I shudder at the image that conjures and Dawn pauses, then goes on. 'The Scorpion was sneaking up on me—which was fine, because I knew she was. Roger was watching her on his drone feed and keeping me updated through my earpiece. The plan was I would taser her when she got close enough—we really wanted her alive, to interrogate. Unfortunately—as it turned out—I had two NCA men covering me from behind a clump of bushes, just in case.'

She pulls a face. 'One of them panicked. He saw the Scorpion draw a bead on me, which didn't matter because *I* was wearing a vest too. Unlike him, the Scorpion didn't have night-vision goggles—so she would have had to aim for central mass. But the NCA guy hadn't worked that out, so he went and shot her.'

All Daisy's hostility has evaporated. It's like watching your child realise the kid they hate has a bigger toybox. 'What sort of taser d'you use?'

'Yours,' Dawn replies with a little smile. 'Alan told us about your equipment cupboard, so... hope you don't mind. There's some wicked stuff in there, by the way.'

'Hmpff. My drones are in the stone-age compared to yours.'

Maybe this would be a good time to bring out the holiday snaps?

'Okay.' I stand, to get their attention. 'So we can go now—to Glasgow?'

Daisy's face falls. I think she'd forgotten and feel bad about reminding her. 'Yeah, we'd best find Alan and see if he's ready to leave. Then everyone can carry on with their lives.'

She gets up too, then glances at Dawn. 'I was right, though—you *were* using us as bait. Weren't you?'

Dawn nods slowly, then flaps her hand. 'Sit down, wilya? Yes, sorry. You *were* the flies on our hook—we knew the Scorpion would come back so long as you and Sam were still here. And yes, we drugged you—couldn't risk you twigging what was going on and interfering. Or worse, getting hurt...'

'How'd you do that?' Daisy demands, sitting again. 'Drug us, I mean—without me spotting it.'

Dawn stands and holds up a hand, spreading her fingers to prove it's empty. She leans over Daisy and reaches behind her ear. After making a show of tugging, Dawn draws back and opens her hand. An old American dollar, complete with golden eagle, lies in her palm.

'Sis is always in demand for kids' parties,' Roger chirps, which earns him a scowl.

'I don't do kids,' Dawn grates.

I believe her

'But it was *you* who slipped whatever it was in our drinks,' Daisy says, looking at Roger.

'She taught me everything I know,' he drawls glibly, indicating Dawn, who rolls her eyes.

'Anyway…' Dawn starts, but Daisy interrupts.

'Look, okay. Thanks… I think. Doesn't matter—where's Alan?'

Dawn smiles. 'Let me finish. We're grateful for your cooperation, albeit you had little choice. Also, Angus has been bleating on about some mobster being as much to blame for his shooting as the Scorpion—if not more so. Of course, we know fine he's simply taken a shine to you both and wants us to intervene on your behalf. Which we've decided to do. Now, pour yourselves another of these excellent coffees and I'll explain what's going to happen…'

20

After they've gone, I turn to Daisy. 'Do you think...?'

She looks dubious. 'Not really—but Dawn seemed confident. Like it was all in a day's work. Dunno, Sam... let's wait and see. They're only asking for twenty-four hours, after all.'

Dare I hope?

DAWN

Roger does a pretend recoil when Dawn turns from the mirror, and she pouts. 'I *was* going to ask what you thought...'

Her brother shakes his head. 'Scary—from a distance, I'd think you *were* the Scarred Spider. Hey, *she'll* get a laugh from this when we tell her.'

Even through layers of makeup transforming one side of her face into a ravaged mess, Dawn's amusement is plain. 'I still can't believe we're mates with the Continent's most feared contract killer. How did that happen?'

'It was my quick wit and repartee that won her over,' Roger says seriously, then ducks as a pillow hurtles overhead.

They're in Dawn's room at Glasgow's premier (and most expensive) hotel. She casts an appreciative eye over her surroundings, then glances through a window and across the Clyde to the SECC conference centre. Finally, her gaze flits to the room's four-poster bed as she curls bare toes into a huge sheepskin rug. 'What a relief to be back in a proper hotel. That place was a slum.'

'It wasn't so bad,' Roger protests. 'Very clean...'

Dawn tuts. 'What would a man who spends most of the year living on his boat know about anything? And that Louis character—I'm glad we didn't try his cooking.'

'They say he's a genius...' Roger murmurs.

'Anyway.' She turns to face him full on again. 'Will I do?'

'Absolutely, Sis. Any word back from Gilmartin yet?'

'No—but I'm not worried. Gilmartin's failed five times to kill Sam and Daisy—although of course he only knows about four of those. The guy has to be getting desperate. He won't turn down an approach from the Scarred Spider—not with her reputation.'

Roger nods. 'Yeah, they say her success rate is 100%. Maybe making friends with her *wasn't* such a bad idea...'

Dawn's phone dings and she lifts it. Then holds the screen out for Roger to see. 'Gilmartin. He'll be there at eight.'

She smiles. 'And so will I.'

DAWN GETS OUT OF THE PORSCHE AND SLAMS ITS DOOR, then looks around. The car park borders Hogganfield Loch, a large expanse of water within striking distance of Glasgow city centre. It's eight pm, and hers is the only vehicle here. Darkness fell several hours ago and LED lights in plastic posts along the boundary with Hogganfield's shore do little to disperse a gloom made creepier by the loch's inky backdrop.

Dawn strolls forward, right to the loch's edge, and enjoys the sound of water licking at grassy banks. It makes the distant yet distinct thrum of traffic seem out of place. She turns in a circle, raking the shadows, but sees nothing—knowing, nonetheless, that Gilmartin's scouts are already here. Watching… waiting…

Dawn hears the car before it appears—a black Range Rover that crawls to a stop in front of her Porsche. An insect buzzes past Dawn's face and she smiles. Then Roger's voice sounds in her earpiece. 'That them?'

'Sure is,' she murmurs as the Range Rover's doors fly open and four men emerge.

The driver stays by his vehicle and Gilmartin's bodyguards make a show of staying one step behind as he swaggers towards Dawn. A barrel-chested man, Gilmartin's jacket strains to suggest it was fitted many gym sessions (or packets of steroids) previously. Over the wool suit he wears a sheepskin coat whose front sags open, as though it was shrugged on in afterthought.

The bodyguards look their parts. Huge and ugly with bulges under their arms—Dawn almost laughs at the stereotyping and wonders whether Gilmartin keeps them around more for show. She strides forward to meet the mob boss halfway, making it plain she's unperturbed when his cold eyes joust with her confident stare. 'Thank you for agreeing to see me,' she grates, her inflection suggesting it's Gilmartin who should be grateful.

Gilmartin holds out his hands, palms up. 'Why here? What was wrong with my office?'

'I'm at the top of several "most-wanted" lists, making discretion essential. Your office is in the city centre, which is full of cameras. I have no desire to be flagged by image-recognition software.'

Gilmartin nods, if grudgingly. 'Alright, but why was it necessary for us to meet at all? It's an open contract—there are no terms to negotiate and therefore nothing to discuss. All I insist upon is being kept informed of progress.'

'I am the Scarred Spider,' Dawn growls. '*If* I take a job, it is on *my* terms. The most important of which is—I require three times the remuneration you are offering.'

Gilmartin laughs, shortly. 'That is a *lot* of money. Why would I...?'

'Because...' Dawn cuts in '... after four failed attempts by the kind of amateurs who work for peanuts, you are in danger of becoming a laughingstock. I mean, really—two young women? Making an absolute fool of *you*?'

'*Four* attempts? You are mistaken—there have only been three.'

Dawn recites them off, counting on her fingers as she goes. Ghostface's attack on Sam, her Panda's brakes failing, then a sniper in Glasgow, and finally Scorpion's thwarted attempt at the hotel yesterday. (She assumes Gilmartin can't have heard about Scorpion's second, ill-fated foray—so yes, that's four.)

Gilmartin shakes his head. 'I don't know anything about an assassin dressed as Ghostface.'

Oh

'*Only* three?' she recovers with a wave of her hand. 'Isn't that enough?'

The gangster's heavy brows corrugate and Dawn patiently waits him out. Finally, Gilmartin turns, hawks, spits at the ground, then nods sharply. 'Alright, if you're good as they say... agreed. But I expect it done quickly.'

'Of course. Now, it's only sensible to confirm, formally, *who* you want me to kill. My understanding is the targets are Samantha Chessington and her friend Daisy, yes?'

'Correct. Do you need access to our files on them?'

'That won't be necessary. I already...'

She breaks off when a dragonfly buzzes around her head and waves both hands to discourage it. When the insect lands on her nose, Dawn sideswipes with a palm. The dragonfly takes off at speed, leaving Dawn to gape in horror at gobs of makeup stuck to her hand. Three safeties click simultaneously and she frowns at the weapons attached to them, all pointed straight at her chest.

'Oops.'

Gilmartin's face is beet red. '"Oops" is right. You aren't the Scarred Spider—remove the gun I assume you're carrying, and slowly.'

Scowling, Dawn reaches to the small of her back and carefully brings out a silver beretta.

'Drop it—good. Now kick it over here.'

Gilmartin turns to one of the bodyguards. 'Check her for listening devices.'

'Don't bother,' Dawn says in a defeated voice. She grabs a pendant hanging from her neck and jerks it, breaking the chain. Then removes a tiny earpiece and holds both out.

Stepping forward, Gilmartin snatches them. 'They weren't working, anyway,' Dawn mutters.

Gilmartin's smile is smug. 'On our arrival I activated a signal-blocking device in my Range Rover, which began disrupting all short-wave radio transmissions within a 500-yard radius. So the "admissions" you so skilfully extracted from me—went nowhere.'

Considering its bulk, the arm not holding his gun moves with surprising speed when he backhands Dawn. The crime lord looks down with disgust at smears of makeup on his knuckles. 'Did you think *I* was an amateur? Who are you—police?'

Even though Dawn rode with the blow, she's seeing shooting-stars. At least, she reflects wryly, he's forgotten to bring the other arm back up. Meaning the gun in Gilmartin's hand now threatens only the tarmac he's standing on. Unfortunately, the bodyguards' guns remain trained on her. But—two is an improvement over three.

'Yes,' she admits, letting her lip tremble. 'This is—was—an NCA sting operation. Look, let's just call it quits and...'

'Where's your backup?' Without waiting for an answer, Gilmartin turns a querying gaze on his driver—who's still standing by the Range Rover. The driver nods acknowledgement, then ducks into the vehicle and re-emerges holding a torch. Turning away from them, he clicks it on and off three times.

Moments later, three answering flashes blink in response. 'No unusual activity, boss,' one of the bodyguards growls, and Gilmartin's hard stare returns to Dawn.

'We knew you'd have watchers already here...' she murmurs, the reluctance in her tone plain '...and positioned the armed response units farther back than usual. They're still only five minutes down the road,' she adds hopefully.

'How long will they wait, after losing radio contact?' He waves his gun menacingly.

'This isn't the first time you've used that signal-blocking trick, so we factored it in as a likelihood. Which is why, if my comms went down, they were to hold back for three minutes—then roll.'

Gilmartin runs a hand over the top of his head. 'Five plus three is eight—yes, they wouldn't expect our meeting to last longer than eight minutes. We've been here—what, three minutes?'

Both bodyguards nod.

Gilmartin's lips retract, showing his teeth. If Dawn knew any good dentists in this neck of the woods, she'd pass on their details. But decides some things are better left unsaid... and anyway, Gilmartin's speaking again. 'So that leaves us five minutes. I can be clear of here in three—leaving two spare. Hm... how to make the best use of those?'

'Um—by giving yourself a little extra leeway with the escaping part?'

Gilmartin's face sets and his eyes harden as he looks her up and down. 'I want to send the NCA a message,' he says slowly.

Yes—our ICE profiler thought you might

'One that will demoralise those in command—perhaps make them think twice about playing foolish games with me in future.'

As Gilmartin speaks, Dawn watches him raise the gun. His face lights up—reminiscent of a heroin addict about to take delivery from his dealer. This is a man who *enjoys* killing—and he means to shoot her.

Dawn moves so fast it leaves Gilmartin and his bodyguards flat-footed. Without warning she leaps sideways, twirls through 180° while still in mid-air, then takes off towards the loch at a flying sprint.

The first bullet whistles by on her right—followed by a second on the opposite side, only much closer. The third...

21

Roger

In the NCA mobile-ops van, Alan screams into a radio-mike. 'All units—GO. Officer down.'

Beside him, Roger stares at a laptop screen where moments before he saw Dawn make her desperate flight from Gilmartin. The same screen that showed his sister buck suddenly, then collapse. Now she's an unmoving shadow on the grass verge, with Gilmartin and his goons pounding towards her.

Roger's fingers rattle on the keyboard, then he breathes a sigh of satisfaction as the gangsters come to a dead stop when 2000 watts of short-arc xenon-generated light turn night into day. Picking up a second microphone, Roger barks: 'Armed police. Get down on the ground—NOW.'

Roger and Alan are thrown back in their seats as the mobile-ops van moves off at high speed.

Alan squints at the live feed on Roger's screen where Gilmartin and his bodyguards are shielding their eyes and probably wondering where the amplified voice came from. Gilmartin takes a tentative step towards Dawn's prone body—and Roger's hand flashes to depress another key.

At Gilmartin's feet, the concrete erupts in a shower of stone particles when a 50mm cartridge slams into it. Roger speaks into the microphone again. 'Down on the ground—NOW. Final warning—the next one goes through Gilmartin's skull.'

Gilmartin gesticulates wildly at his men and all three drop to their knees. So does Gilmartin's driver, at his station by the Range Rover. Alan sighs loudly. 'Good—they bought it.'

Roger turns and Alans shudders at the sight of those normally liquid-brown eyes frozen in amber. Then shivers at the tone in Roger's voice when he says: 'I wasn't bluffing.'

His gaze back on the screen, watching the gangsters intently, Roger asks: 'Will we get there first?'

'Should do.'

'Good. I don't want anybody else going near Dawn. If another unit beats us to it, make sure they know.'

Alan gapes at him. 'But surely the sooner...'

'Make sure they know,' Roger grates, and Alan transmits a group-wide message.

Dawn didn't lie when she told Gilmartin the armed response units were five minutes away. She also neglected to mention the NCA ops van, bedecked with colourful plumbing logos, was parked at a nearby golf clubhouse. So Roger's fears are unfounded because it only takes them *two* minutes to reach the scene—ahead of everyone else—during which time the gangsters make no further move.

The van shudders to a stop and Roger dives through its side door. He dashes to Dawn while Alan and a group of Kevlar-clad colleagues rush to handcuff Gilmartin and his bodyguards. When that's done, Alan looks across to Roger—who's on his knees with Dawn's wrist grasped in one hand. 'I've got a weak pulse,' he calls in answer to Alan's unspoken query.

Alan's about to reply when a black transit screeches into the car park. Two white-clad paramedics leap from it and Roger yells—'Over here.'

The paramedics shoo Roger away and he wanders back to Alan, who's still gawking. '*What* is that?' Alan demands.

'An ICE emergency medical unit. We always have one standing by during hazardous missions.'

'Wow,' is all Alan can think to say as the paramedics roll Dawn onto a stretcher and rush her to their van. Then he puts a hand on Roger's shoulder. 'How bad is it?'

Roger drops his eyes. 'Bad, Alan. I... don't know if she's going to make it.'

'I saw her take a hit to central body mass,' Alan says, hesitantly, into the sudden silence.

'AND a head shot,' Roger adds in a shaky voice.

'I didn't see *that*.'

'Neither did I. But if you remember, she was at the edge of our panoramic drone feed when the first bullet struck and we lost sight of her until I repositioned it.'

'So how do you know... Oh.' Alan throws a guilty glance at the spot where Dawn lay. He stares at it for a long moment, then mumbles: 'Do you think the video on its own will be enough to convict Gilmartin? Without any sound?'

Then catches himself. 'Of course, that's moot now after him shooting...'

Unexpectedly, Roger smirks. He holds out his hand and whistles a single note.

Alan starts when a dragonfly lands on Roger's palm. Then leans in and squints at the insect. 'Is that...?'

Roger nods. 'Yep, the latest in insect-drone surveillance technology. Not even *technically* a drone, because it has working wings. Long and short, Alan, the *overhead* drone captured almost everything on video—while this little beauty recorded a matching soundtrack. So when I download its memory, we'll have those "admissions" Gilmartin thought the scrambler blocked—particularly his announcement he was going to shoot Dawn—all verifiable using voice-print analysis.

Roger slips the dragonfly in his pocket and Alan gawks—seemingly lost for words.

Then finds some. 'Em... wasn't that the insect responsible for breaking Dawn's cover?'

Roger dips his head. 'I only got the thing last week and yes, maybe I could have piloted it better. Anyway, what're you trying to say? *I didn't pull that trigger, you know.*'

Alan looks like he wants the ground to swallow him. 'No... that's not what...'

Both men snap their heads sideways when the ICE medical van's rear door opens. A paramedic walks over, slowly—too slowly—and Alan's expression tightens when the man shakes his head. 'We tried—but she didn't stand a chance. Not with a head wound like that.'

Roger lets out a low wail, which slowly increases in pitch while Alan stands helplessly alongside. Hesitantly, the NCA officer drapes an arm over his grieving colleague's shoulders. 'I'm so sorry,' he says, knowing how useless that sounds.

WITHIN MINUTES, THE CAR PARK COMES ALIVE WITH flashing blue lights. Swarms of policemen, some armed, mill about in black uniforms—easily distinguishable from a second squad of white-suited scene of crime technicians.

A group of particularly burly officers haul Gilmartin and his men to a police van and throw them in its rear compartment. When several of them follow the prisoners in, Alan shouts: 'Guys! I need them in one piece—alright?'

A sergeant turns and nods sharply. Alan can only hope they'll be careful not to leave marks.

Another ambulance, with conventional white livery, pulls up beside the ICE vehicle. Alan touches Roger's arm and his voice is gentle when he says: 'Roger—may my people take her now? This has to be done by the book if we're going to make a murder charge stick.'

Roger grimaces. He signs to the ICE paramedics, then watches silently while they transfer a body bag between the vehicles.

When it disappears into the second ambulance and its doors clang shut, Roger pulls roughly away and stalks to where Gilmartin and his men were standing. He scoops the centremost pistol – Gilmartin's – from the ground and stares at it.

Alan bounds over and breathes a sigh of relief when he sees Roger has gloves on. 'Roger,' he hisses. 'You shouldn't be touching that—it's evidence.'

'What... oh, right. Only... this is the gun that...'

Roger groans and doubles over, then slowly draws himself straight. Alan holds out a plastic bag and Roger drops the gun inside. 'Sorry...'

Alan shakes his head. 'Forget it, I understand. No harm done. Roger—Gilmartin will go down for this. I promise you. And after murdering one of our own, I guarantee he'll never see the light of day again.'

22

Daisy stares back at me, slack-jawed, her eyes glistening. I feel my own well up and Alan looks uncomfortable. 'So, tragic news—but you're both safe now. No need for witness protection any more—Gilmartin won't be a threat to anyone ever again.'

When Alan knocked at the owners flat door ten minutes ago, just as we finished breakfast, I couldn't have imagined what he was about to say.

Daisy sniffs. 'But surely Gilmartin's successor will carry on where he left off?'

Alan shakes his head. 'No. Gilmartin ruled with a fist of iron—I don't know what drove him more, narcissism or paranoia, but he had an ample supply of both. In his mind, only *Gilmartin* could do things the way *he* wanted them done—which is why the blighter was so averse to delegating in any shape or form. But Gilmartin was also terrified of being usurped—with good reason, in his dog-eat-dog world. He guarded his power zealously—with the result none of his underlings have the authority to do *anything* now he's gone. We're already hearing reports about Gilmartin's territories being annexed by rival gangs. No, ladies—you're free and clear. Thanks to Dawn and Roger.'

'But at what a price,' I mutter and Alan shrugs.

'They knew the risks,' he mumbles, going to leave. Then hesitates. 'I'm so glad this worked out for you,' he says quietly. 'Even after...'

He grits his teeth and closes the door softly behind him. My mind is a mass of conflicting emotions. Some of me is ecstatic we have our lives back—but the bigger part mourns a woman I totally misjudged and feels a crushing sense of guilt our freedom cost her what it did.

Daisy sums it up. 'Beggar,' she snaps.

I nod and she bumps me with her shoulder. We're sitting on the sofa, which is just as well—if I'd been on my feet, that was hard enough to send me spinning.

'I'm devastated about Dawn—and poor Roger,' she adds, biting her lip. 'But we've got our lives back, Sam. We don't have to leave everything... and everyone.'

'Wish I could muster more enthusiasm. But I can't.'

Daisy drops her head. 'No, neither can I.'

Then we sit in silence for a minute, until it's broken by a tap at the door. Daisy goes to see who it is and returns a moment later with Angus trailing behind.

He looks much better. In fact, you wouldn't know there was anything amiss if it weren't for the extra care he affords every movement.

When I tell him to sit down, it comes out in a stutter. His friend died, for *us,* and I feel a curious mix of responsibility and embarrassment.

Angus eases himself into the armchair opposite our sofa, grimacing as he wraps an arm around himself to cushion his cracked rib. He looks from me to Daisy, then back again. 'I'm leaving soon, ladies. In fact, Wilf's waiting for me in the car park. He's giving me a lift tae the station. But I need a wee word first—about what happened.'

'Angus,' I blurt. 'I'm so, so sorry.'

'Me too,' Daisy adds, looking awkward as I feel.

'Actually,' Angus says, 'I was *told* tae speak with ye—and what tae say. Now—let's get straight tae the point. Alan's just been telling ye how Miss Dawn died—I'm here tae let ye know she did nothing of the kind.'

'What?' Daisy sits upright. 'But Alan saw her getting shot—and the body being taken away.'

'What Alan saw was a bullet hitting the Kevlar vest Miss Dawn was wearing under her coat. Then he watched her being carried intae the ICE emergency medical van...' Angus laughs '...no that there's any such thing. The corpse they then transferred tae the proper ambulance wasn't Miss Dawn's—that was the Scorpion.'

'The Scorpion,' I repeat, disbelievingly.

Angus chuckles. 'Aye, after cartin' her body out the other night through poor Louis' kitchen, they loaded it in that same "emergency ambulance"— which is really the cleanup team's van. It was when she realised they had a spare body that Miss Dawn came up with her plan.'

He lowers his voice, confidentially. 'They used tae be con artists, ye see—good ones. Still are...'

My mind spins as I try to picture the scene, and one aspect in particular horrifies me. 'How could Dawn be sure Gilmartin wouldn't shoot her in the head? What a terrible risk she took...'

Angus smiles tightly. 'No' really. It was dark, and she was running—in those circumstances even a crack shot will aim for centre mass.'

Daisy slaps her thigh. 'So you're saying they set Gilmartin up? Framed him for—Dawn's murder? But the Scorpion would look nothing like Dawn, surely—and anyway, the ballistics won't match.'

'Yer first point—the Scorpion *did* take a bullet through the head, and its exit wound rendered her features unrecognisable. Fortunately...' he winks '... nobody found that bullet, so there's nae ballistics from *it* tae compare.'

He glances at me. 'If ye remember, the two women had much the same colour of hair and were a similar build and height. Now, back tae ballistics. The second bullet, which went in between the Scorpion's shoulder blades—that was delivered post mortem from a gun Mr Roger switched with Gilmartin's at the scene. You already know how good he is at that sleight-of-hand stuff.'

Daisy nudges me. 'Like Tina had Liam do to her dad, remember?'

'Who are Tina and Liam?' Angus asks, and Daisy's fingers make an arc in the air.

'Oh, nobody—only some wasters who pulled a similar trick.'

Angus' eyebrows shoot up. 'My. Ye do lead interesting lives, the pair of ye.'

Daisy stares at Angus. 'But why? Why would they do that—risk so much—to help us?'

'Because they believe in justice,' Angus says softly.

Then he winks. 'If ye ask me, this little caper was just what they needed. So—I'll away and leave ye tae enjoy yer newfound freedom. By the way, I found that bottle of Lagavulin ye left in my room. Thanks for that—I'll drink a toast tae ye when I open it.'

Angus heaves himself up but after two steps, stops and turns. 'Oh, before I go. Miss Dawn said tae tell ye Gilmartin didnae know anything about the knife attack at Halloween. He had no reason tae lie, so either one of his "contractors" didn't keep him informed—which seems unlikely, considering all our intel says Gilmartin's a control freak—or ye've got somebody else after ye.'

WE NEED SOME AIR.

I'm planning a wee chat with Jodie if she's around, but decide to accompany Daisy to the detective agency first. She wants to check what Rebecca's been doing—and reclaim the helm now we're not going anywhere.

Outside, it's bitter cold and a light drizzle spatters us as we walk through the hotel's rear grounds. But for me, it could just as well be the south of France in June. As the news sinks in we aren't mob targets anymore *and* Dawn's alive, it feels like I'm walking on air.

Glancing sideways, I see Daisy wearing a stupid grin. There's something that needs saying. 'Daisy—NO more gangsters, understand? From now on, we stick to missing persons and wandering spouses.'

'Um... the whole mess with Dobson started when Liam went *missing*. Remember?'

'Yeah, but then we took on a kidnap case. I'm serious, Daisy—my nerves can't stand any more. If you want to play at Charlie's Angels, do it without me.'

'You don't mean that.'

'I DO.'

We walk on in silence, then Daisy stops dead and whirls on me. 'We aren't out of the woods yet. Angus says Gilmartin had nothing to do with the Ghostface attack.'

'Ah. So he did. And I've just thought, Alan was going to ask Wilson about letting Ricky out on bail. With this new information, they'll probably revoke that.'

'Mm—I'll give Kat a ring and see what's happening. But meanwhile, we're left with an unsolved murder attempt—*yours*. Still saying I shouldn't get involved in criminal cases?'

'Yeah, well, obviously... but this is the last. Comprende?'

She agreed too easily—but I'm not really in a position to push it

I spread my arms. 'But WHO would want to murder ME?'

'No idea—but we'd better find out before they try again. Let me think about it—meanwhile, keep your wits about you. And don't go anywhere alone.'

She strides off and I trail behind, my mind working furiously. Why *would* anyone come after me? I'm the least likely target imaginable. The only argument I've had lately was with the dairy over Louis' milk deliveries. Even that was resolved amicably...

When we enter the detective agency, Liz is sitting at the front desk. 'Rebecca, they're here,' she shouts.

Rebecca comes tearing out of the office and wraps me in a hug. Then she turns to Daisy, hesitates, and pats her shoulder instead. 'Alan told me—oh, I'm so excited. This is wonderful news.'

Aww—after that, I can't even be sarcastic about her turning up to work in a filmy négligé. It does go all the way down to her ankles, after all. And maybe it's just a trick of the light, making it *seem* transparent...

'Never got a chance to thank you for those macaroni pies,' Liz puts in. 'They were brill—weren't they, Rebs?'

'Mmm.' Rebecca smacks her lips. 'How did you know about that shop, Liz?'

'Liz used to work in Glasgow,' Daisy explains.

'Really? You never said...'

'It wasn't for long.' Liz grins. 'I don't tell you everything.'

Rebecca looks like she's about to say something else, but Daisy's more interested in status reports on the cases she left her assistant overseeing. Which is my cue to leave.

'Be careful,' Daisy calls after me and I promise to be.

'Why does she need to be careful?' Liz asks. 'I thought...'

'She worries about me,' I mutter quickly, making light of Daisy's comment. Then head out swiftly before they ask any more awkward questions.

I want to savour having my life back just a little longer before starting to worry about who's still trying to take it.

23

Jodie answers the cottage door and I feel cut to the quick when it's obvious she's nervous about my being here. Her eyes flick over my shoulder as she checks the road beyond. 'It's all over, Jodie,' I blurt. 'The mob isn't gunning for us anymore.'

Her head tilts to one side. She must think the stress has sent me to cloud cuckoo land. 'No, really,' I insist. 'Can I come in and tell you about it?'

The reluctance clouding her eyes only lasts a moment. I don't know if it's because Jodie realises I'm serious (and compos mentis) or whether her policewoman's curiosity has taken over, but she stands aside and beckons me in.

'Where's Alanna?' I ask, following her into the sitting room.

Jodie points at a baby alarm on the coffee table. 'Gone for her morning nap—at last. Oh, thanks for being thoughtful enough not to ring the doorbell—that would definitely have woken her. I presume you inherited that monstrosity from Doctor Frame—it's ghastly.'

Rossini's "William Tell Overture"? My pride and joy? Obviously, Daisy isn't the only philistine around here. Luckily, Jodie doesn't wait for an answer. 'Want some coffee?'

'Yes, please. I took pot luck you'd be here. Wasn't sure if you would be, after having Thursday off.'

'Our weekends are on a different rota to the monthly days. Right, take a seat—I won't be long.'

When we're settled with mugs of instant (but the good stuff that comes in a silver tin) I tell Jodie what Alan told us. Of course, I keep mum about Angus' revelation—that was for Daisy's and my ears only.

Jodie slumps back in her armchair and whistles—loudly.

'Watch you don't wake the baby.'

'Oh, cripes.'

She slams a hand over her mouth and stares at the baby monitor for ten seconds, then sighs. 'Nope, got away with it. Wow, Sam—this is incredible news. Gosh—it's like something out of a Nelson DeMille novel. That poor woman, though...'

Pretending to be grief-stricken over Dawn while knowing she's right as rain is hard. I've never been much good at acting but maybe I'm improving, since Jodie seems fooled by my crocodile tears. Feeling she's entitled to know, I fill her in on the other bombshell Angus dropped—that Gilmartin had nothing to do with the first attempt on my life. (Which, of course, he only knows about from listening to the recording Roger's "surveillance-bug" made.) 'So there's still something afoot,' I confess. 'But at least the mob isn't after us any more.'

She frowns. 'Hell of a coincidence—is Angus certain Gilmartin wasn't lying?'

I shrug. 'He had no reason to. Gilmartin thought he was talking to a fellow killer. But I've no idea who else would try to murder me.'

Her lips tighten and she leans forward. 'I'm sure you'll track them down soon enough. After surviving the Glasgow mafia, whoever's left should be a dawdle by comparison. But—would you mind if we stayed here until then? For Alanna's sake? Just to be safe while you catch up with this other murderer.'

I nod. 'Of course—in fact, I've got a proposition for you.'

She looks intrigued. 'Go on.'

I take a deep breath. 'Daisy has been *told* this kind of nonsense has to stop—but we *are* running a detective agency, so it's hard to guarantee trouble won't ever follow us home again. What I wondered—how would you feel about doing a permanent swap? You stay here—and we'll move back to the owners flat.'

Her face lights up, then falls. 'Oh Sam, that would have been brilliant. Living in the flat isn't ideal with a wee one, and buying a cottage around here *is* our long-term plan. We need a garden for Alanna, and somewhere that's only a quick stroll down the road for Logan when he's working late. But—the reason our plan's long-term is because it'll take ages to save up a deposit. And we can only put that sort of cash aside by staying in the hotel—paying rent would add years to our plans.'

Yes—I'd guessed all that

'You know, Jodie, when we moved to the cottage I expected it to enhance our lives in so many ways. But recently I've come to realise the opposite happened, for the simple reason Daisy and I are workaholics. The maintenance involved here—cutting the grass, tending Doctor Frame's roses, cleaning a house that's far too big for us—has turned into a major pain. We just don't have time to do it properly. All things considered, I see now the owners flat suited us better. So how about you stay here—rent free—until you're ready to buy? At which point, you can have it for whatever the valuation is.'

May have overstated our motivation slightly, but I need her to agree—we owe them this much

Jodie gasps and runs a hand over her face. 'Oh, but that wouldn't be fair. We'd have to pay you something...'

I shake my head. 'Uh-uh. Don't want it—put the money in your deposit fund. After all, it's our fault you have to move Alanna somewhere safe—and anyway, we'll be getting the owners flat rent free.'

'But what about all the equity you have tied up in this?'

With my arms spread wide, I explain. 'Jodie, I won't be needing it for anything in the foreseeable future—and there's no better investment than property. So, what do you say? Deal?'

In answer, Jodie springs out of her chair and dives at the sofa—then grabs me in a hug. 'If you're sure...? Oh Sam, I can't believe it. Wait till I tell Logan.'

My heart lightens, seeing how happy this makes her. I've been feeling *so* guilty about bringing danger down on our friends and, as a side-issue, honestly think moving back to the flat *will* be better for Daisy and me.

Daisy—oops. Just remembered—I haven't told her yet

AT THE HOTEL, I CLOSET MYSELF IN MY—CLOSET? I HAVE A so-called "office" in a partitioned extrusion into surplus space at one end of the snooker room, entered via a door from the residents lounge. At some point, we need to think about a back extension with proper administrative offices. There again, when Daisy and I lived in the owners flat before, it doubled as a management suite. Okay, maybe I'm getting carried away there, but it was a place I could spread out to do the books in comfort and also afforded a private (and comfortable) venue for business meetings.

I wonder how Daisy will react when she finds out we're moving back

Thinking about building work reminds me of Davy—I haven't spoken to him since Thursday. We've exchanged loads of texts, but it's past time for a proper chat. He still doesn't know about our brush with the Glasgow underworld—*that*'s going to blow his mind.

Plus, in Davy's last message, he was waiting to hear *when* his employer plans on releasing him. It isn't impossible my fiancé could be home this weekend—for good.

Reaching for the phone, I snatch my hand back when it rings.

Spooky

Lifting the handset, I glance at caller ID and see "Geraldine". It's Davy's mum.

Still spooky

Geraldine lives in Skye and speaks with a rich, northern accent. She's a busybody, no two ways about it, but I love her. She was my rock when Davy was recovering from his accident.

'Geraldine—how are you?'

'Fine, dear. What's this I'm hearing about that son of mine finally seeing sense?'

'About Glasgow, you mean? Yes, he's chucked it in to come back here. Between you and me, I couldn't be more pleased.'

'Me neither, lass. It wasn't fair of him to put you in that position. Not when he knows how much Cairncroft means to you. Just out of interest—what *would* you have done?'

I wish people would stop asking that

'Honestly, Geraldine—I wouldn't like to say. Davy is everything to me—but so's my life here.'

She cackles, reminding me of the three witches from Paisley. 'At least you're honest, luvvy. Unlike the hussy that caused all this bother.'

'Leslie? You know her?'

Geraldine knows Leslie?

'Aye, from when she got her hooks into him back when Davy and her were at university. Off her rocker that little madam is. Pestered poor Davy for months after he finally grew a pair and broke up with her. It didn't surprise me when I heard she'd popped up again—her type's the perennial bad penny.'

'I take it Davy told you about Leslie overstating his qualifications to the company in Glasgow. Why do you think she did that?'

'I should have thought it's obvious. She's run out of men and having to give the ones who dumped her another try.'

'It's just hard to believe anyone would…'

'No' if ye know her, it isn't. That lassie's bonkers.'

Geraldine doesn't beat about the bush. She'd get on well with Daisy. (Actually, she does—though neither of them will admit it.) 'Thing is, Leslie's so pretty—and personable. I don't understand why she would need to…'

'Aye, the men come flocking alright, but then they find out how crazy she is. Yon Leslie's like an iceberg—the bit everybody sees on the surface is only a tiny wee part of her.'

I'm tempted to try and get more out of Geraldine—but it feels a little underhand. So instead, reluctantly, I head off her rant. 'Okay, I'd better go. I want to give Davy a ring.'

'Don't waste your time. He's out propping up a skyscraper in East Kilbride—I caught him on his way out. He'll probably call you tonight, though—but I've been warned not to say why.'

With that, she makes a quick exit. Geraldine's self-aware enough to know the chances of her keeping schtum about what Davy wants to tell me are minimal, and it sounds like he's looking forward to breaking the news himself. He must have a date for leaving Glasgow.

After saying our goodbyes, I put down the phone and try to psyche myself into tackling a pile of paperwork awaiting attention. Which is when the door flies open and Daisy beckons with both hands. 'I've just spoken to Kat, and she's got Ricky with her right now. We need another chat about his case, but it's also a good chance to find out what's happening with Murder-Meals—and whether we're on our own with the murder mysteries next week. You coming?'

'You bet,' I trill, grabbing my bag and rushing past the box of VAT invoices she just gave me an excuse not to sort through.

24

Although the village is only a short walk away, knowing Kat and Ricky are waiting prompts us to take my "courtesy car".

'Thought you'd have heard about the Panda by now,' Daisy comments when we're underway.

'I phoned Arthur yesterday and he said they're still figuring out the cost of putting it back together—then the insurers will give their verdict. Arthur reckons I'll hear by Tuesday at the latest.'

'I know what that crafty weasel's up to,' she grins. 'It was obvious how taken you were with the Fiesta. Betcha Arthur's dragging this out on purpose, so when he announces Panda's defunct but surprise-surprise, the courtesy car's for sale— you'll bite his hand off. Beggar probably knew poor old Panda was a write-off the minute he saw it.'

'Do you think so? Surely not...'

Oh blimey, she's spot on. That's exactly how Arthur's mind would work. I'd have realised myself if it weren't for the distraction of being parachuted into a "shoot-em-up" movie.

Approaching the T-junction where we turn right onto the main thoroughfare through Cairncroft, a canary-yellow Peugeot comes flying towards us and Daisy tuts. 'Shouldn't they be slowing down for the passing place?'

This road's too narrow for two-way traffic, hence the provision of "passing places". I inhale sharply when the Peugeot barrels past the only one between our cars. 'What's he doing? He was supposed to pull into that.'

Then I gasp. 'He's speeding up—and headed straight for us.'

'Don't brake,' she shouts. With my foot poised to stamp the pedal, I pause.

'Why not? Daisy, I have to...'

'No—that's what he wants you to do. This smells of an intercept. Keep going, Sam—play the beggar's chicken game right back at him.'

My imagination instantly conjures up a picture of armed thugs jumping from the Peugeot—which is enough to stay my foot on the brake. 'But he isn't slowing—what will I do?'

'Um... brace for impact?' she mutters as the gap between us and the Peugeot shrinks to nothing.

I'm so close to the grass verge our wheels skiff against it, jiggling Daisy and I into each other like a pair of castanets. At the last moment, when collision seems inevitable, the Peugeot veers sideways. I wait for the now all-too-familiar sound of buckling metal, but with mere millimetres separating our vehicles the Peugeot somehow gets past without a scratch.

'Don't stop,' Daisy yells as I finally hit the brake. 'That's what they want.'

I shake my head, watching the rear-view mirror. 'No, they aren't even slowing—nearly out of sight, in fact.'

With the Fiesta stationary, I slump back in my seat. 'Daisy, will this ever end? Suppose it's too much to hope you got their number?'

'Nope,' she says, sounding frustrated. 'I did notice it had L plates, though.'

'D<small>O YOU THINK IT COULD SIMPLY HAVE BEEN A LEARNER</small> driver who panicked? Maybe pressed the accelerator by mistake?'

We entered Kat's office looking like the fugitives our various attackers are turning us into. She was quick to produce mugs of strong coffee and is now being the "voice of reason". 'After all,' she goes on, 'all that's happened lately must have sensitised you both. Could it be you're hearing zebras instead of horses?'

Daisy shrugs. 'Kat might be right. A car that ancient—it was at least twenty years old—and displaying L-plates? Hardly the first choice of any self-respecting hitman.'

The coffee's calming me a little and I'm inclined to agree. Who could blame us for becoming paranoic, after all? And yet... for all my many trips along that road, I've *never* experienced anything like that. A deep breath—quick gulp of coffee—and I make myself nod firmly. 'Maybe we read too much into it.'

From the third client chair, Ricky just *has* to say: 'Kat, it's the "all that's happened" which makes it *less* likely this wasn't another attack.'

Kat glares at him from behind Mr M's desk, which she's using in his absence. 'If it *was* an ambush, why didn't the other car simply stop at an angle and block the road?'

Daisy waves both hands. 'This is getting us nowhere. Right, Ricky—so you're still out on bail? I was worried they might have pulled you back in since Alan told Wilson the stabbing was nothing to do with Gilmartin.'

Ricky reaches down and drags up a jeans leg, exposing the bulky plastic box shackled around his ankle by a metal cuff. 'I'm having to wear this, though,' he mutters indignantly. 'So they can find me if I do a runner.'

Kat tuts. 'Don't moan—you're lucky to be out at all. Although I think we've got a strong case. After all, who in their right mind murders someone in front of a packed audience? Still, an alternate theory to give the jury *would* help.'

'You mean the "some other dude did it" defence?' Daisy pipes up, and Kat nods.

'Yeah, exactly. Which leads me to—any more on that blonde girl Ricky saw?'

Daisy pouts. 'Sorry Kat, nothing. We're working on it, though. Ricky, did you get my text asking whether any of the other "Ghostface" actors were responsible for scaring Sam on Monday night?'

'Yes, and I've checked with all of them. I was going to message you back—anyway, the answer's no. Nobody admits to flying head over heels when their "victim" bent down to tie a shoelace.'

'Beggar—so Sam *was* being targeted.'

I feel a flutter in my chest. Daisy told me she was getting Ricky to find out about that and I hoped it'd turn out to be one of his actors who accosted me—proving me wrong about *that* knife being real. No such luck, though. 'What's happening with Murder-Meals?' I ask, forcing my mind onto business matters. 'Specifically, will you be putting on murder mysteries for all these guests we're expecting next week?'

'Not a problem,' is Ricky's answer—to my great relief. 'A few of my actors have walked, understandably, but manpower-wise that balances out with the clients who cancelled. So long as the police don't haul me back in, your shows are going on as normal.'

'Let me know if you come up with anything else,' Kat says as Daisy and I get up to leave.

'Will do,' I promise. 'Seeing as it looks like I was the real target, we can assure you The Cairncroft Detective Agency is *very* motivated to solve this case.'

Daisy glances around Mr M's office, as if she just realised where we are. 'Isn't it time Mr M sprung for your own room, Kat? Where is he, anyway?'

Obviously a sore point. 'I'm *supposed* to be getting the file room next to Miss Dobie's. When he finally agreed to let me digitise our records, it became redundant. Needs gutting first, though. I keep asking, but the lazy so-and-so hasn't gotten around to doing anything about it. As for where he is now—your guess is good as mine. I *presume* out with his fancy woman again.'

'It *is* Saturday,' I remind her.

'It's *always* Saturday for him these days,' she retorts.

She shakes her head, then: 'You going to the fireworks display in Donstable tonight?'

I'd forgotten today's the 5th of November. Somehow, the prospect of loud bangs doesn't excite me. 'No, think we'll give it a miss this year,' I mutter, looking at Daisy.

She nods grimly. 'Yeah—we've already had enough fireworks to last a lifetime.'

After a moment's silence, Daisy looks thoughtful and murmurs: 'Didn't you specialise in criminal law, Kat—down in London?'

'That's correct. My, you were thorough with that background check.'

Daisy grimaces, but plows on. 'Are you planning to do much of that here?'

'Hoping to—we're near enough Aberdeen that I can cast a net in those waters. I've already taken my Scottish Law Society exams, obviously, but still have a bit to do before they give me advocacy rights. However, in the meantime, I intend to get started as an instructing solicitor.'

The snort is loud. 'I don't have the foggiest what half that means, but my point is you'll need an investigator for criminal work. No?'

Kat wags a finger. 'Yes, and I've already got you earmarked—if that's where this is headed.'

Daisy looks taken aback. 'Oh, excellent. Well, you know where we are...'

I thought we weren't DOING criminal cases any more

MR M'S OFFICE IS ONE FLOOR UP, OVER THE CUPPA TEA. ON our way downstairs, the man himself appears— uncharacteristically beet-faced and puffing as though he's run a marathon. 'Hello, girls… sorry, can't stop…'

He pushes past and we turn to watch him disappear through the glass door above. 'What's eating him?'

I shrug. 'No idea—maybe his new girlfriend dumped him?'

Daisy sniggers. 'Looked more like she was *chasing* him.'

At the street door, Daisy sticks her head out first and checks both ways. 'Nope, no sign of any Mr M-starved hotties.'

'Don't be rotten.' Which loses most of its impact when delivered through a giggle. When we reach the car, Daisy stops but makes no move to get in. Jingling my keys, I ask: 'What?'

'I'm wrestling with where we are—or aren't—on "The Ghostface killer". Ricky just confirmed she *was* after you. We know it's a "she" because Ricky and the witches saw her—but that's *all* we know. *He* can only describe the back of her head. As for Agatha's crew, *they* were too busy debating the colour of her aura to notice what she actually looked like—I've seen better identikit pictures in the Beano. Where the heck do we go from here?'

Checking my watch, I see it's nearly five. 'What about Donstable, to pick up a Chinese?'

25

The Chinese was yum. Marred only by me, in a burst of celebratory bonhomie, letting Daisy get chopsticks. Still, this jumper was due for a dry-clean...

On our way up, Daisy diverted to the residents lounge bar where she appropriated two bottles of wine. I saw Colin's expression when she wittered something about "quality control" over her shoulder—won't be long before *that* starts wearing thin.

One of the bottles is Colin's/Roger's Cabalié 2021 and, having opened it first, I see why Colin lobbied so hard to make me order some. And why Roger's face lit up when he tasted it. Daisy smirks. 'Mm... makes our usual stuff from the Co-op look silly.'

Maybe this would be a good time. 'Daisy, there's something I need to tell you.'

When I've finished, she gapes. 'We're moving back here?'

'Yes. Like I said, all things considered, it's the decent thing to do. I'm sorry about not consulting you first, but...'

'But you were worried I'd talk you out of it?'

Oh-oh

'Not at all—it was spur of the moment. And anyway, I thought...'

To my relief, she giggles. 'You thought right. Sam, the cottage is fine—but it makes sense us living here. Not to mention we can eat and drink like lords and ladies again—alright, just ladies. Naw, suits me.'

Whew

'You really don't mind?'

'Which part of "suits me" didn't you understand? Honestly, Sam—I'm totally with you on this. A family will make much better use of the cottage than we ever did—and Alanna needs a garden of her own.'

This from someone who, best I can gather, spent her childhood on an upper floor in a concrete tower block. Despite being a hard little besom, she's paradoxically (if occasionally) selfless. Endearingly so.

Daisy stares at the ceiling. 'We could be like Dawn. Roger told me she spends most of her time in swank French hotels, living off room service, even though they've got a ritzy pad in London.'

'Hmm—you liked Roger, didn't you? And incidentally, the Cairncroft Hotel—sorry, The Murder Hotel—doesn't offer room service.'

'Maybe it should?'

She could have something there. Logan would definitely jump at any chance to upgrade the hotel's "posh factor". Of course, the logistics *are* daunting. But she's ducking the key question—although I know better than to push it. No point, anyway—Roger lives in a different world and Daisy will probably never see him again.

Unless she decides otherwise

'And Sam—shouldn't you get together with Logan to change the hotel's name back? It seemed a good idea at the time, but everybody around here still calls it "The Cairncroft Hotel".'

Maybe

Daisy pats the couch we're sitting on. 'What are we doing about getting the furniture swapped over?'

'Jodie and I are going to arrange for a "man with a van". Oh, and she'll be popping in and out to shift smaller stuff as and when. I said we'd do the same.'

'You'll have to do something about those attic stairs. Before Alanna starts toddling.'

She's right. Ages ago, I set up a sewing station in the cottage attic while Daisy had grand plans to turn the remaining space into a games room. The stairs up are scarily rickety, but since I only ever got around to finishing two pairs of curtains—and Daisy forgot all about the pool table and whatever else *she* was planning—we haven't been up there in months. As they say, out of sight... 'I'll get Davy to organise something. No rush—Alanna won't be walking for a while yet.'

'What about Logan, though?' Daisy deadpans, making me laugh.

Actually, she has a point...

'So, back to Ghostface and the attack. Any thoughts on who might want you dead?'

Talk about a conversation stopper. But living with Daisy, you get used to it. 'No, honestly. I've wracked my brains, but can't think who would hate me that much.'

Daisy frowns. 'Isn't there anyone who would *benefit* from you being out of the way? C'mon—however slightly, even if it sounds ridiculous. We're just brainstorming here.'

I shrug. 'Logan, I suppose, if I'm really scraping the barrel—our partnership insurance would make him sole owner of the hotel.'

'Nah—Logan couldn't run this place on his own. He knows that.'

'True. In that case, nope. I'm stumped. Anyway, it might not only be me. Maybe they planned to do both of us. Anybody watching would know you were coming down the path next. Alan mentioned that—remember?'

She wrinkles her brows. 'Who'd want to hurt me? Okay...' she grins '... let's rephrase that. Who'd benefit from getting rid of me?'

'Who?'

'Exactly. Nobody I can think of. You might be onto something, though. If we were *both* being targeted, I suppose it *could* be somebody with a grudge against the detective agency—as Rebecca said.'

Which is when it hits me—if this were a cartoon, there'd be a huge lightbulb popping on over my head. 'Daisy—it has to be Lena.'

'Lena? Don't be daft—she's banged up.'

Lena, AKA the Bus Stop Killer, came close to ending our lives a little over six months ago. But Daisy's right—Lena's in a secure psychiatric facility somewhere down south. And yet... 'Dressing up as Ghostface to kill someone—doesn't that just smack of Lena? And we haven't come up with anyone else. What if she's escaped?'

Daisy shakes her head. 'We'd have heard... but I see where you're coming from. That stunt *has* got "Lena" written all over it.'

'She isn't blonde, though.'

'Wigs—dye?'

Deciding, I whip out my phone. 'I'm going to call Jodie—get her to check if Lena's still safely in custody.'

'Can't hurt,' Daisy agrees, as the ringtone sounds.

Then: 'Hi, Sam.'

The miracle of caller display

'Jodie, I need a favour.'

'Just ask—something to do with the flat?'

'No—you remember Lena?'

I explain my epiphany, and Jodie snorts. 'Sam, Rampton Hospital has a "high secure" categorisation. Which is why they sent Lena there, all the way to Nottingham. And in the unlikely event she'd broken out, they'd have told us.'

'That's what Daisy said, but could you check with the hospital? Just for my peace of mind?'

She puffs. 'Oh, alright—I'll have to clear it with Wilson first, but can't see him having any objection. I'm in at work tomorrow, so I'll give you a bell after speaking to Rampton.'

'Thanks, Jodie.'

Daisy fidgets while Jodie and I exchange some logistics on our respective dwellings—soon as I hang up, she blurts: 'Well?'

I explain we'll hear tomorrow and her face falls.

'That's no good—I want this cleared up now.'

She frowns, then: 'I know—Alan should be able to find out straight away.'

'Didn't he change his number...'

Daisy nods, tapping her phone as she speaks. 'No idea why he'd do that, but I made Rebecca give me his new one. Alan—yeah, it's me. What... oh, from Rebecca. Why'd you change it, anyway? Never mind—need a favour.'

She holds the phone at arm's length for a moment, then returns it to her ear. 'Look, buddy. You still owe me—no, you *wouldn't* have got that promotion without me. Doesn't matter—this is a legit request.'

She explains quickly, exchanges a few more words, then hangs up. 'He's promised to call back within ten minutes. Says the admin offices at

Lena's place will be closed now, but he can use his super-duper NCA computers to access its inmate list.'

I breathe a sigh of relief. I *know* how unlikely it is that Lena's involved—but still want it confirmed she isn't.

'So,' Daisy goes on. 'In case Lena *is* where she should be—what do we have on this phantom Ghostface, again?'

'Mm. Two eyewitnesses—Ricky and the witches. Which actually makes four.'

'*Eye*witnesses? A blind man's dog could tell us more than that lot did. But they're all we've got. No point in going back to Ricky, 'cos he only saw her from behind. But the witches—maybe we should have more words with *them* in case they've remembered anything else. No good doing it on the phone, though—there's three of them, and what one says could jog another's memory. So it means another trip to Glasgow— well, Paisley, actually.'

'People sometimes remember things a while after the fact,' I suggest hopefully.

'*Those* weirdos are more likely to forget the little they *did* remember. But it's worth a try—and we can show them a pic of Lena. See if it rings any bells.'

Heck—Glasgow! I completely forgot. 'Daisy, I have to phone Davy. He was out earlier and we haven't spoken properly since Thursday.'

She nods, and I wait.

Daisy looks quite settled—sips her wine.

'So—I'll go through to my bedroom if that's okay. And ring him.'

She waves a hand. 'Of course. No problem.'

'Only thing is, there's no phone extension through there.'

'You've got your mobile. Haven't you?'

I'D REALLY RATHER USE THE LANDLINE BECAUSE ITS SOUND quality is much better. But since my rhinoceros-skinned friend doesn't look like moving anytime soon, and not relishing the thought of a three-sided conversation when I phone Davy (she'd probably make me put it on speaker), I give in gracefully and grab my mobile on the way out.

Of course, Geraldine said Davy would likely phone me himself tonight, but what if he forgets? After all, I almost did. Or maybe it's just, having remembered, I can't *wait* to hear when he's coming home.

Davy answers on the first ring. 'Sam—I was about to call you.'

'Great minds think alike, obviously. So—any news?'

'You bet. Guess what—they're releasing me immediately. Well, Wednesday—which is only four days away.'

'Wow, that's terrific. Did you tell them *why* things haven't worked out?'

Momentary silence. Then: 'Not exactly—I didn't want to land Leslie in it. Just said there'd been some confusion over my CV.'

'Oh, Davy. They'll think it was you who lied—and that won't do your reputation any good.'

'Doesn't matter—I don't intend applying for any more jobs. It's strictly self-employment for me from now on. I've already spoken to my contacts out our way and they're happy to take up where we left off.'

I consider carefully first, but decide it needs saying. 'You've still got a soft spot for Leslie, haven't you?'

He takes so long to answer, I wonder if that upset him. When his response finally comes, I realise he was just taking time to think it through. 'Leslie's—complicated. Okay, she's a bit of a nutter. But we were close for a while all those years ago and Leslie can't help who she is. To be honest, rather than having a soft spot, I feel sorry for her. I reckon she's got enough problems without me adding to them.'

Good answer, you big softie. Knew there was a reason for me wanting to marry you

Attempting to lighten the mood, I ask: 'Hey, did you try that café yet—the one with those scrumptious pies? Remember? You were going to pass it on the way to a job.'

'I did—and you were right. They do a brilliant bridie. Word's obviously getting around about them—place was queued out the door when I went. Not bad, considering they've only been open three months.'

When I go back through, it's in something of a daze. Daisy takes one look and tops up my wine glass. 'Here—so, what's happened now? Has Bob the builder signed up for a gig in Outer Mongolia?'

'No—Davy's coming home next Wednesday. They gave him early release from his contract. It isn't that—he went into Liz's pie shop and got talking to the owner. Daisy, that place has only been open for three months. Before that, it was a launderette.'

Daisy's jaw drops. 'Three months? But...'

'Yep, Liz said she used to go there—when she stayed in Glasgow. But three months ago, Liz lived in Donstable. No way could she have commuted.'

Just then, Daisy's phone blasts out the theme from "Hunger Games" (the loud bit) and she answers it.

When she hangs up, Daisy's lost some of her colour. 'What now?' I breathe.

'That was Alan. He can't find Lena on the list of inmates at Rampton Hospital.'

26

Next day, we're both still reeling. Last night was a double whammy. 'Maybe it's a clerical error,' I suggest, grasping at any straw that would mean Lena isn't on the loose.

Daisy shrugs. 'Can't see it, but Alan's going to check further and get back to us tonight.'

'Tonight?'

'Yeah, I know—he's tied up all day with something crucial to national security. So *he* says. Anyway, we don't need him—I phoned the witches. We can show them Lena's picture and ask if they recognise it.'

'When?'

'Unfortunately, today's out—they're busy. Tomorrow, though, they have a shopping trip to Glasgow planned and Agatha agreed to meeting up then. I suggested the café in Cowcaddens, seeing as it's not far from Sauchiehall Street. She was fine with that and promised to be there at three.'

'Okay. Paisley's not *so* much further, but I'd rather go somewhere familiar. And it means I can visit with Davy while we're there. Um… did you think of sending them the pic electronically?'

'Duh—yes. None of them have a smartphone—they sound even more technologically challenged than you.'

'I am *not*…'

She isn't listening. 'Lena's only half the problem, though. *What* about Liz?'

'I can't believe she sold us out,' I mutter, yet again.

Daisy puffs. 'It's not that surprising. After all, when we met Liz, she was posing as a nanny to rob our safe.'

'I know, but… we put that down to her pickpocket boyfriend's bad influence. She seemed so full of remorse afterwards…'

'All an act to make us take pity on her. The woman's a con artist—but unlike Dawn and Roger, has no scruples. It's obvious, Sam—she sent us to that pie shop knowing the mob was lying in wait.'

'We can't prove it, though…'

'Wanna bet?'

Right on cue, there's a knock at the door. I go to answer it and return with Wilf. 'Daisy, Wilf says you've a job for him.'

'I have.'

After Daisy briefs Wilf, which also serves to fill me in on her plan (I'm always last to know), she puts her phone on speaker and hands it to Wilf. He sits at the coffee table, where Daisy's laid out a row of "prompt cards" to guide him. She and I sit on the sofa and Wilf presses a preprogrammed autodial button. Moments later, Liz's voice says: 'Cairncroft Detective Agency. How can I help you?'

She sounds almost excited by Wilf's call. Of course—we open on a Sunday to accommodate punters from Saturday night's murder mystery, but this week's performance was cancelled. Liz and Rebecca are probably bored out of their minds.

Wilf clears his throat. 'Mr Gilmartin asked me to have a word. We need to know where the targets will be this afternoon.'

There's silence—then Liz whispers: 'But I thought that was all over. Mr Gilmartin's in jail—isn't he?'

'*Was*—you surely don't think those dummies at the NCA got the better of Mr Gilmartin? I'll call again in an hour—make sure you have the information then.'

'No, wait. I don't want to do this anymore.' She's still whispering—Rebecca must be in one of the other rooms.

Wilf accesses his inner Brando. 'Crossing us would be a big mistake, missy. Nobody does that and keeps breathing.'

I glance at Daisy, who's wearing a grim smile—and wonder if that last didn't stretch credibility a bit *too* far.

No—obviously it didn't. 'Alright, I'll try. Could take more than an hour, though. They haven't come in yet.'

'Two hours,' Wilf barks. 'Then you'd better have what I want.' He stabs the "end call" button and grins. 'How'd I do?'

For a moment, neither of us can speak. We're too shocked. Despite the evidence, I still hoped we were wrong about Liz.

But we weren't—she took everything we gave her and chucked it right back in our faces.

'Your Oscar's in the mail,' Daisy says in a flat voice. 'Brilliant performance, Wilf.'

'What you gonna do now—call the rozzers?'

Daisy shakes her head. 'Not yet—not till *I've* finished with her.'

WHEN WE STROLL INTO THE DETECTIVE AGENCY, IT'S HARD TO return Liz's cheerful smile. I expected her to look strained—but she gives every impression of not having a care in the world. From what sounds like a kettle boiling in the staff room, I deduce Rebecca's brewing up. Presumably Hector's through there with her—and won't be in any hurry to show his face now Daisy's here.

'Rebecca,' Daisy calls, striding towards her office. 'Keep an eye on the front for a minute, will you? Liz, it's time for your evaluation. Follow me.'

Looking surprised, Liz gets up and the three of us traipse through. Daisy goes behind her desk and motions to Liz she should take the client chair. I slip around to sit in my usual seat at one end. Liz smiles brightly. 'Evaluation?'

'Yes, you remember we employed you on a trial basis?' Daisy says, somewhat officiously. 'So it's time to decide whether your performance warrants a permanent contract.'

'Only a formality, I hope?' Liz suggests, looking a little puzzled.

'We'll see. Now, I want to go back over your employment history. Specifically, the period you worked in Glasgow. I notice you didn't mention that on the application form.'

Liz looks relieved—this is just a paperwork issue. 'Oh, I wasn't giving much thought to filling the form in. You'd already said I could have a job. But alright, I was in Glasgow for six months, working in... um... retail.'

'When?'

'Let me see... a year ago? Slightly more?'

Daisy smiles for the first time—she even manages not to make it scary. 'Stroke of luck being close to that brill pie shop. Mm—those bacon pasties were to die for.'

Liz titters. 'Their macaroni pies were awesome—that's why I asked you to pick some up. Used to go there every lunchtime.'

Daisy's smile metamorphoses into the expression "Jaws" wore just before he clamped his teeth on an unwary swimmer's leg. 'Sure it wasn't Doctor Who you worked for in Glasgow?'

'Pardon?'

'Well, there had to be time travel involved—seeing as the pie shop only opened three months ago.'

'No, that can't be right...'

Daisy stands, smacks both palms on the desk, and rears forward. Liz's cheeks burn and she recoils. 'I can explain...'

'Please do. And make it the true version—like how you sold Sam and me out to mobsters. You're going down for this, lady—for a long time, if I've anything to do with it.'

Liz's face drops into her hands and her shoulders shake. 'I... I'm... sooo sorry. It wasn't my fault.'

'Wasn't your fault?' Daisy repeats, incredulously.

Raising her head, Liz gulps several times then forces her eyes to meet Daisy's. 'I had no choice. They threatened Pete.'

'Pete? The pickpocket? But you and he split up...'

'That doesn't mean I don't still love him,' Liz snaps. Then: 'Sorry. But Pete's in jail—he got caught lifting somebody's wallet. A horrible man came into the café in Donstable where I was having a coffee and told me somebody called

Gilmartin would have Pete killed—and painfully—unless I did what he asked.'

'You just said Pete was in jail,' I remind her.

'Yes, that's the whole point. The man described in gory detail what Gilmartin could make happen to someone in jail. I didn't want to do it, but... they were going to hurt Pete. Kill him. What else *could* I have done?'

'You should have told us straight away,' Daisy growls, but the ferocity's gone out of her.

'I wish now I had,' Liz wails. 'But I was so scared... Pete and I have been together forever. He'll come back to me eventually—he always does—and the idea of those thugs doing what the man said they would put me in a panic. Oh, I just realised—the phone call earlier? Was that you?'

Daisy nods, then gives me a helpless look—which I return with one of my own. Liz's actions are inexcusable—but maybe also understandable? What if it had been me and Davy? It's easy to say I wouldn't have made the choice Liz did—but none of us really knows how we'd react in such an impossible situation.

Finally, Daisy slumps back in her seat. 'Alright. I don't agree with what you did—not at all—but suppose I can understand it. You can't stay, of course—you're fired, effective immediately—but we won't tell the police what happened.'

Liz wails again. 'Thank you, I'm so grateful—and terribly sorry.'

Daisy flaps her hand at the door. 'Just go—and don't come back.'

'Wait a minute.'

Liz turns to me and I fix her with my hardest look. (I've been practicing in the mirror.) 'I'm not having you living with Rebecca after this. On your way out, tell her you're leaving Donstable—because you are. Then make sure all your stuff's out of the flat before Rebecca finishes work—and don't ever contact her again.'

Liz's eyes widen, but she nods. 'Alright—if you say so.' She trudges to the door and closes it softly behind her.

Daisy gives me a slow handclap. 'Sam, you never stop surprising me. You're becoming a real hardass.'

I feel a little embarrassed about it now

'I just didn't want her corrupting Rebecca. The poor girl's worked hard to turn her life around. She doesn't need that sort of influence in it. Oh, Daisy—how could we have been so stupid? Taking Liz on in the first place.'

Daisy grins. 'We took the same chance with Rebecca—and look how she turned out. Hey, we're batting one for two—not such a bad average.'

A FEW MINUTES LATER, REBECCA BURSTS INTO THE OFFICE. She looks distraught. 'Liz has GONE,' she gasps.

Getting up, I guide her to the client chair. 'Did she tell you why?'

Rebecca shakes her head. 'Only that she had to leave immediately—an emergency of some kind—and would put her keys through the flat's letterbox. What's going on, Sam?'

So we tell her what Liz did—watching Rebecca's jaw drop as her eyes bulge more than Marty Feldman's ever did. At the end of Daisy's damning diatribe, Rebecca slumps in her chair and gasps like a beached goldfish. 'I can't believe she would... Sam, Daisy, she didn't just leak information. Liz actually *participated* in sending you to that pie shop, knowing...'

'We don't *know* what she knew,' I intervene quickly. 'Maybe she thought they were only going to deliver a warning.'

That pacifies Rebecca slightly. 'But why? *Why* would Liz *do* that?'

Daisy explains about Pete, and Rebecca sits bolt upright. 'What a load of twaddle. Pete isn't in prison—he called round the other night, trying to borrow money from her. Not that she had any to give him,' Rebecca adds in a tone that reminds me of Caron, Liz's former flatmate.

Daisy looks helplessly at me. 'The cheeky mare. She conned us—again.'

I nod, my initial surge of anger changing to something approaching amusement. 'Yep—right pair of Wally's, aren't we?'

'Are you going to report her to the police? Now you know that?'

Daisy answers. 'Naw, not unless she's got the cheek to ever come back. Then all bets are off. But what you tell Alan is your affair, Rebecca.'

Rebecca sniffs and pulls a hankie from somewhere. Which is quite a magic trick, considering how scant today's outfit is—there's barely room for *her* in it. 'No, I think we'd all rather just forget about Liz. The *besom*. She's left me in a right mess.'

'How so?' I ask, suddenly concerned.

'Liz still owes me last month's rent—in fact, last month's everything. All this nonsense about our having a shopping fund—would have been a fine idea, but Liz never got around to putting in her share.'

Rebecca dips her head. 'And she borrowed some money from me—said her auntie was sick and couldn't afford taxis to the hospital for treatment.'

Daisy smacks her forehead. 'The little... she had us all fooled. We should have seen through her sooner.'

I'm still standing beside Rebecca and reach down to touch her arm. 'What about the flat? Will you be looking for someone else to share with?'

'Oh, Sam. I'm broke—up to my ears in credit card debt. I mean, it's not like I'm normally any good at managing my finances. But when you add in the money Liz owes me—what am I going to do? The rent's too expensive to keep on paying by myself. But the thought of getting a new flatmate scares me, after Liz ...'

What she's saying doesn't come as a complete surprise. I've wondered before how Rebecca can afford the likes of Abercrombe & Fitch on her salary. Daisy suggested it was because there must be a limit to what even a designer can charge for handkerchief-sized scraps of material...

I can't help feeling slightly responsible for Rebecca's woes. It *was* us who brought Liz in. Bending over, I place a hand on each of her shoulders. 'Rebecca, you and I are going to have a tutorial session on managing money. Meanwhile, I'll front you a wee loan to clear your debts—that's a *loan*, mind—and if you want it, your old room in the staff corridor's still free.'

She springs up and gives me a hug. 'Sam, I can't thank you enough. That's *so* good of you. I'll get on to the landlord now and tell him. I'm pretty sure he'll let me move out straight away, without notice...'

I wonder why? Maybe because he'd rather have tenants who actually PAY their rent?

'Rebecca,' Daisy says in a serious tone. 'You need to be on your guard until I say otherwise. There's a possibility Lena's on the loose.'

'Lena? How...'

'We don't have any details yet—it's not even confirmed—but meantime, lock the door anytime you're here alone. Don't open it until whoever's there has identified themselves. I'll let you know more when we do.'

'Okay.'

Spontaneously, Rebecca hugs me again—then bounds out of the office. One thing about her—she never stays down for long. Daisy throws me a quizzical glance. 'You're too soft. She'll never learn if you keep bailing her out.'

I put the argument that we were partly to blame (for the "Liz" element of Rebecca's problems) and Daisy laughs. 'Rubbish. Rebecca doesn't need any help to land herself in debt. Just a department store.'

'Well, anyway—she's all the staff we have left, so it seemed a good idea to ensure *she* stays.'

'Mm... when you put it like that. Think we'll hold off on replacing Liz, though—I'm wondering if a receptionist is really necessary. After all, we can divert the landline to our mobiles...' she hesitates '... probably better make that *my* mobile. And we don't get many people walking in off the street—which figures, seeing as we aren't on one. So long as somebody's here the day after murder mysteries, is there any need to have the place manned constantly?'

She's got a point. Hmm, I'm supposed to be the business brain—did I fall asleep on the job?

Not really. Daisy's right—I am too soft, and was more concerned with giving Liz her second chance. Time I hardened up a bit.

After telling Daisy I intend doing just that, she looks askew at me. 'Naw. Don't change, Sam. You're fine as you are.'

27

Neither of us feels like lunch. Daisy decides to help Rebecca move back into her old room in the hotel's staff corridor, and I attack the dreaded VAT invoices.

An hour later, Hazel taps at my cupboard door. 'Somebody to see you,' she coos. Sticking my head out, I spot a flustered-looking Mr M pacing the residents lounge.

'Could you bring two coffees, Hazel?'

Hazel trots off obediently while I reluctantly (hee-hee) abandon my unpaid work on behalf of Customs & Excise and wave to Mr M. 'Over here—Hazel's getting us some coffee.'

He joins me at a table, his normally placid expression more reminiscent of an 18th century French nobleman en route to the guillotine. 'Samantha. So glad I've caught you.'

While we wait for Hazel, I bring Mr M up to date on the warzone that's been my and Daisy's lives lately. He's heard most of it from Kat and Jodie, but listens raptly regardless and is obviously delighted that our problems with the Glasgow underworld are resolved.

Hazel reappears in double-quick time with two mugs of steaming Jamaican. She pops them in front of us, then returns to reception. Mr M waits until she's out of hearing. 'My dear, I owe you an apology.'

'No problem, Mr M. Um... what for?'

'Yesterday,' he says sadly. 'The "almost" vehicular collision. That was me—in effect.'

The Peugeot—was Mr M? 'I didn't even know you drove?'

'I have a licence, but decided some time ago the costs involved in running a car were out of proportion with my modest usage. So I sold my old BMW.'

'Then whose is the Peugeot?'

'Em... I suppose it's Miss Dobie's now. It *was* her sister Enid's, but she can't drive anymore.'

This isn't making much sense. 'Mr M—*what* are you talking about?'

He holds up a palm. 'Sorry, let me start again. Miss Dobie's sister is in poor health and needs taking care of. To that end, Miss Dobie has to visit her in Alford twice a day.'

'Uh-huh,' I say, sympathetically, but still not getting it.

'Miss Dobie, courtesy of her sister, now has a car—unfortunately, she does not have a driving licence.'

A ray of sunlight twinkles through the mist. 'Ah—you're teaching her to drive?'

'I am.'

'So that was you and Miss Dobie yesterday? In the Peugeot?'

'That's what I'm trying to tell you,' he says patiently.

'What happened?'

Mr M takes a huge swallow of coffee. 'Miss Dobie confused the brake and accelerator pedals—she does that a lot. How we got past unscathed is a mystery to me—perhaps she has some latent driving skills after all. Either that, or a well-developed survival instinct.'

'But why didn't you stop afterwards?'

'My dear, we were another mile down the road before Miss Dobie re-identified the brake pedal.'

He pulls out a silk handkerchief and mops his brow. 'She is not an easy pupil.'

Struggling to keep a straight face, I realise this explains Kat's suspicions. Mr M hasn't been off with some fancy woman—he's been teaching Miss Dobie to drive. (Or trying to.) It's also the reason he looked so harassed yesterday.

If we'd only realised that was Mr M and Miss Dobie, it would have saved us a great deal of angst—but everything happened so fast.

Then something Kat said a while back pops into my head. 'Miss Dobie's sister was in hospital a few months ago, I remember that—but Kat told me it was just ingrowing toenails.'

'Since then, poor Enid fell and broke her hip. Unfortunately, "routine" surgery to repair the damage turned out to be anything but, leaving her with severely compromised mobility. A longstanding distrust of outside agencies compounds the problem in that Enid won't allow carers in her home, only accepting assistance from her sister. I found all this out when Miss Dobie handed in her notice a month ago. She was devastated to do so—that job, you must understand, is her life—but Miss Dobie saw no alternative due to the time involved in travelling back and forth from Alford. So, rather than accept her resignation and as an interim measure, I have been driving Miss Dobie to and from Enid's until she passes her test.'

Which, if yesterday's anything to go by, won't be anytime soon

'I think it's wonderful—what you're doing for her.'

'Miss Dobie has provided me with many years of faithful service and it gives me great pleasure to repay her in kind. But I cannot continue being her chauffeur indefinitely—yet frankly despair of ever getting the woman through her test. She really is the most abysmal driver. Anyway, that's why yesterday happened. I had no idea who we'd nearly forced off the road until Kat told me today.'

Of course—he didn't recognise the Fiesta

Finishing his coffee, Mr M goes to stand. 'You have both my and Miss Dobie's sincere apologies. Now, I have kept you from work long enough…'

I raise a hand. 'Wait up, Mr M. Maybe I can help…'

'You did what?' Daisy asks, incredulously.

'I offered to give her some lessons. It's nearly fifty years since Mr M passed his test—he's probably telling the poor woman all wrong.'

Daisy smirks. "You aren't known for having nerves of steel."

'Don't be silly—Miss Dobie just needs some proper instruction and she'll be fine. I remember what it was like learning to drive, and the difference a good instructor made.'

'When's the first lesson?' she asks, rolling her eyes.

'I'm picking her up at five. That is, I'm driving around to her cottage, then we'll go out in the Peugeot.'

'Okay.'

Daisy pretends to ponder. 'Personally, I'd rather face the Glasgow mafia... which reminds me, keep your eyes peeled for Lena.'

Miss Dobie lives in a row of former farm cottages at the far end of Cairncroft. She's surrounded by little-used country roads, which are ideal for assessing what stage her driving's at. Mr M will ferry Miss Dobie to Alford later for Enid's "bedding down"—we agreed it best her first lesson with me should be restricted to local roads.

When I pull up behind Miss Dobie's Peugeot, she's already halfway down the garden path. I get out and meet her at the gate. 'Samantha, this is so kind. Thank you.'

'Not at all, Miss Dobie. You might find it easier having lessons with another woman.'

She titters. 'Mr MacLachlan tries very hard, but gets *so* upset when I do things wrong. I think that might be putting me off.'

'I'm sure it is. Learning to drive should be a relaxed experience. The trouble with men is they need to be in control all the time. While it *is* important you do as I ask, there's no need for any sort of strained atmosphere.'

She puts both hands together under her chin. 'Oh, I think this is going to work out famously. With your help, Samantha, I'm sure it won't be long before I pass my test.'

We get into the Peugeot and I run through a few basics. 'Alright, I presume you're familiar with the controls?'

'Just remind me, dear—which one is the brake pedal?'

A little numbly, I point. She nods. 'Yes, of course. I must try and overcome my mental block about that.'

Hm—Mr M DID mention that was a problem

'I'm fine with the clutch,' she adds cheerily. 'Probably because my left foot only has *it* to contend with. But having *two* pedals to control with the right foot is terribly confusing.'

'Do you have any stickers in the house?'

Miss Dobie rakes in her pocket then brings out a pad of post-its. 'Will these do?'

Somehow, I'm not surprised her pockets are full of stationery supplies. 'Ideal.'

I rip one off and slap it on the dashboard. 'There, see—I've put it on the left, same side as your brake pedal.'

She squeals with delight. 'What a clever idea. Mr MacLachlan never thought of that.'

We both fasten our seat belts. Then Miss Dobie turns the ignition key. 'No need to rev it quite so much,' I suggest gently. 'Now, mirror, signal... Miss Dobie? *What* are you doing?'

'Driving, dear. Isn't that what we're here for?'

'You can't just take off like that. Didn't Mr M tell you about checking the mirror?'

'It's fine. At precisely the correct angle.'

'I don't mean that—you're supposed to *look* in the mirror before pulling out, in case anything's coming up behind. And signal.'

'Signal?'

'Your indicators.'

'Oh, I thought they were for turning corners.'

'Miss Dobie, be careful…' I grab the steering wheel and twist it sharply, bringing us back to our side of the white line.

'Did I let it wander again? I'm so sorry. Mr MacLachlan gets awfully upset when I do that…'

Glancing over my shoulder at a roadside tree whose intimate acquaintance we came within inches of making, I feel my heart thump. 'Miss Dobie, it's not necessary to look at me when you're speaking—keep your eyes on the road at all times.'

Gingerly, I remove my hand from the wheel and return control to my pupil. An instant later, I yelp: 'Slow down, you're going too fast. Press the brake—Miss Dobie, you're still speeding up.'

'Sorry, dear. I'm getting them mixed up again.'

Her eyes dart from side to side, obviously searching for the post-it, and I grab the wheel. After forcing us around a bend, I gape in horror at the rear end of a tractor toddling along in front. The gap between us is closing rapidly—*too* rapidly. 'BRAKE, MISS DOBIE. BRAKE.'

'Ah, there it is.' She taps her nail against the post-it, then plunges her foot on the brake pedal. The car shimmies wildly and we screech to a stop inches behind the tractor. The Peugeot's engine stutters violently, then stalls.

Miss Dobie tuts. 'Tractors are terribly slow— shall we wait until he's gone, or would you like me to overtake him?'

'Um… I think that's enough for today. Let's change seats and *I'll* take us back…'

Miss Dobie gives me a peeved look when I turn the Peugeot around, but tough. I wasn't expecting her driving to be *this* bad—although the near miss yesterday *was* a clue. But there is no *way* my nerves could survive another lesson with this woman. And yet I promised…

As we draw up to Miss Dobie's cottage, she fixes me with a glare. 'Mr MacLachlan always took me out for at least an hour.'

'We can build up to longer lessons,' I mutter, scrabbling for time to think—because I have the glimmer of an idea.

'Would you like a cup of tea?' she asks as we get out, said in that way people do when they expect a refusal.

'Could murder one,' I tell her.

'Oh… lovely. Come on in, then.'

'Just tea, though,' I say firmly, remembering the trolley-borne spread she magicked up last time Daisy and I were here. 'I'll be going back for my evening meal, you see…'

When Miss Dobie disappears (literally—how does she do that?) to the kitchen, it gives me a chance to polish my inspiration. Yes—this might be the answer.

Miss Dobie can't help herself—she comes in pushing a trolley loaded with plates of scones and biscuits. 'I didn't make sandwiches,' she apologises. 'After what you said.'

The scones are warm? I start to wonder if she's got some kind of "Willie Wonka" style baking factory through there. 'Miss Dobie,' I begin. 'Mr M told me about your sister—I'm so sorry to hear about her difficulties.'

'Enid is struggling terribly. If I don't get my driving licence, it'll mean giving up work to look after her.'

'Mr M said. I was thinking—could it be you're going about this the wrong way?'

She drops her biscuit back on its plate and fixes me with a challenging glare. 'How so?'

'At the moment you're shooting over to Enid's at least twice a day. Why not bring Enid to live here? Then there won't *be* any travelling to worry about.'

She opens her mouth to speak, then changes her mind and lifts the biscuit. Takes a bite of custard cream and chews thoughtfully. 'Enid—live here?' she says, without blowing a single crumb.

'It's the ideal solution. All that time you would have spent going to and fro is better used looking after Enid. And it means you can keep working.'

She scratches her head. 'You know, I never thought of that, but now you mention it—yes, that makes perfect sense. Enid might be funny about moving, though... she's very strong on independence and won't give up her house easily.'

'No need for that at this stage. Put it to her as a temporary arrangement until her condition improves. "Just for a month or two".'

Her face sags. 'I can't see Enid improving now...'

'Yes, but she probably hasn't accepted that yet. Dressing it up as convalescence will ease her into the whole idea and also give *you* a trial period—in case things don't work out.'

'Mm. I think you could be onto something. Insist she comes to stay for a while—just until she feels better—then let nature take its course? Oh, and it means I don't need to have any more driving lessons. What a relief.'

You and me both

28

'Stop laughing—it isn't funny.'

'Yes it is.'

Daisy makes her way to the drinks table (when did she set that up?) still shaking with mirth. She returns with a large brandy and holds it out. 'Here—you probably need that.'

'I do.'

Sipping gratefully, I watch her open a bottle of beer before flopping on the sofa beside me. 'You look whacked,' I comment.

'Oh, it's that whole Liz thing. Really knocked the feet from under me.'

'Me too. How was Rebecca when you left her?'

'You know Rebecca—takes a lot to get that one down. We made a couple of trips and got most of her stuff moved back.'

'Did you remember the cat?'

Daisy throws a hand over her mouth. 'Blast. *Knew* there was something I'd forgotten...'

'Hm. You might, but Rebecca wouldn't. I feel sorry for her. She was getting on so well, what with moving out to the flat and all...'

Daisy shakes her head. 'If you ask me, Rebecca's happier here. It's what she's used to.'

'You could be right. Did Alan get back to you—about Lena?'

'No, not yet. Which I'm fuming about—and the beggar isn't answering his phone. Hey, have you heard from the garage?'

I nod, still not sure how I feel about that. 'Yep, Arthur phoned, and would you believe Panda's a write-off—and the Fiesta's for sale at a knock-down price?'

'Define "knock-down".'

'Sky-high whittled down a touch. Part of me's in mourning for the latest car I fell in love with, but the Fiesta's winning me over. It goes like a wee bomb...'

Daisy throws up her hands in mock horror. 'Here, steady on—maybe we'd better get you measured for a crash helmet. So I take it you're keeping the Fiesta, then?'

'Provisionally. I want Davy to look it over first and advise on the price. Arthur isn't best pleased about that—Davy got him down three hundred on the Panda if you remember—but Arthur was too desperate for the sale to put up much of a fight.'

'Talking of Bob... sorry, Davy... did you say he's back on Wednesday?'

'Yep. Can't wait.'

'Great—Wilf knows a man with a van who'll shift our and Jodie's stuff. The guy's available next weekend—and I said Davy would help him with the heavy lifting.'

'I'll ask him,' I tell her pointedly, but she only smirks.

'He won't mind,' she asserts confidently, just before my phone rings.

'Jodie,' I murmur, answering. Daisy frowns, and I hear her muttered aside.

'Better late than never—which is more than *Alan's* managed.'

Hopefully, Jodie didn't pick that up

'Hi, Sam. Sorry I couldn't get back to you sooner—it's been crazy here today.'

Oops—maybe she did

Daisy wanders off towards the kitchen, presumably to satisfy an attack of the nibbles—though *attack* is the wrong word for a chronic condition—and Jodie says something that has me sitting up straight. 'Hold on,' I interrupt. 'That can't be—Daisy spoke to Alan and he said she wasn't listed as being at Rampton.'

Jodie's "tut" makes the receiver vibrate. '*She* doesn't know the meaning of "patience"—and *he* has a reputation for going off half-cocked. I was on the phone with Rampton earlier on—and they *were* puzzled at first, because Lena didn't show up on their computer. Even though the woman I was talking to had seen her in the exercise yard ten minutes previously. Turns out whoever inputted Lena's details spelt her surname wrong. Well, with a name like Bartholomew, it's hard to blame them. Long and short, Sam, Lena's accounted for at Rampton and won't be getting out anytime soon.'

When Daisy comes back through, still chewing, I fill her in. Her jaw freezes, mid-mastication, then she talks through what's left of her cheese sandwich. 'Flippin' Alan—I'll kill him.'

I can't decide whether I'm relieved or disappointed. Lena, I did *not* fancy tangling with again—but there was a certain comfort in knowing who we were up against. A bit of the "devil you know." Now we're back to square one. 'You'd better tell Alan.'

An evil expression flares in her face. 'Naw—he can find out for himself.'

I shake my head. 'What about the witches—do you still want to meet up with them tomorrow?'

'I think we should talk to them again, but it obviously isn't as big a deal knowing Lena's accounted for—I was hoping it'd be simple as showing the witches her pic, but now we're grasping at straws. The other thing is, Rebecca took in a new insurance case on Friday. The usual—someone claiming an accident at work left them crippled, who somebody else saw up on a roof fixing loose tiles. Shouldn't take long to get some photographic evidence documenting his miracle recovery, but this is a firm we haven't dealt with before and I'd like to impress them with a quick turnaround.'

'So you want me to go and talk to the witches on my own?'

'Would you?'

'Sure—and the bonus is I'll be able to see Davy again.'

She sniffs. 'Why bother? You can see him *anytime* after Wednesday.'

'Daisy, we're engaged. It's snatched moments that keep the romance alive in a relationship.

Anyway, why aren't you sending Rebecca to get photos of your insurance fraudster?'

'I'm worried in case he's back on the roof and falls off when Dolly Parton strolls by. Naw, actually I sort of said she could have a couple of days to finish moving in down the corridor.'

'What a kind thought. You can be, sometimes.'

Ignoring her aggrieved look, I hold out my glass. 'More, please. Think Miss Dobie's left me with a nasty case of post-traumatic stress disorder.'

Daisy's phone rings. 'Aren't you going to answer that?'

She glances at the screen, then tosses it aside. 'Naw—it's only Alan.'

NEXT DAY, FOR SAFETY, I SET OFF EARLY. OVER AND ABOVE driving time per se, you have to allow for the inevitable roadworks and a whole myriad of other disruptions now endemic to today's motorways. Then there's getting through Glasgow city centre, not to mention finding somewhere to park. As a rule of thumb, I look up my "journey duration" on Google—and double it.

Yet somehow, often as not, I'm still late.

Today, I'm forty minutes early. You can't win!

Trying not to dwell on the charges accumulating with every minute my new Fiesta sits in that multi-storey car park, I pass some time in a couple of department stores. Which reminds me why I so much like living somewhere that doesn't *have* any big shops.

Feeling battered as a front-line player in last week's Scotland vs Australia match at Murrayfield, with my ears ringing from a combination of "Muzak" and imbecilic shrieks from other customers who've found something they don't need marked down by 10%, I almost welcome the traffic noise on my way to meet the witches. At least Whitney Houston's no longer screaming "Feels so good", although I just passed somebody in heated debate with a parking warden who was doing a pretty fair impression of Lennon's "You can't do that."

Agatha, Bertha, and Gertha are already there when I reach the café. They're settled with drinks at a window table and send flurries of waves my way while I fetch a macchiato from the counter.

'Hello ladies—thank you ever so for agreeing to meet.' I sink into the fourth chair and my feet (foot) scream(s) their (its) appreciation. (Outdoing even Whitney.)

Agatha gives me a piercing look. 'You have a powerful aura today, dear. I see such strength hidden within that feeble frame.'

I'm not sure whether to be insulted. Probably safest if we get right down to business. 'Have you remembered anything more about that woman? The one you saw leaving after the murder.'

They all glance at each other, as though to confirm something. Then, as usual, Agatha speaks for the group. 'Sorry, nothing.'

Daisy told me to try this. 'Did she remind you of anyone? An actor on television, for example, or somebody famous.'

Bertha adopts a thoughtful expression. 'She *was* a bit like that lady who presents the weather on TV.'

Nice call, Daisy. Now we're getting somewhere

'Which weather girl is that, Bertha?'

She looks at me blankly. 'I told you—the one on television.'

'Yes, but—which channel?'

'I can't remember. She's blonde, though.'

Oh dear

After Gertha tries to liken the suspect to someone "in a film I once saw" and which, on being pressed, she remembers was about "people on a boat"—I'm ready to give up. These are lovely ladies, but their memories have more holes than a colander. Agatha seems transfixed by something outside, and I follow her gaze. To my surprise, Davy gets out of a car that just stopped with its hazards flashing.

It's not the sight of Davy that surprised me—we arranged to meet here and he's bang on time. Anyway, surprise isn't a good word for what I'm feeling, horror being a better description of my reaction when I realise Leslie's in the driving seat. There's something different about her—ah, she's started wearing specs since I last saw her.

Whoever helped her choose those frames needed glasses themselves

Agatha taps my arm. 'Do you know that person?'

'What—oh, yes. He's my fiancé—Davy. We're taking the chance of a quick meet-up.'

Agatha shakes her head. 'No, not him. The driver.'

'Just somebody he works with. Why?'

She shrugs. 'Because that's her. The girl we saw on Allhallows Eve—isn't it?' she asks the other two.

They both stare, then nod excitedly. 'Yes, that's definitely her.'

DAVY OFFERS TO SIT AT ANOTHER TABLE UNTIL I'VE FINISHED with Agatha & co, but they've already given me what I came for. Agatha looks first at Davy, then me, and raises her eyebrows.

A brief shake of my head tells her I don't want to discuss their identification of Leslie in front of Davy and she gives Bertha and Gertha meaningful glances that freeze them into silence. My thoughts are racing, trying to make sense of this new information. It was *Leslie* who dressed up as Ghostface to try and kill me last week?

So she could have Davy to herself?

Davy described Leslie as being "a bit of a nutter" and Geraldine said the girl was "bonkers". She added that, underneath, Leslie isn't who she pretends to be. But Davy still cares for her—he's made that plain. Not in any romantic way, I'm now confident, but they do have a history—and knowing Davy, he probably never stopped feeling guilty for dumping her all those years ago. I'm not ready to tell him about this latest development—need some time to think it through first.

I realise everyone's looking at me and jerk myself back to the present.

'I said, we'll toddle off if you've finished with us.'

'Sorry, Agatha—I was miles away. Yes, thank you ladies—this has been most helpful. I may have to contact you again...'

Agatha nods knowingly and hustles the other two out of the café. Davy drops into the seat opposite and smiles too broadly. 'So—sounds like your meeting went well?'

Maybe he thinks I didn't see who was driving

Glancing quickly out the window, I confirm Leslie's car has disappeared. 'Davy, was that...?'

He reddens. 'My own car's in for a service—seemed daft not to take the chance while I'm still handy for a main dealer. There's usually a spare van or two knocking about the yard and I planned on using one of them to get here. Except, for some reason, there wasn't—they'd all been booked out. So what happened was Leslie heard me phoning for a taxi and offered...'

'When's she picking you up?' I ask, not even trying to filter a layer of ice from my tone.

'She isn't. Leslie decided to take the rest of the week off and went straight home. That's the good news, Sam—since Wednesday's my last day, I won't see her again.'

'Where's she going for her holidays? Somewhere far away, I hope.'

He frowns, which annoys me intensely. 'I don't think she has anything planned. It's more a case of having to take the days they owe her or lose them. Leslie's always been a workaholic.'

The term I used to Jodie regarding Daisy and me—and it jars hearing him describe Leslie the same way. Illogically, I hate the thought of having even *that* in common with her. But... he won't be seeing her again? That's an enormous relief—especially considering what I just found out.

I'm sitting stiffly, with both palms on the table. Davy puts a hand over one of mine. 'Sam, is there something on your mind? Or was it Leslie appearing that upset you?'

Forcing a smile, I shake my head. 'No more than usual. And I'm not miffed about you accepting a lift from Leslie—but after what you've said about her, she freaks me out a little.'

'I maybe shouldn't have told you,' he murmurs, and it takes a moment for me to process that. It isn't what *Davy* told me that's fried my brains…

With an enormous effort, I talk about his imminent return to Cairncroft and convince him nothing else is bothering me.

If only

Finally, enough time elapses that I can offer him a lift back to work. To my relief, he refuses and calls a taxi. 'I know what you're like driving somewhere new,' he says with a grin. 'You'd probably get lost and end up in Kilmarnock.'

When the taxi toots, I follow him outside. Davy hugs me, then delivers a lingering goodbye kiss. For a moment, I even forget about Leslie.

Standing on the kerb, waving after his cab, I wonder what to do next. Realising that isn't an easy question, I go back into the café and order a double-shot—then sit down again.

I need time to think

Okay, so the facts are that Agatha and her crew were pretty sure it was Leslie they saw leave in a hurry after the incident last week. I remember they were definite it was seven o'clock—

something to do with a TV programme Bertha was missing—which ties in perfectly with the attack. Slightly circumstantial perhaps, but I'm in no doubt now that Leslie tried to stab me behind the hotel. Whether she planned her Ghostface impersonation in advance, or just turned up and winged it—no, she must have worked everything out beforehand, because her knife was exactly like the one Ghostface uses in his movies.

So Mr Fortescue's—Joe Booth's—stabbing *was* an accident. Leslie simply dumped the knife in Dinner-Death's dressing room to avoid being caught with it. It probably never occurred to her what could happen—the yanks would call that "culpable homicide", which to me describes her crime better than the "manslaughter" charge she'll likely face.

And, of course, she tried to murder me—no "accident" there.

This is going to kill Davy. Not only is his uni sweetheart going to prison, but he'll be overwhelmed with guilt because of bringing her to my door. I remember how long it took him to get over not being around to protect me from Jake—despite the fact Davy was in hospital when Jake tried to do away with me.

What will I do?

I should tell Wilson what I've discovered—and there's Ricky to think of, too. He's facing charges for what Leslie did, so keeping quiet isn't an option.

Impulsively, I make a decision. I'm going to have a little chat with Leslie. Maybe I can convince her to hand herself in. It won't stop Davy tumbling into a spiral of guilt over what *might* have happened—but for Ricky's sake, if no other reason, this can't be covered up. And getting Leslie to confess is the cleanest solution all around—so far as Davy's concerned it's ripping the plaster off so we can put all this behind us, as opposed to the long-drawn-out process that would ensue if *I* dob Leslie in and she denies it.

Of course, I'm talking about confronting someone who tried to murder me—but remembering how easily I was able to physically intimidate her last time we met, there really isn't any risk involved. Leslie was only a threat when she was sneaking up behind me with a dirty great knife in her hand.

To be honest, I still feel a little guilty about that previous confrontation when I used a painful aikido hold, one Daisy taught me, and brought the lassie to her knees.

Right—decided. Davy said Leslie intended going straight home after dropping him off. Picking up my phone, I call Rebecca. The good news is Daisy won't be around to cause complications—she's out chasing her insurance malingerer—and Rebecca should be able to get me Leslie's address in no time flat.

29

After paying what feels more like a ransom demand to the multi-storey car park's mechanical representative, it takes me twenty minutes to find Giffnock—the Glasgow district in which (I now know) Leslie lives.

Then another fifteen to locate her house.

Faced with a trip into uncharted territory, I remembered what Daisy said about needing satnav and downloaded an app to my phone. During this last stage of the journey, in Giffnock itself, it's been invaluable—without the robot voice giving me directions, I might have spent hours driving around. (Even if it *did* try to turn me down several one-way streets at the wrong end.)

I forgot Daisy had given Rebecca today off so she could settle back into her staff bedroom, but the canny lass brushed off my apologies and dashed down to the detective agency. Once Rebecca had access to our online database services, she found Leslie's address in minutes.

Davy's old flame must be high up in HR because the red sandstone terrace she lives in won't come cheap. Not in that sort of nick and this close to town. Also, I seem to recall Giffnock being a "desirable" area. I'm relieved to see they allow street parking—no permits or even payment required—and pull in two doors past Leslie's house.

Taking a moment to gather the disorganised thoughts that brought me here, I mentally run over my objectives. In short, I intend giving Leslie an opportunity to turn herself in—and a time limit for doing so. If she gets stroppy—well, I'm no Daisy, but neither had I any problem subduing Leslie at our last meeting. I don't anticipate that sort of aggro, though—not from bubbly, catwalk-ready Leslie. Sucking in a huge breath, I get out of the car and walk back to her house.

A six-foot-deep flagstoned area separates Leslie's building from the pavement. Bounded by a low wall, the "front garden" thus formed is full of pots containing evergreens. Tall hedges on either side disguise the fact it's terraced—from the gate I could be looking at a detached property.

Right—let's get this over with. I march up the path and jab Leslie's doorbell.

Too soon after, it opens.

'Oh.'

Not an unexpected reaction. 'Leslie, we need to talk. May I come in?'

She simply nods, then turns around and I follow her into a spacious lounge. Her suite comprises two Chesterfield settees, facing one another across a coffee table. She motions me to sit. 'Would you like coffee?'

Hmm... her tone's not overly friendly, unsurprisingly—but neither is it overtly hostile. And whilst coffee isn't top of my wish list at this moment, I *do* want to encourage a civilised exchange. So I say: 'Thank you, that would be lovely.'

Sitting down, I nearly break my spine on the sofa's low back. It escapes me why Chesterfields are so popular—they have to be the most uncomfortable furniture design I've ever encountered. Well, except for Donstable police station's waiting area—but not by much.

Leslie bustles in with a tray and we spend a minute sorting out drinks. Then she sits opposite and gives me a wan smile. 'I'm so glad you've come, Samantha.'

You are?

Taking a gulp of coffee, I gather my thoughts. 'Leslie, let's not beat about the bush. I know it was you who tried to stab me at Halloween.'

Her eyes widen. 'Samantha, I am *so* sorry about that. I wasn't well—and can only think it was some kind of psychotic breakdown. That isn't who I am—honestly.'

'Hm. The fact remains, a man died because of your actions that night.'

Both hands go to her face. 'Oh, don't remind me. I'm so ashamed, *really* I am. But I didn't mean to...'

Holding up a hand, I cut her off. 'I realise that wasn't part of your plan, but it happened all the same. Leslie—*why* did you want to kill me?'

She pouts. 'You know the answer to that. Davy explained he was so much in love with you that coming back to me was out of the question. So...' she shrugs '...getting rid of you seemed the only option.'

'But you see now how... insane... that was?'

'Of course. In retrospect, it's hard to believe I did that. Will you ever be able to forgive me?'

Is she for real?

'It doesn't matter what I think. You committed a crime—and someone else is in danger of carrying the can. Leslie, would you consider giving yourself up to the police? Honestly, it'll go far better for you than the alternative—which is me spilling the beans.'

She tilts her head. 'Yes, I see that. Alright, I will.'

I did *not* expect it to be this easy, but she seems truly repentant. I put my cup down on the coffee table and somehow manage to spill half its contents. 'Oh, I'm so sorry...'

'Don't worry,' she trills, springing up and darting towards the door. 'I'll fetch a cloth.'

I look at my fingers, which suddenly feel as though they belong to someone else. And my head's swimming...

'Samantha. Are you feeling alright?'

She's back, standing over me and peering curiously. Strangely, I don't see a cloth in her hand. 'Yes, I'm just a bit...'

Leslie splits in two, as does everything around her. The double vision only lasts a few seconds before being replaced by a blanket of grey, which slowly turns to black...

SCATTERED IMPRESSIONS SKITTER THROUGH MY MIND. FIRST, being thrown about like a sack of potatoes—then the sound of a car engine—and finally, I'm vaguely conscious of being dragged over grass. But my awareness throughout is fleeting and it's hard to care, or even show interest. It reminds me of trying to watch a movie after (far) too much red wine.

An eternity later, consciousness seeps back. Unfortunately, as the fuzziness dissolves, a sledgehammer starts pounding inside my skull. Winding my eyelids up is harder than raising rusted shutters clear of a shop window, and I wince when bright lights stab my retinae. There's a damp, musty stink in the air.

After a moment, the illumination dials down and I realise it was never more than normal room lighting. As the photophobia recedes, my vision resolves from coloured blobs and everything around me comes into focus.

I'm slumped on a sofa upholstered in something that feels suspiciously like horsehair, and doesn't smell nice either. Coarse anaglypta blotted with Rorschach-shaped globules of mildew clings gamely to the walls on every side. Now my eyes have adapted, I realise the light given off by an ancient ceiling fixture is far from being bright—and so yellowed it's reminiscent of looking through the cellophane wrapping from a "Quality Street" toffee penny. (Didn't everybody do that as a child?)

Cautiously turning my head to one side reveals the naked glass of a fairly wide window, which tells me everything is pitch-black outside. The movement makes my brain rattle, but gritting my teeth I check the other way and spot a narrow door. It's behind and between what looks like two kitchen worktops doubling as a room divider. The worktops have rows of overhead cabinets looking down on them, creating a view through the space between that's cropped top and bottom—so when motion draws my eye, all I see is someone's torso.

Until she steps into the opening linking the rooms.

Watching Leslie smile benignly kick-starts my memory. 'You drugged me?'

'Sorry.'

She comes over and puts down a mug, filled (half-filled) with Nescafé going by its aroma, on a stained table in front of the sofa. 'Here—drink this. It'll help clear your head.'

Experiencing a sudden and overwhelming Daisy-like desire to hurt this woman, I go to get up. That's when I realise. 'Where's my leg?'

She laughs. 'Have you any idea how comical that sounds? Sorry—it's outside in the car. After last time, I wanted a little advantage in case you decide to attack me again.'

My head's clearing at a rate of knots, albeit in inverse proportion to the throbbing that threatens to split it open. But if Leslie thinks hobbling me will keep her safe…

I'll wait until she comes within reach, then grab her. Once I have Leslie on the floor, being half-a-leg short won't stop me throttling the besom.

But she reads my mind. What looks like an extra-long barbecue fork sporting a too-thick plastic handle rests against the sofa's matching armchair, and Leslie picks it up. 'Do you know what this is?'

She assumes (correctly) from my silence that I don't and answers for me. 'It's an electric cattle prod.'

'What—is that the same as a taser?'

'No. Being only 6000 volts, it doesn't immobilise you like a taser would. All this does is cause pain.'

She grins, and for the first time I notice her eye teeth have pointed tips. 'A *lot* of pain. Quite excruciating, actually. But you'll find out firsthand because a demonstration is essential. I need you to understand the consequences of any misbehaviour.'

I brace myself, but she shakes her head. 'Oh, not right now. That wouldn't be very fair when you're still coming round from the Rohypnol I laced your coffee with. No, silly...' she laughs when I turn an accusing glare on the mug in front of me '... not that one. The coffee I gave you back at my house in Giffnock.'

With the return of my senses, I'm becoming more and more alarmed. On second thoughts, make that terror-stricken. And this latest piece of news isn't helping. 'Where are we?' I gasp.

'Just outside Dumbarton, on the West Coast. Haven't you realised this is a static caravan? On a holiday park?'

No, I hadn't actually—I'm still struggling to remember who I am. But that revelation gives me a burst of hope. A holiday park? Even at this time of year, surely there'll be people about—all I have to do is get their attention.

Leslie holds a finger to her lips and pretends to chew the nail. 'Full disclosure. Craigview Holiday Park went bankrupt six months ago. Their caravans are so old and dilapidated, the liquidators didn't consider it worthwhile employing a watchman. Or, for that matter, putting in place *any* kind of security. So—it's just you and me, Samantha. We're out in the wilds—our nearest neighbour is five miles away—and I'm afraid escape is quite impossible.'

30

"Escape is impossible," Leslie says. But escape from *what*?

Why has she brought me here? (Or are those both the same thing?)

Casting my eyes ceilingward, seeking inspiration, something occurs to me. 'You said the caravan park was closed. Where's the electricity coming from?'

'What a bonus, eh? I loaded up the car with candles and a camping stove on the assumption there'd be no power. Luckily, I decided to make sure. There's a proper bricks-and-mortar building at the park entrance—it was a site office and shop. So I broke in and tried turning on the mains electric switch.'

Leslie holds out her hands, like she's checking for rain. 'Bingo. Couldn't believe my luck—they left the leccy connected.'

Candles—camping stove—whatever Leslie's up to sounds likely to involve days rather than hours. Which is good news in one sense, since she obviously doesn't intend killing me. The *bad* news, of course, will be what she *does* intend. 'Leslie—why did you bring me here?'

Stroking her chin, she pretends to think. 'Samantha, you were never in any danger when I crept up on you at Halloween. Know why?'

I shake my head and Leslie goes on. 'I couldn't do it. At the last moment, I wasn't able to make myself stab you. Yeeuch—that isn't who I am at all.'

'There was also the small matter of your falling over me...'

She dismisses that with a slash of one hand. 'Which only happened because realising my inability to kill in cold blood distracted me. There's no way I could have gone through with butchering someone. I know that now.'

Sounds promising

'How did you manage to plan that, anyway? By conning inside information out of Davy?'

She giggles. 'It wasn't really *planned* as such. Not like this little adventure. But yes, Davy told me enough to inspire the knife purchase. Then I just turned up and played things by ear. All those people milling about made it easy to avoid you—the only person who would recognise me. I kept tabs on you, though. I was banking on you going outside, having already filched a costume from the actors' room and stashed it in some shrubbery.'

'Leslie, I don't understand. Having stated you aren't capable of murder, what am I doing here? And this is all carefully plotted out, that's obvious—but how could you know I'd come to Giffnock?'

Her expression turns smug. 'Let's deal with the second question first. When Davy—because we still speak, the poor man's too nice not to—when he told me you were coming through to Glasgow, and on the day he'd booked his car in for a service, I saw my chance. Getting my days-off arranged at short notice was easy—I *am* in HR—as was sending some of the lads off on wild goose chases so there were no vans left for Davy to use. Luckily, I was around at the last moment to offer him a lift.'

She giggles. 'As to how I knew you'd come to Giffnock, well—I didn't. I parked in the nearest multi-storey, guessing you had too, and waited—there was a clear view of the street from my parking bay. Then I followed you. I was hoping you would go somewhere else before leaving

Glasgow, ideally another cafe where I could spike your drink—but if not, I'd have cut in front and made you stop. I had a whole other story prepared for that eventuality, but—imagine my surprise when you led me to Giffnock. You were obviously headed for my house, so I zipped ahead and was there to welcome you.'

'Okay, fine. But you already admitted to being incapable of murder. So back to my first question—*what* do you hope to gain by bringing me here?'

Leslie looks thoughtful and sounds far away when she answers. 'I'm not capable of "active" murder, but a "passive" approach is something else altogether.'

'You've lost me.'

'Oh, it's simple. I won't actually *kill* you. I'm going to *let* you die. According to Google, someone deprived of water can't go on living for much more than three days. And I've got the whole week off. So I'll wait until you expire naturally—then there'll be nothing to stop Davy and I getting back together. Oh, and I hope you enjoyed that coffee—because it's the last fluid you'll ever intake.'

MY THROAT IS DRY AS DESERT SAND—I THINK SOME OF that's down to the drugs Leslie gave me. After revealing her crazy plan to kill me by dehydration, she went to bed.

Can you only survive three days without water?

Unfortunately, that sounds about right. There's no running water to the caravan—it must be turned off at the main stopcock. And of course, Leslie didn't turn *that* on.

The chemical toilet she brought in from "the" car and installed in a second bedroom (there wasn't room in the pokey bathroom) does have a water tank for flushing, but... that's definitely a last resort. Apart from the yuck factor, it could have chemicals in it. Bleach, for example.

("The" car—turns out the besom used *my* Fiesta to bring us here.)

Leslie's using bottled water for herself and keeping careful tabs on it. She only brings in one bottle at a time. And, of course, took that through with her when she retired. Along with a small halogen-lamp heater which up to then had maintained a bearable temperature in the living area—but now my teeth are chattering.

Leslie's parting words were a warning not to try and sneak up on her during the night, claiming she has a "door handle alarm."

I've heard of them. They're meant for people staying away from home—as in hotels. Basically, it's a little gadget you hang from the door handle. If anyone tries to enter, it detects vibrations and sets off a built-in siren. So, like Leslie says—no way will I be able to surprise her while she's asleep.

That's alright—I don't need to. Earlier, after the heater had been on for a while, Leslie removed her coat and carelessly tossed it over the coffee table. Then, while she was making herself a bedtime cocoa, I filched her (my) car keys from it. She remembered to take the coat away when she went through—but didn't think to check its pockets.

My hastily conceived plan assumes Leslie forced the caravan door to gain entry, meaning it can't be locked, so my initial task is going from here to there (it's in the kitchen area) with only one working leg and, vitally, making no noise while doing so.

Then I'm out—and away.

To whichever house is nearest, where I'll raise the alarm. That's five miles, according to Leslie.

But getting outside—silently—is my immediate objective.

I can't hop—that would be too noisy. But I still have two knees—and am able to crawl. So I'm currently becoming more intimate than is comfortable with the caravan's manky carpet—a literal case of "get down and dirty"—as I edge my way towards the outside door. I have to be careful because, without my prosthetic's stabilising influence and in this weakened state, it would be easy to slip sideways and land in a clatter—which Leslie would hear.

Once I'm on the kitchen floor with its smooth vinyl, this becomes more of a concern—but somehow, I resist the overwhelming urge to hurry. Picture book images of hares and tortoises flash through my mind, provoking a wry smile.

And—yes—I'm there. Now—mustn't make any noise pulling myself upright, which makes this a slow and tedious process, but... hurrah... finally, I'm standing at the door holding its handle. Triumphantly, I press down—carefully, so as not to let it click.

And... it's locked? How can that be?

Smacking myself around the head, I realise what should have been obvious. Leslie broke into the site office to turn on the power—and that gave her access to the caravans' keys. From vague memories of a childhood holiday, there was probably a big wall board putting the things on prominent display. Meaning she *didn't* have to break in here—and was able to lock the door.

While I'm thinking nostalgically of Daisy and the lock picks she carries everywhere (*and* knows how to use), a voice at my shoulder startles me. 'I'm a very light sleeper, Samantha.'

Using the kitchen worktop for support, I wheel around. Leslie's standing behind me, and doesn't look pleased. Worse, she has that cattle prod in her hand.

She waves it in front of her. 'Remember me saying I needed to demonstrate this—so you'd be motivated to behave? Then deciding to leave it till morning because you were still recovering from the drug? Well, it seems my consideration was a mistake.'

She lunges, there's a crackle, and—my shoulder explodes in agony. I scramble to get away, but the door's behind me and when I move sideways,

Leslie moves with me. Just when I think this torment will never end, she yanks the cattle prod back. Sobbing, I slide down the door and crumple on cold vinyl. The car keys slip from my hand.

Leslie laughs. 'Remember your little judo trick at my hotel in Donstable? You've no idea how much I've looked forward to this moment.'

That was aikido—not that it matters

She stares down at me and her eyes blaze with pure hatred. Then scoops up my keys and stalks back to the bedroom.

My shoulder's still on fire and it feels like I'm trying to swallow sandpaper. Those euphoric moments of imminent escape made me forget how thirsty I am. Curled in a corner formed by the locked outer door with a kitchen cupboard, exhaustion and pain making it hard to even think—my outlook is bleak.

31

The next couple of days go past in a blur.

Now it's day three of my captivity—I think, but it's like the difference between counting fence posts or the gaps between them. I arrived here on Monday and this is Wednesday—would you call that two or three days? The only certain thing being that my time is running out fast, at least according to Leslie's Google research on dehydration.

The Rohypnol must still have been in my system because, after that abortive escape attempt on Monday night, I eventually went to sleep—and slept through half of yesterday.

Leslie constantly studies me, like I'm some sort of lab rat. At first it was unnerving, but sometime last evening I stopped noticing. Too much else to think about.

I have chapped lips and my throat feels as though it's lined with cardboard. In addition, the symptoms of dehydration appear to mimic an acute case of 'flu. Dull headache, sporadic dizziness, profound weakness that makes everything an effort—and I'm so befuddled, time is passing without my noticing it go.

It's now Wednesday midday, as confirmed by my watch. Despite a lowered awareness of anything outside the locus of my suffering, I've noticed Leslie become progressively agitated today. Something tells me that might be worth playing on.

'Leslie,' I grate, in a voice that's alien even to me. (It's how you'd expect a Dalek to sound—one that could use a hefty gargle of WD40.) 'You must realise Davy wouldn't give the time of day to anyone he suspected of being involved in my death.'

She smiles, but her bouncy demeanour has flatlined. 'He won't. Suspect me, I mean.'

I wave a hand at our surroundings. 'Get real—your DNA's all over this place.'

Leslie shakes her head and takes on the role of my old maths teacher as she wags a finger. 'Nobody will know you died here. See, I'll dump your corpse miles from anywhere—where there's no phone signal. Then leave your car nearby, after syphoning all its petrol out. They'll think you ran out of fuel and wandered in circles for a couple of days before collapsing. It'll look like a tragic accident. Of course, people might wonder what you were doing away out there—but, hey? It won't be the first time you've done something unexpected, from what I hear.'

'So how are *you* going to get back—from this isolated spot, "miles from anywhere"?'

'Oh, I'm well into camping and hiking—that's my alibi for this week, as it happens. I'll make my way to the railway station in Dumbarton and go home. Where I'll wait for the news to break—then be there for Davy when he needs comforting.'

All day yesterday, I was sure Daisy would turn up and rescue me. The fact she hasn't means there's nothing to connect Leslie with this place. It's looking more and more as though this monstrous woman's insane scheme will succeed. With a shudder, I wonder if Davy *might* eventually succumb to her charms when he recovers from the initial shock of losing me.

Then I remember how Davy dismissed Leslie as a "nutter"—and more to the point, Geraldine's opinion of his first love. Even if Leslie were to win Davy around, Geraldine can be relied on to set him straight.

No—Leslie won't be getting lovey-dovey with Davy, despite eliminating me. While that affords a certain satisfaction, in a curious sense it makes my suffering seem more tragic since, ultimately, there'll be no point to it.

I ponder whether to play the "Geraldine" card in an attempt to convince Leslie she's risking life imprisonment for nothing. Tell her what Davy's mother thinks of her.

Then I decide it's too risky. Forewarned, Leslie isn't above repeating this exercise with her prospective mother-in-law.

Also, if I push the wrong switches, Leslie could make things even more uncomfortable for me. For example, she could tie me up outside the caravan to hasten my demise—I woke briefly at dawn today and, glancing through the window, saw a blanket of frost over everything.

But *would* it be? More uncomfortable? Unbelievably, I find myself wondering if that might actually be preferable—because I remember reading somewhere that hypothermia is a quick and painless death.

If only it wasn't so HARD to think... Putting together the simplest conjecture feels like that Greek guy—Sisyphus?—must have while pushing his boulder uphill. It's yet to be seen whether my own modest collection of rocks is also doomed to roll back—always assuming I reach a high enough point to set them in motion

Leslie's sprawled in the armchair opposite my sofa. Suddenly, she jumps to her feet and stares at me for a long moment. Then nods. When she speaks, it's as much to herself. 'Yes, you're pretty far gone now—surely it's safe to pop out for a little while? My supplies of *everything* are running low—and anyway, I'm going stir crazy in here.'

Gosh, Leslie—have I been inconveniencing you?

But for the first time since the "car keys" incident, hope flares in my chest. I have a plan—which depends on Leslie leaving me alone for a while.

I was starting to think that just wasn't going to happen...

Leslie skips off down the corridor, then reappears wearing her coat and carrying a canvas bag. Trills: 'Be good,' and unlocks the main door.

I hear a click when she relocks it from the outside, then listen for her car starting. Gritting my teeth, I force myself to wait another ten minutes—in case Leslie sneaks back to check on me.

Finally, I decide—it's now or never.

32

In my mind, I leap from the sofa—in reality I *roll* off and get on my hands and knees, being too weak to hop. Then crawl towards the hall cupboard.

The journey seems to take forever—especially since it feels I'll pass out at any moment. But at last I'm there, and reaching up to grasp the handle. Yanking open the door, I grab a long-handled brush—the same one Leslie brought out yesterday to sweep up shards of crockery after dropping a mug.

Getting upright takes an interminable amount of time and ironically brings me to the point of collapse. I manage, though, then ram the brush head under my arm. The disappointment is intense—my makeshift crutch is too long to be effective.

I feel frustration—but not despair. Because I have a backup plan for this eventuality—just hoped it wouldn't be needed.

The brush helps me keep my balance as I hop back to the kitchen area, using it like a punting pole. I have to try three drawers before unearthing the serrated bread knife Leslie used to cut her bread.

The poor love was furious at discovering she'd bought an unsliced loaf by mistake, but finding this knife saved the day for her—as I hope it will for me. The point's far too blunt to be any use as a weapon—Leslie checked before returning it to the drawer—but that isn't what I want it for.

Okay. I've laid the brush on the worktop, handle-end protruding on this side while the brush head extends into the living area, and rammed it tight against a metal pole supporting the upper cupboards. Now I'm sawing into it with the bread-knife. An effort that uses more strength than I have left and is making lights flash at the centre of my vision.

Panic stirs within as I expect Leslie to appear at any moment, but she told me Dumbarton is half-an-hour away. Surely that means she'll be gone for a minimum of ninety minutes—probably more? Which still leaves me at least an hour, I reassure myself.

Saw—rest. Saw—rest. Saw…

When the blade's about a third through the brush handle—it sticks. There is *no* chance I'll get it moving again. My hands shake as I reposition the brush.

The fridge is below the worktop, leaving an inch-wide gap into which I feed the broom handle while ensuring the notch I cut stays uppermost—that latter made easy by the breadknife still stuck in it. Now I carefully jiggle the handle in and out until the notch is aligned with the fridge front.

Gripping the brush head with both hands, I slam all my weight down and into it. The theory being—there should be sufficient leverage to break the handle where I've weakened it.

The reality is—nothing happens.

A gargled scream rips free from my acrid throat. A red mist descends and adrenaline rushes to bolster spent muscles as I push against the brush head with all my might—a frenzied effort doomed to burn out in seconds.

CRACK

The handle breaks and I go down hard, my nose losing a fight with the vinyl flooring. I feel a trickle of blood on my upper lip, but who cares? Because I just manufactured myself a custom-made crutch.

Getting upright again takes ages. I have the brush gripped in one hand while my other claws at the worktop—then suddenly I'm back standing, like an ungainly crane. Leaning my bottom against the kitchen units, raising my left arm to receive the brush head, I slip my improvised walking aid in place.

YES. It works—perfectly. I can—sort of—walk again. During long months of rehabilitation after the car accident, I spent a lot of time learning to use a crutch before my stump healed sufficiently to be fitted with a prosthetic—and became quite the expert.

Happily, my muscle memory remembers as though it were yesterday.

Breathing in quick gasps, aware of the darkness crouched ready to pounce at every edge of my fragile consciousness, elation thrums through me and re-energises my battered body as I move freely about the caravan. Right—by my calculations, I still have a minimum of forty-five minutes.

On to stage 2

Although a gross exaggeration, it *feels* like I hurtle down the back hallway. Then into the second bedroom. Skirting the chemical toilet with a grimace of distaste, I stop at the window. Then unlatch both its levers, one at a time.

Oh, joy—the window opens easily. It's on a central hinge, presumably to make cleaning easier. The glass swings horizontally so half of it is outside, half in—and above and below, clear gaps ooze air that reek of freedom. The bottom gap is plenty deep enough for me to ease myself through.

Sticking my head out, I examine the ground about ten feet below. Even landing on grass I'd break something—probably my neck.

Already thought of that

There are two narrow beds in here. I go to the first and yank off its mattress. Being "caravan-sized" the mattress isn't heavy, although in my weakened state it feels like a sheet of lead. After dragging what is essentially a rectangle of foam to the window, one-handed, I feed it through the gap. Watch it drop to the grass.

Then repeat the process with bed number two.

Right. Now, I toss my precious crutch clear of the mattresses—then follow it through the window, head-first.

This is the bit that worries me. There was no way I could manoeuvre out feet- (or foot-) first and if I land on my head, it's game over. But—I'd rather take the risk than die slowly and painfully.

The fleeting seconds as I drop through freezing air, twisting desperately to protect my head, stretch out until every nerve is at breaking point. Then the impact. A sickening thud, followed by horrific pain as my shoulder flattens the thin mattresses and crumples against ungiving terra firma immediately below—but still there's more joy in my scream than hurt.

After all, my neck's not broken...

And even if my shoulder's fractured, it's the right-hand one—which I can manage without.

I don't think it is, though—after gingerly testing the joint while sobbing through bolts of agony unleashed by moving it, I nevertheless conclude the bones are still intact.

Alright—that's the least of my worries. *Focus*, Sam.

I scramble off the mattress. Then grab my makeshift crutch (with my left hand) and yet again go through the long process of raising myself upright.

Made doubly difficult now my right arm's useless.

My battered body has run out of adrenaline and must be running on empty, but *somehow* I manage.

Taking a well-deserved moment, I cast a curious gaze around. From my vantage, there are about twenty caravans scattered in all directions on either side of a dirt track that presumably is the site's main thoroughfare. From Leslie's tyre marks, it's clear which way she came and went—telling me which direction the exit's in—and I set off, hoping she won't return early.

Hey—I really *am* good at this walking-on-a-crutch lark. A sudden burst of optimism cajoles my depleted adrenal glands back into action until it seems as though I'm whizzing along.

Of course, reality is somewhat different—but after two (or is that three?—still haven't decided) days of hopping around on one leg, my snail's pace *feels* like an Olympic sprinter's.

It probably takes another ten minutes to reach the main road, by which time my latest injection of adrenaline has well and truly dissipated. I'm shivering now—the temperature can't be far above freezing. Struggling to draw breath, I stare at a signpost. It says simply "Dumbarton" with an arrow pointing to the right. From the fact it gives no indication what lies the other way—I deduce "not much". However, there must be some*thing* out there—isolated dwellings, farms—some*where* with a phone.

That's all I need.

There's no choice—I have to turn left, or risk meeting Leslie returning from Dumbarton. My imperative is to get so far down this road, it'll be impossible for her to check every nook and cranny along the way. Then I'll hide, rest, and wait for dark—when it should be safe to look for help.

It was a good plan in theory—but about twenty minutes later, I'm spent. My shoulder's killing me and everything's swimming in and out of focus. I can't go any further.

I *won't* be going any further.

And I'm nowhere *near* far enough away yet.

Okay—my only chance is to hole up like the wounded animal I am and hope Leslie doesn't find me. I didn't take temperature into account, and my mind wanders longingly to the quilts I discarded from their mattresses in the caravan's second bedroom. If only I'd thought to bring even one of the cotton sheets—I'll have to try and stave off hypothermia with dead leaves or some other form of natural insulation.

Wryly, I think back to those previous fatalistic thoughts—at least hypothermia is supposed to be painless, I remind myself.

But before any of that matters, I need to find a hidey-hole.

There's a hedge on either side of the road and if I could crawl into one, it might give me *some* protection from the cold. Problem is, they both look too tightly knit for squeezing into.

Maybe I could lie in the ditch? Then, if Leslie gives pursuit in her (my) car, she'll drive right past without knowing I'm there—but after hobbling over, I immediately see it's half full of water.

WATER. For a moment, I envisage drinking the muddy liquid—lapping at it with my tongue, like a cat. Even in this state, I know that isn't a good idea. Nonetheless, I'm going to do it... have to, because my base instincts just outvoted whatever conscious volition remains.

But before figuring out how to get myself down there, I hear the growl of a car engine—coming up fast behind me.

It can only be Leslie.

There's no fight left in me—I'm finished. As my limp body hits the dusty tarmac, I realise with sickening certainty—it's over.

33

My head buzzes like a hive of bees and it takes a moment for me to make out the words in her triumphant yell. '*There* you are.'

Dimly, I register the vibration of feet galloping towards me. Hands seize my shoulders and pull me into a sitting position. I don't care anymore—Leslie can do what she wants. I can't stop her.

'Sam. SAM.'

Except—that isn't Leslie. A cataclysm of emotions explode in my chest as I recognise the voice.

Daisy!

For just a moment, I'm conscious of her panicked face scrutinising me—then my vision fades to a snowstorm of white static. At least the bees quieten, letting me hear what Daisy says to someone else.

'Don't stand there like a Wally—call an ambulance.'

Is that Davy now? Sounding as though he's struggling to form his words?

'Yes, ambulance—no, I've no idea what's wrong with her except she's in a bad way.'

Then Daisy again, talking in a strangely calm if forced tone.

'Tell them Sam's eyes look sunken and there's crusting on her lips. Looks like exposure… or dehydration? And her pulse is rapid but thready—Davy, make it plain they need to hurry.'

I wink out then, for I don't know how long. The sound of sirens wakes me and next thing I'm being rolled onto something, then lifted. I fade in and out of consciousness during a bumpy road trip before lights appear overhead—lots of them, buzzing like the bees in my head did—and I have a sense of hurtling under and through their cold glow. Footsteps ring out all around, then… nothing.

'ABOUT RUDDY TIME.'

Blinking, I struggle to get my bearings. I'm propped up on pillows in a (hospital?) bed. When I try to move, an IV tugs at the back of one hand and my shoulder erupts in pain. Shaking my head to clear it is a mistake I instantly regret. Pressure on the hand that doesn't have a tube attached draws my gaze and I follow the fingers squeezing mine, right up to their owner's face.

'Wha...?' I croak, and Daisy frowns.

'Don't try to speak—here, want some ice chips to suck? They said you can't have water yet—it would make you sick.'

The ice is heavenly against my parched lips. As it melts, the tantalising trickles taste better than anything ever has before. A figure peeks out behind Daisy and reaches around to squeeze my leg through the quilt. 'Davy?'

'You had us worried, Sam. They say you'll be fine in a few days, though.'

A grunt from Daisy. 'More like a few *weeks*.'

'My shoulder...?' I manage to croak.

Daisy brings her face close to mine. 'It's okay—just bruised. Well... actually, *very* bruised, but your X-rays are clear.'

A nurse bustles in and checks my vitals. She tells me to use the call button if I need anything, then scoots out again. 'Where am I, Daisy?'

'Hospital, dopey. What the blazes happened to you?'

'Leslie,' I murmur, before a bout of dizziness sends me slumping back on the pillows. 'She kidnapped me—held me without food or water.'

In my side vision, Davy doubles over as though he's been punched in the gut. 'How did you find me?'

'Wasn't easy,' Daisy mutters, fumbling in her pocket before bringing out a silver pen. 'Remember this?'

I shake my head (very carefully). 'No.'

'Roger's emergency signaller—he gave you one, too. We hit a dead end, Sam. I spoke to the witches and guessed Leslie was behind your disappearance—but she'd vanished, too. Then, this morning, I remembered the signaller. On the off chance it was still in your bag, I called Wilf—and he contacted Angus. Ten minutes later, Roger phoned back with your exact location. Well, the signaller's location—but I was gambling it didn't get to Dumbarton on its own.'

Davy comes around the bed to put a gentle hand on my good shoulder. It's obvious he's struggling to stay composed. 'I drove down here with Daisy, and Roger's coordinates led us to the caravan park. We figured out from the open window and mattresses that you'd escaped—leaving your bag behind, with the signaller inside—but had no idea where to.'

I almost laugh—almost, but not quite. If I'd just stayed where I was...

'How did you track me down from there, then?'

'That was me.'

Daisy looks smug as she cuts in. 'It wasn't so hard. You'd obviously make for the main gate after that Houdini act and, assuming your kidnapper had gone off somewhere—which would most likely be Dumbarton—I reckoned you wouldn't want to risk meeting them on their way back. So we drove along the road, *away* from Dumbarton, and... there you were.'

Looking from one to the other, I feel my eyes well up. 'I really thought that was my end.'

Daisy's voice is softer than I've ever heard it. 'I know, lovey. Listen, you're pooped. Get some rest—Davy and I aren't going anywhere. We can talk some more later.'

She looks up at Davy. 'Go'n' find us some coffee, eh? Just for you and me, of course. Oh, and see if they've got any biscuits...'

IT FEELS LIKE I SLEEP FOR DAYS, BUT DAISY TELLS ME IT WAS only overnight. 'Where's Davy?' I ask, looking around, relieved that moving my head doesn't hurt any more.

'Sent him for a walk—he was getting on my nerves. Poor guy's still worried sick, but the medics say you'll be fine. Nice timing, by the way, 'cos Alan's coming in to see you.'

'Alan?' I repeat, surprised.

'He's NCA, and I suppose kidnapping's more their thing than the local flatfoots'. Or maybe Rebecca's nipping his ear. Anyway, he's due anytime.'

'Did they arrest Leslie?'

'Not yet. Tell you what, for her sake—they better catch her before I do.'

I can't help a grin, because she isn't joking.

'You decent?'

Alan's face appears around the door and his smile falls away as he takes in my appearance. 'Oh heck, Sam. You look awful.'

Cheers for that

He sidles in and approaches me as though I'm radioactive. 'Boy, she really did a number on you.'

Okay—got it, thanks

It's slightly easier to talk now, but I still don't sound like me. 'Did you get her—Leslie?'

He shakes his head. 'She must have come back and found you gone—probably passed the ambulance on her way. Besom torched the caravan with a can of petrol, so our DNA evidence went up in smoke. We caught up with her at home, and her immediate response was: "I've been away—camping rough near Dumbarton for a few nights. I love camping—ask anybody. *Really*? What a coincidence..."'

Daisy's incredulous. 'And you believed her?'

'Of course not—but I can't do anything without evidence, and there isn't any. It's Sam's word against hers. Sam, did she say *why*?'

I explain (as best you *can* explain the unexplainable) but another part of my mind panics. If Leslie's still on the loose, I'm back to looking over my shoulder. Then a thought occurs.

'Leslie brought us here in my Fiesta. What did she do with *it*?'

Alan frowns. 'It was left parked outside Dumbarton railway station—keys in the ignition, and wiped clean of prints.'

Daisy looks thoughtful. 'Anything found in it? Like Sam's leg, for instance?'

Shaking his head, Alan says: 'Nada.'

'Have you checked for strands of hair, fibres— DNA even—that would link Leslie to the car?'

With an exaggerated frown, Alan flicks a hand. 'Too circumstantial—Leslie only has to claim Sam gave her a lift somewhere, sometime, and we're back to it being one's word against the other's.'

But Daisy isn't finished. 'Thinking about the leg—Leslie's scheme to make it look like Sam got stranded in some remote spot wouldn't have flown if she wasn't wearing her leg. Ergo—Leslie must have brought it along. She would have left it outside in the Fiesta, of course—last thing she wanted was Sam getting ahold of that. So where is it now?'

Alan shrugs. 'I'd guess she burned it with the caravan.'

Her eyes glow, and it's Daisy's turn to shake her head. 'Think about it, Alan. She came back to find

Sam gone—after passing an ambulance going in the opposite direction with its siren blaring. I reckon she'll have been in an absolute panic. And an almighty rush to get herself out of there—grudging every second it took to set the caravan on fire. The question is: did she forget about the leg? It won't have been in plain view—she went shopping in Dumbarton, remember. The leg will have been stashed away out of sight—after all, it's the sort of thing that would stick in the mind of any passer-by who noticed it.'

'Yeah,' Alan says, looking puzzled. 'But even if that's right, she obviously did something with it before leaving Sam's car at the railway station—because it wasn't in the Fiesta. She probably dumped it on the way there.'

Daisy's bobbing up and down now. 'No—she *wouldn't*. That leg would have forensic evidence on it. And while you can wipe prints, DNA's harder to eradicate—so Leslie couldn't risk somebody finding it. The besom's a psycho, but a clever one—she'd know that. Heck, everybody with a Netflix subscription does. I think she *had* to take the leg home with her.'

Alan snorts. 'Okay, that's all very plausible—but since then, she's had another fifteen hours to clean and dispose of it.'

'Put yourself in her shoes. First, how could Leslie be sure she'd removed every skin cell of trace evidence? A prosthetic's got loads of wee nooks and crannies. Meaning she still can't risk it being found. Second, how does she know you aren't watching her—following her, even? Which you might have been if the NCA were smart enough to figure out what I just did... No, if I was her, I'd... bury it in the back garden. That way, if the police came to search her house, they wouldn't find it.'

Alan laughs shortly. 'Daisy, you're reaching. This is starting to sound like an episode of "Sherlock". You'll be bringing out a crystal ball next.'

She scowls. 'I don't hear you coming up with a proper counter argument. Look, why not just get a warrant and check?'

I've read about spontaneous combustion—Alan looks as though he's about to give us a demonstration

'It's not that simple. Yes, I could get a warrant on the basis of Sam's statement. But if I go in like a bull in a china shop, it becomes that much harder to pursue future leads. Sheriffs don't sign warrants willy-nilly—they expect the first one to stick. And I don't want to screw up my options for such a hare-brained theory.'

Daisy takes a step towards him and for one horrible moment, I'm sure she's going to hit him. Alan must think so too, from that nippy backstep he just executed. But she draws a deep breath instead, and her tone turns pleading. 'Look, what if *I* were to take a wee gander? Unofficially, like. And if *you* then got an anonymous tip-off—would you follow-up on it?'

'What sort of tip-off?' he scoffs.

'Don't know yet, do I? Okay, for example—because *my* scenario makes sense to *me*—if you heard there was a patch of freshly turned-over earth in Leslie's rose bed, would that persuade you to go have a look. Officially?'

Reluctantly, Alan nods. 'If... someone... got sight of incriminatory evidence and tipped me the wink, then yes... I'd follow up.'

'Great.'

She leaps at him but the panic that blossoms on his face is unfounded since she merely pushes Alan towards the door. 'Alright, leave it with me. Now, scarper—I need to make a phone call.'

I meet Alan's gaze over Daisy's head and we both roll our eyes at the same time. 'Fine,' he says, making his exit as Daisy pulls out her phone.

'Rebecca? Get over here now—in the Audi. Yes, Dumbarton—pick me up at the hospital. No, right now... I don't care... and listen, there's a coupla things I need you to bring.'

As she wanders through the door, still speaking, a wave of weariness washes over me and I let my eyes close.

34

Two days later, the hospital discharges me. I'm weak and my arm's in a sling, but the doctor says everything should be back to normal in a few weeks.

Davy picks me up and we head straight for Cairncroft. Looking at him hunched over the wheel, I can read his mind. 'Davy—don't.'

He glances sideways, startled. 'What?'

'You're on a guilt trip and frankly, I could do without it. I don't blame you for what happened—so don't blame yourself.'

'But it was because of me she...'

'NO. Leslie's sick—and that's not your fault. Please—having to tiptoe around you is *not* what I need right now. TLC, on the other hand...'

After some brow wrinkling, he grins suddenly. 'Okay, see your point. We'll make a deal. You get oodles of TLC—and I'll consider myself off the hook.'

'Done.'

Thank goodness for that

He snorts. 'Knowing she's locked away makes it a lot easier to put that crazy bitch behind us.'

'Alan says they've ordered psychiatric assessment—Leslie will probably be committed indefinitely instead of going to court.'

I gasp at the irony. 'She might end up sharing with Lena.'

'So how exactly *did* Daisy come up with the goods?'

Oh, of course—Davy wasn't there when Daisy delivered her victory speech. 'She sent for Rebecca and her Audi—remember I told you we had it fitted with tinted windows?'

Davy grins. 'Yeah—I can see where Rebecca couldn't do surveillance jobs without them.'

'Precisely—Rebecca's nothing if not memorable. Not that Leslie's ever met Daisy or Rebecca—but she was snooping about on Halloween and could have seen them then. So, they staked out Leslie's house. When she left to go shopping, Rebecca followed her while Daisy went for a nosey around. It meant Daisy had all the time in the world, knowing Rebecca would phone and warn her when Leslie was on her way home.'

'So Daisy broke in…?'

I shake my head. 'She didn't have to. Remember I told you about Daisy's off-the-wall theory that Leslie buried my leg in her back garden? Well, that's where Daisy went first—and, would you believe it, found a square of turf on Leslie's lawn that had been recently cut, then put back.'

'And the leg was buried under that?'

'Yep—Daisy was spot on. Right enough, I've never known her miss an episode of "Criminal Minds"—she *should* be an expert on profiling by now. Anyway, she checked the leg was there, then replaced everything the way it was and rang Alan. Who went straight for a search warrant, then arrested Leslie. Just to put some icing on the cake, they found one of my earrings in Leslie's car—it had gone down behind the rear seat, so she wouldn't have noticed it. I can't even remember wearing earrings that day—but my memory's still fuzzy.'

'So, faced with all that—did Leslie confess?'

'Not immediately. Alan said Leslie seemed almost catatonic when they brought her in. It was like she couldn't accept they'd got the goods on her. Eventually, though, she broke down and admitted everything. Which doesn't surprise me because Alan pulled Inspector Wilson in to run the interview. I've seen him in action—he makes the KGB look tame.'

'Suppose she didn't have a lot of choice—not after they found evidence to back up your story.'

Poor Davy—this has turned his world upside down. In a softer voice, I say: 'Despite what she did, I'm just so glad Leslie's going to get proper care.'

'Long as she's locked up while they deliver it,' he says darkly.

I can't help nodding my agreement.

'Sam, how on earth did Leslie hold down such a high-powered job when she's crazy as a loon?'

'According to Daisy, the technical term is "organised psychopath".'

He sniffs. 'Yeah, she should know. Did I mention she's got me helping a "man with a van" move your furniture tomorrow? Not that I mind—but she only told me this morning.'

Then he grins and nudges me. 'Welcome home, Sam.'

Watching familiar sights like "The Cuppa Tea" spin past, my spirits soar. 'This *is* my home,' I tell Davy sincerely. 'Don't you go looking at any more jobs in Glasgow—or anywhere else.'

He shakes his head. 'No worries—I've learnt my lesson. It's true what they say. Nobody appreciates what they've got until...'

'Just remember, not everybody gets a second chance. *Don't* blow this one.'

'Yes Ma'am,' he quips, as we arrive at the hotel. Daisy's standing in a huddle with three other women outside the main door. Who look like...?

'Isn't that those weird biddies you were telling me about?'

'The witches? Mm, you're right. Wonder why *they're* here? It's a long way from Paisley.'

Davy parks, then helps me out. The hospital supplied me with a proper lightweight-aluminium crutch, but remembering my makeshift brush I feel quite nostalgic. Davy frowns. 'Did Alan say when you'd get the leg back?'

'Could be months—they have to keep it as evidence. Don't worry—I've got an appointment in Aberdeen tomorrow to be fitted for a new one. Past time I had the cast updated, anyway.'

Daisy rushes forward. Before we can hug, the witches gather round and Agatha leans right into my face. 'Didn't I tell you—about those powers I sensed? They certainly came to the fore when you needed them. And I hear you used a broomstick to escape that horrible woman.'

It was a BRUSH

Although, thinking back in disbelief to all I accomplished three days ago, Agatha's crazy assertions about my "inner strength" suddenly don't sound so daft any more. 'What are you doing here?' I ask. 'Not that it isn't nice to see you all,' I clarify hastily.

'They're moving to Cairncroft,' Daisy answers for her. 'Seem to have taken a shine to us.'

Agatha draws herself upright. 'There is much untapped power within the fabric of this region,' she says in a low voice. 'We have already identified several undocumented ley lines. Yes, relocating to this area will serve our work well.'

She leans in and whispers. 'Our little getaway last week was also an exploratory mission.'

'They're looking at cottages,' Daisy pipes up. 'I was telling them there's one for sale at the far end of Donstable...'

Agatha shakes her head. 'We'd rather find something closer to Samantha. So we can assist in the freeing of her true self from its corporeal shackles.'

Oh, no—this is all I need

'I've hired a car and we're going to drive around—check out what's available,' Agatha goes on.

I'm curious. 'Are you looking for *three* cottages, then?'

'Only one, dear. We all live together. Take care, now—we'll see you soon.'

She fumbles for her keys, walking towards a beaten up old Mini that smacks of Arthur's "Executive Car Hire." Daisy pulls some sort of gadget from her pocket. 'Allow me,' she trills, pressing a button, and the Mini's lights flash.

Agatha spins, her face a picture. 'What magic is that?' she gasps.

Daisy smiles modestly. 'It's a frequency analyser.'

Oh, right—she had that in Glasgow

The witches get into their Mini and drive off, looking befuddled. Davy points at Daisy's gadget. 'A *which*?'

She tuts. 'When Agatha arrived, this clever little machine figured out what frequency her car key was on. Then, just now, I had it broadcast an identical signal. Brill, isn't it?'

I'm not listening. Because seeing how easily she can get into any car has reminded me of something. In fact, it struck me like a thunderbolt. 'Daisy... do you remember Wilf telling us he still had his dead father's prosthetic? In a cupboard under the stairs.'

Daisy puts the tip of a finger to her lips. 'DID he? No... I don't remember that...'

The Donstable Gazette

16TH NOVEMBER, 2022

HOTEL OWNER NARROWLY ESCAPES HORRIFIC DEATH

Following last week's firearms incident at the Cairncroft Hotel (see recap on page 3) part-owner Samantha Chessington underwent a horrific 3 day ordeal.

Ms Chessington was abducted and held without food or water. Details of her rescue have not yet been released and neither has the kidnapper's identity. Our usual spokesperson at The Cairncroft Detective Agency claimed some of the credit when she told us: 'As usual, I got lumbered with the leg work.'

PUBLISHED EVERY WEDNESDAY
BY DONSTABLE PRESS LTD

NEXT IN SERIES

Things that go bump in the night...

... seem louder on Allhallows Eve

But when spooky turns to murder at the Cairncroft Hotel's Halloween party...

... you just KNOW who they're gonna call

ALSO BY A.J.A. GARDINER

THE SAM & DAISY MURDER MYSTERIES

THE MURDER HOTEL

THE CAIRNCROFT DETECTIVE AGENCY

MURDER & MAYHEM AT THE CAIRNCROFT HOTEL

MURDER AT THE CAIRNCROFT FAIR

THE DAWN & ROGER THRILLER SERIES

THE CON WOMAN - KIDNAP IN CANNES

THE CON WOMAN - THE SCAM

THE CON WOMAN - THE BLUFF

MARK ROGERS - OPTOMETRIST

EYES UP

COMICAL SHORT STORIES

AUTHOR'S NOTE

Thank you for choosing this book—I hope you enjoyed reading it as much as I enjoyed writing it.

The best way to be kept informed of new books etc is to join my readers' club—when you'll get a free eBook called "When Sam met Daisy", a short story telling how the girls met—it's yours by typing the following into your browser:

https://ajagardinerwriter.co.uk/free%20book/

You can mail me by writing to: ajagardiner@mail.com - I check this mailbox at least once a week. Or better still, visit my website where you can see ALL my books, sign up for newsletters, AND contact me.

www. ajagardinerwriter.co.uk

Thanks so much for reading my book - if you liked it, puh-lease tell your friends! 😃

I look forward to our next meeting.

AJAG

PS if your free book doesn't appear, check the SPAM folder. No joy? Mail me at alistair@ajagardinerwriter.co.uk – & I'll sort it for you!

This is a work of fiction. Names, characters, places, and incidents either are the product of the author's imagination or are used fictitiously. Any resemblance to actual persons, living or dead, events, or locales is entirely coincidental.

Copyright © 2024 by A.J.A. Gardiner

All rights reserved. No part of this book may be reproduced or used in any manner without written permission of the copyright owner except for the use of quotations in a book review. For more information, email alistair@ajagardinerwriter.co.uk

First paperback edition January 2024

ISBN: 9798874443177

(Front cover design by Addison-Wright Publications)

Printed in Great Britain
by Amazon